The Dutiful Duke

"Usually when I am alone with an attractive woman I am singing praises to her glorious hazel eyes, not discussing impressionable young minds," Wyatt said.

Nia felt her cheeks glowing with embarrassment. "Nonsense, my lord, I am a governess, not an . . . an attractive woman."

Her answer amused Wyatt. "I was not aware that being a governess precluded being attractive," he drawled.

Nia rose to her feet. "With your permission, sir, I will be retiring to my rooms."

A half-smile played about his lips as he watched her cross the room.

"Miss Pringle?"

"Yes, Your Grace?"

"Your hazel eyes *are* glorious."

Other Regency Romances by
Joan Overfield

The Dutiful Duke

JOAN OVERFIELD

AVON BOOKS NEW YORK

THE DUTIFUL DUKE is an original publication of Avon Books. This work has never before appeared in book form. This work is a novel. Any similarity to actual persons or events is purely coincidental.

AVON BOOKS
A division of
The Hearst Corporation
1350 Avenue of the Americas
New York, New York 10019

Copyright © 1994 by Joan Overfield
Published by arrangement with the author
Library of Congress Catalog Card Number: 93-91662
ISBN: 0-380-77400-3

First Avon Books Printing: February 1994

AVON TRADEMARK REG. U.S. PAT. OFF. AND IN OTHER COUNTRIES, MARCA REGISTRADA, HECHO EN U.S.A.

Printed in the U.S.A.

RA   10   9   8   7   6   5   4   3   2   1

For Leona

Chapter 1

⚜⚜⚜

London, 1816

"That beast! That hateful, monstrous, selfish beast!" Miss Thomasina Pringle's hazel eyes glittered behind the smudged lenses of her spectacles as she stood in the center of the neat, book-lined study. "Well, he needn't think he will get away with this, because if it's the last thing I do, I vow I shall make him pay!"

Mrs. Alvira Langston, headmistress of the Portham Academy, glanced up from her books, her face paling at the dramatic pronouncement. *Not again*, she thought, sliding open the top drawer of her desk and fumbling for the bottle of smelling salts she kept tucked inside. "Who won't get away with what?" she asked, praying her youngest and most difficult teacher didn't mean what she feared she did. "To whom are you referring?"

Nia, as her late father had dubbed her, gave her employer an impatient look before casting herself upon the nearest chair. "The duke of Tilton, of course," she responded, scowling as she stuffed a strand of mahogany-colored hair beneath her prim linen cap. "What other hateful, monstrous, selfish beast have I the misfortune of knowing?"

Mrs. Langston closed her eyes, her worst fears confirmed. "Oh, Nia," she wailed, raising the salts for a restorative sniff. "You promised!"

Nia shifted uneasily, her conscience pricking at the despair in her employer's voice. She'd been raised

1

believing her word was her bond, and she could not like the knowledge that she may have compromised that belief. Shoving her spectacles back with a slender finger, she searched her agile mind for some acceptable justification of her actions. "I promised Miss Portham I wouldn't contact the duke by post," she said at last, knowing her defense was shaky at best. "And you needn't think I've gone back on my word, because I haven't. *I'm* not the one who wrote the wretch a letter."

All too familiar with Nia's tendency to manipulate the truth, Mrs. Langston allowed herself another sniff before pressing for more information. "Then who did write His Grace?" she asked, steeling herself for the answer.

Nia shifted again, toying with the idea of lying before deciding to make a clean breast of the incident. It was only a matter of time before the headmistress knew the whole of it, and she thought it might be best if she learned the details from her. "Amanda," she admitted at last, her eyes dropping to the toes of her scuffed slippers. "She wrote him a letter asking him to visit her for her birthday."

"Amanda!" Mrs. Langston's fingers closed about the bottle. "But she is only a child!"

"She will be seven in a few months," Nia corrected, leaping spiritedly to the defense of her favorite pupil. "And she has the loveliest hand of any pupil in the school. Why, only yesterday Miss Leeds was praising her letters, and Miss Cummings said her grammar was quite superior for a child her age."

"I wasn't questioning Amanda's scholastic abilities, Miss Pringle. I was questioning why you encouraged her to contact the duke when he has made it more than obvious that he desires no such contact." Mrs. Langston spoke coldly, deciding it was past time she took a firmer hand with Nia and the situation involving Amanda Perryvale. In the past she'd allowed Miss Pringle far too much leniency with the child, but she could see that would have to change. The last thing the academy needed was to make an enemy of the powerful and haughty lord.

"But Amanda is his niece!" Nia protested, her feeling of righteous indignation flaring back to life. "It is his duty to care for her!"

"That may as be," Mrs. Langston conceded, for privately she shared Miss Pringle's opinion of the duke's appalling neglect of the lonely little girl, "but as I have already explained, one cannot force another person to do that which he has no intention of doing. By persisting in this folly you have endangered not only your position at this school, but the rest of us as well. Or have you forgotten His Grace's threat to bring action against us if you contacted him again?"

Nia's cheeks pinked with color as she recalled the cold missive from the duke. She'd written him out of desperation, hinting rather broadly that his reputation could suffer if it became known that he'd abandoned the only child of his late brother to what was in reality an orphanage.

The duke's response had been a blunt threat that if she even attempted to go to the newspapers, he would see the school brought up on charges of blackmail. The entire fiasco brought the founder of the academy, Miss Arabelle Portham, to the school, and she had made Nia promise not to write His Grace again. At the time Nia had truly meant to keep her vow, but then last week Amanda had come to her crying because the other children had been teasing her.

"But they say if he was really and truly my uncle he would at least visit me!" the girl had sobbed, her violet eyes bright with tears as she gazed up at Nia. "Why won't he come, Miss Pringle? Doesn't he like me?"

The memory of the painful scene made Nia's throat tighten even now, and she cleared it uncomfortably. "I am well aware of his lordship's blustering threats," she said crossly, "but it was Amanda's desire to write her uncle and invite him to visit her for

her birthday. I know I probably should have put her
off with some foolish story, but I thought perhaps if
he heard from Amanda directly he would change his
mind."

"And I take it he did not?"

"The only answer came from his solicitor." Nia removed the crumpled letter from the pocket of her
apron and handed it to the older woman. "I haven't
had the heart to show it to her."

Mrs. Langston smoothed out the sheet of paper,
her eyes widening in horror at what she read. "Oh,
my heavens, he ... he is saying ,she is a ... a ..."

"A bastard." Nia said the hateful word stonily, her
full lips tightening with fury. "He states quite clearly
that there is some legal question regarding her parents' marriage, and until such time as the matter can
be resolved, she cannot be considered a legitimate
member of His Grace's family. He even hints that she
is breaking some obscure law by using the Perryvale
name."

"What are you going to do?" Mrs. Langston asked,
eyeing Nia with concern. Ordinarily she would have
sent for Miss Portham, but the lovely heiress had recently married the earl of Colford and was rusticat-
ing at her husband's country estate.

"I don't know." The admission all but choked Nia.
"But I do know I can't let Amanda know. It would
shatter her, and God knows the poor child has suffered enough."

"But won't she wonder when there is no reply?"

"I could tell her His Grace is out of town," Nia
suggested, wincing at the thought of lying to the girl
she adored as if she were her own child. "She'll be
disappointed, of course, but it's far kinder than telling her the truth."

"Yes, that is so, but ..."

"But what?" Nia pressed when her voice trailed
off.

"But I cannot help wondering if perhaps it would
be best if you told her the truth ... or at least most

of the truth," Mrs. Langston amended, shuddering at the memory of the solicitor's cruel words. "By encouraging her to hope for some future reconciliation with the duke, you are only setting her up for further heartache."

Nia paled at that. "I am?"

"Yes, you most certainly are," Mrs. Langston said firmly, grateful to see she had finally managed to penetrate Nia's unshakable resolve. "Amanda is young yet, and with patience and love she will forget her uncle. You can see how attached she has become to you, and with time she will accept her lot. Now admit it," she added, lifting a warning finger when Nia would have protested, "she scarce spoke of her uncle until you began prattling on about his duty toward her. Isn't that so?"

Nia's expression grew bleak at the headmistress's words. She recalled the many times she had mentioned His Grace in the girl's presence, and Amanda's curious questions. She'd never meant to hurt her, but the duke's irresponsible behavior had made her so angry . . .

"You're right," she admitted quietly, her shoulders slumping in defeat. "Amanda barely knew of His Grace's existence."

"Then you can see the folly of encouraging her to hope for a reconciliation?" Mrs. Langston asked, pressing home her advantage despite the look of misery on Nia's face. "You won't allow her to write His Grace again?"

"I won't."

"And you won't write him yourself or attempt to force your way into his home?" Mrs. Langston added, recalling an earlier incident. "You give me your word?"

Nia considered for a long while before slowly nodding. "I won't write His Grace or attempt to gain entry to his home," she intoned solemnly. "And I promise I shall never speak his name to Amanda without your permission."

"Then you may go," Mrs. Langston said, relief washing through her at the easy victory. "And if you will pardon my saying so, I trust this has taught you a lesson. No good ever comes from interfering in people's lives; I hope you will remember that."

After leaving Mrs. Langston's study, Nia stopped to check on her students before slipping up to her room for a moment of quiet reflection. The other teachers all shared quarters, but because one of the instructors had left to take another position, Nia had the small room tucked beneath the eaves all to herself. It was a situation she had never appreciated more than at this moment. Drat and bother, she brooded, staring out her casement window with a scowl, what the devil was she going to do now?

The pledge Mrs. Langston had wrenched from her placed her in the awkward position of being unable to keep her word to Amanda that her uncle would visit her for her birthday. She knew it had been foolish of her to make such a promise, but she'd been unable to bear the tears shimmering in the little girl's eyes.

Nia's father had been a physician in the army, and she'd been raised to believe that duty was sacred above all things. It was the duke's duty to care for his niece, and she was certain he could be compelled to do the right thing if only she could convince him. But how could she convince him of anything when she couldn't so much as write him a letter?

It was a pity she wasn't a member of the *ton*, she thought, idly tracing a pattern in the fog lacing her window. Then at least she might be able to corner him at a soiree and argue him into submission. Or she could threaten a scene; men hated scenes, she knew, and surely he would promise anything to be spared a fit of the vapors. She'd seen several officers' wives employ such tactics, and she reasoned if they could keep battle-hardened soldiers in line, they should prove equally as effective with a spoiled and pampered lord. But the fact remained she was *not* a member of the *ton*, and if she wished to contact His Grace, she would have to think of something else.

She could infiltrate his household disguised as a serving maid, she supposed, but that would mean breaking her word to Mrs. Langston. Or she could hang about his doorstep hoping for a chance to confront him as he climbed in his carriage, but that was dubious at best and she would have the watch to worry about as well. Still, there had to be something she could do, she thought, and then it came to her.

There was another sort of female who might have contact with a duke; one whose presence, while it might raise a few eyebrows, would never be questioned. She's seen several of these sad creatures in her travels with her father, and their bold and to her mind desperate actions were more or less ignored. Men would be men, after all, and who would think to stop a doxy from climbing into a man's carriage for an assignation? It was the perfect solution.

She froze as the thought took hold. It was outrageous, her logical mind argued. Unthinkable. She would lose her position at the school and her reputation would be forever tarnished, were she caught. She didn't even know if His Grace was the sort of man who went to such women. And yet ... She bit her lip. And yet, what choice did she have?

Desperate times called for desperate measures; she'd heard the general in command of her father's regiment say that. Of course he had been talking of war, but Amanda's happiness was every bit as important to her as the outcome of any battle. If the men who fought and died for England had been willing to sacrifice all, could she do any less for Amanda? The answer, of course, was no, and with that in mind Nia turned from the window, her small chin set in resolve.

"Hell and damnation, Royston, what the devil do you mean I've had enough?" Wyatt Perryvale, the duke of Tilton, demanded with an outraged roar, his midnight-dark eyes narrowing as he glared at the elegant man standing before him. "Who do you think you are? My nursemaid?"

"Your friend, your very good friend as a matter of fact, and I'm not about to let you make a fool of yourself with half the *ton* looking on." Ambrose Royston replied calmly, his blue eyes cool as he met the duke's furious gaze. "I know you miss Christopher, Wyatt, but you'll not find him in the bottom of a brandy bottle however hard you may try."

The mention of his younger brother sent a fresh shaft of pain stabbing through Wyatt. It had been over a year since he'd received news of his brother's death at the futile and tragic battle for New Orleans, and yet the pain was as fresh and raw as if it was yesterday. He glanced away from Royston, struggling against the grief that was his constant companion.

"I don't know what you're talking about," he denied thickly, his hand clenching his glass. "My wanting a drink has naught to do with Christopher. I merely felt like having a bit of fun. And for your information, sir, I've had but four glasses!" This last was added with a defiant scowl.

"Which is two more than is your habit," Ambrose answered, his manner as composed as ever. He and Wyatt had known each other since their days at Eton, and he knew his friend almost as well as he knew himself. He'd spent the last year watching Wyatt's silent anguish, but tonight was the last straw. Even if he had to break a table over the duke's hard head, he would not allow him to make a public spectacle of himself.

"Then perhaps 'tis time I was acquiring new habits," Wyatt replied with a sneer, lifting his glass in a mocking salute. "All true Perryvales are known for their prodigious thirsts, Royston. Didn't you know that?"

"Wyatt . . ."

Wyatt muttered another oath, annoyed by his friend's persistence. He knew he was behaving like a foolish schoolboy, but he couldn't bring himself to care. He didn't even like the taste of brandy, but tonight he'd felt the need to lose himself in the sweet mists of oblivion. Unfortunately the fiery liquor wasn't providing him with the escape he so desperately craved, and he could see no sense in continuing the useless endeavor. Perhaps a different sort of oblivion was what he needed, he decided, his dark eyes growing speculative.

"Very well, Royston," he said, setting his glass on a table with exaggerated care, "perhaps you are right. Getting bosky in such august company would never do. If you will excuse me, I believe I shall be taking myself off."

"Where are you going?" Ambrose demanded, deciding he didn't care for the wild glitter in Wyatt's eyes.

"Why, to find a different sort of company, of course," Wyatt drawled, giving him a wolfish smile. "And if you are thinking of coming with me, I shouldn't bother. Three in a bed is one too many, to my way of thinking."

After making his excuses to his hostess, Wyatt retrieved his hat and cloak from the butler and went out into the cool, damp night. There was a long line of carriages waiting in front of the Pettingtons' elegant townhouse, and it took him several minutes to find his own coach. The delay hardly improved his already black temper, and his jaw was clenched with displeasure as he climbed into his conveyance.

"You might at least have made yourself known," he grumbled to the footman holding his door. "It would have been damned embarrassing if I'd entered the wrong carriage!"

"More embarrassin' to some than to others, I reckon," the footman replied with a cheekiness that would have startled Wyatt had he been in a frame of mind to notice. With the exception of his valet and housekeeper, his staff usually treated him with almost painful formality.

"Just see it doesn't happen again," Wyatt retorted, still scowling as he settled onto the plush seat. "Tell Coachman to take me to Cleveland Street. He knows the address."

"Right you are, Yer Grace!" The footman was smirking as he gave a mocking bow. "You'll be wantin' us to go the long route, I takes it?"

"Have him take whatever route he pleases," Wyatt snapped impatiently, the servant's odd behavior finally registering. "Just get me there."

The footman bowed again, slamming the door and leaping onto the top of the highly sprung carriage with a chuckle. The whip cracked and the carriage started with a lurch that sent Wyatt flying forward. He managed to catch himself and sat back in his seat with a muttered oath. That was when he saw the woman.

"What the devil . . . Who are you?" he demanded incredulously. "How did you get into my carriage?"

"Your footman let me in," the woman replied in a voice that was surprisingly cultured. "I wish to speak with you."

"Well, he can just let you out again," Wyatt snapped, ignoring the last part of her statement. "I don't pick up doxies off the street. Be off with you!"

Nia stiffened at the crude words. "I am no doxy, sir," she denied hotly, scowling as she struggled to bring his blurry image into focus. She'd left off her spectacles to convince the wary coachman she was a lightskirt, and she could scarce see a thing in the darkened coach. The first chance she got she'd slip them on again, and then she'd do something about her scandalous décolletage. No wonder prostitutes lived so short a life, she thought, giving the bodice of her gown a discreet tug. The poor creatures doubtlessly succumbed to pneumonia!

The action drew Wyatt's eyes, and he studied the tempting display of creamy flesh with predatory interest. Why should he trouble his latest mistress with his lusts when he had a willing and nubile female already at his disposal, he thought, brandy and his own black mood destroying his usual reserve. He reached out and grabbed the woman's waist, pulling her onto his lap with a powerful tug.

"Sir!" Nia gave a startled cry, her hands flying up to push ineffectively at his shoulders. "Release me at once!"

The tones of starchy outrage in her voice amused Wyatt. "Afraid I shan't pay the piper?" he teased, bending his head to inhale her delicate fragrance. Unlike most prostitutes, who doused themselves in heavy scent, she smelled delightfully of powder and roses. "Don't worry, sweet," he added with a chuckle, brushing a soft kiss against her slender neck. "I am a generous man. You may ask any of my mistresses. They'll tell you I pay cheerfully for services rendered."

Nia wasn't so green that she failed to take his meaning. How could she not, she wondered desperately, when she could feel the hardness of his body beneath her thighs? For the first time since approaching his coach the dangers of this insane masquerade became real, and she realized the full extent of what she was risking. She began struggling in earnest, and her frantic movements made the bodice of her gown slip even lower, exposing the curve of her breasts to her captor's touch.

Wyatt was quick to take advantage of what was offered, his mouth sliding lower to taste the sweetness of her soft flesh. She felt incredible in his arms, and he was eager for more. His hand slid up her body to cup her breast, and he moved his thumb teasingly against the nipple until he felt it bead in response. Another movement of his hand bared her breast completely, and he lowered his head to pull the turgid peak between his lips.

The feel of his mouth closing over her sent alarm shooting through Nia. Alarm and a burning excitement that horrified her almost as much as what he was doing to her. For a moment her mind went blank with panic, and then the instructions her father had given her flashed into her mind. She forced herself to relax, and when he began lowering her to the bench, she pretended to acquiesce. He moved to cover her completely, and the moment he was vulnerable, she brought her knee up with all her might.

Pain exploded through Wyatt, and for a moment he literally saw stars. With his body bending in agony he had no choice but to release the woman, and she scrambled away from him to the opposite bench. He managed to grab a handful of her voluminous cape, but when he raised his head he found himself looking down the barrel of a pistol.

"This was my father's," Nia warned breathlessly, her chest rising and falling as she fought to control the shivers racking her. "I learned to shoot when I was a child, but even if I wasn't a crack shot I could hardly miss at this distance."

The lingering effects of passion and the brandy he had ill-advisedly consumed vanished under a wave of cold fury. "If this is a robbery, young woman, you have sadly underestimated your victim," he said between clenched teeth, taking care not to make any sudden moves as he slowly drew back. "I suggest you give it up before you end up as Tyburn fruit."

"Dangling from a gibbet, you mean?" Nia gave a shrug, although inside she was quaking with fright. "I am hoping it won't be necessary to shoot you, but one never knows. As for my lifting your purse, I am no more a thief than I am a doxy."

Since she had just used a weapon to defend whatever virtue she possessed, Wyatt decided to concede her the point. "Then what are you?" he demanded, furious at being put in so ridiculous a position. His eyes were adjusting to the darkness, and in the poor light he could see details of her appearance he had been too distracted to notice earlier. Despite the fact that her gown was half off her shoulders and her brown hair was curling widly about her face, there was something in the set of her mouth and the proud

tilt of her small chin that made him wonder if he had
mistaken her character.

"I am a schoolmistress."

"What?" Her cool answer had Wyatt shaking his
head in disbelief. He couldn't have heard aright.

Nia hesitated, and then decided she had nothing to
lose by telling the truth. "Your Grace," she began at
last, "I give you my word that I mean you no harm.
All I want from you is but a moment of your time.
Do you promise you will listen?"

The novelty of having a woman assure him his
person was in no danger, especially after all that had
passed between them, struck Wyatt as bordering on
the farcical, and for a moment he was tempted to
test the veracity of her statement. Then he remembered the conclusion to their passionate interlude,
and his brows met in an angry scowl.

"Very well, madam," he said, inclining his head
mockingly, "say whatever it is you have come to say.
As for having my undivided attention, you had that
the moment you aimed that pistol at my heart."

"It's not as if I wanted to bring the wretched thing
with me," Nia grumbled as she cautiously lowered
the gun. "But I thought it might be the prudent
thing. 'The readiness is all,' you know."

The literary reference had Wyatt arching his eyebrows in amusement. "*Hamlet*, madam? Hardly a reassuring quote, considering the gentleman was
contemplating murder, but I take your meaning. You
felt it best to be prepared against any eventuality. A
wise decision for anyone entering a life of crime."

"I am not a criminal!" Nia shouted, deciding she'd
had quite enough of the duke's sardonic accusations.

Her hot denial brought a wry gleam to Wyatt's
dark eyes. "Yes, I'd forgotten that," he drawled in a
voice meant to give offense. "You're a schoolmistress,
aren't you? Tell me, madam, just who is it you instruct? Highwaymen?"

There was a hiss of air as Nia drew in her breath.
Another silence ensued before she said, "I teach or-

phans, Your Grace. Specifically orphans of soldiers who have fallen in gallant defense of their country, and kindly stop calling me 'madam' in that odious manner. My name is Miss Pringle."

"My apologies if my manners offend you, Miss Pringle," Wyatt returned, amused by her indignant tones. "But this is the first time I have ever been held at gunpoint, and I am afraid I am not up to all the niceties. Where is it you teach?"

"The Portham Academy, of course," Nia answered, feeling another stir of unease. "Don't you recognize my name?"

"I am afraid not." For some odd reason he felt compelled to apologize. "Although I admit the Portham Academy sounds vaguely familiar." He gave the matter some thought before adding, "It was started by the countess of Colford, was it not?"

"Ha! As if you didn't know!" Nia declared, furious he could keep feigning innocence even now.

His amusement vanished at the accusation in her voice. It was one thing to humor a woman holding a gun on him, but quite another to allow her to question his honor. He straightened in his seat, his eyes narrowing as he studied her shadowy figure. "I warn you, *Miss Pringle*," he began, his tone dangerously soft, "my patience is wearing thin. Unless you are truly prepared to use that weapon in your hands, I suggest you not test it any further. What is it you want with me?"

"What I want from you, Your Grace," Nia replied, determined to match his cool control, "is that you do your duty. Nothing more, and nothing less."

"What the devil is that supposed to mean?" he demanded, struggling to decipher the cryptic words. "What duty have I failed to perform?"

"Your duty to Amanda, naturally!" Nia snapped, deciding she'd had enough of his silly games. He could pretend all he liked, but he knew precisely what she was talking about. She'd seen the letter bearing his crest arrive at the school, so he could hardly claim to be an innocent in any of this. "Why else would I have gone to the bother of seeking you out like this?" she continued in an exasperated tone, indicating her mussed clothing with an impatient wave of her hand. "Do you honestly believe I'd have gone to such lengths had you left me any other choice?"

"Who the devil is Amanda?" Wyatt snapped, beginning to fear a madwoman was holding him captive.

"You know very well who Amanda is!" Nia retorted, hating that he could be so single-mindedly selfish. "And what is more, you can tell that hateful solicitor of yours that he needn't waste his ink penning any more threats. Amanda is most assuredly your niece, and what is more, I have all the evidence it will take to prove the matter in court! Unless you want the greatest scandal of the season, my lord, you will cease shirking your duty and admit to the truth. Amanda Perryvale is the daughter of your late brother, and you know it!"

Chapter 2

There was a charged silence in the carriage, and in the faint light filtering through the glass Nia could see the shock on the duke's face. *"What?"* he gasped, his tone harsh.

For the first time since sneaking from the academy, Nia knew a moment of indecision. Slipping into His Grace's coach posing as a doxy hired by an undisclosed "friend" had been an inspiration, and when she'd succeeded, she'd thought the most difficult part of the night was behind her. While waiting for the duke's return she passed the time marshalling her arguments, and she was confident of her ability to counter any opposition he might offer. The one thing she hadn't planned on was that he would deny any knowledge of either her or Amanda.

"I don't know what you're talking about," he said furiously. "Christopher is dead. He couldn't possibly have a child!"

"I beg to differ with you, Your Grace," she said, gentling her tone as she sensed the confusion behind the fury. "But Amanda is indeed the issue of your brother's marriage to a Miss Miriam Jensen. I have her birth records and a copy of their marriage lines, if you'd care to see them."

"There is no need for that," Wyatt said slowly, struggling to comprehend what he was hearing. "I'm well aware of Christopher's marriage to Miriam. I did my best to talk him out of it at the time, but he wouldn't listen."

"Yes, I'd heard there was some opposition to the

16

match," Nia said coolly, some of the pity she'd been feeling fading at his distracted words. "But I hardly think that any reason to label an innocent child a bastard."

Wyatt stiffened, his hands clenching into fists. "I have never labeled any child a bastard, Miss Pringle, nor am I likely to do so, especially if there is even the slightest possibility that child could be my brother's daughter."

The menace in his voice made Nia draw back into the shadows. "Very well, Your Grace," she said, wondering at his vehemence. This wasn't at all the reaction she had expected, and she wondered if perhaps she'd misread the duke and the situation.

"Good." He gave a curt nod. "As for my opposition to the match, that had nothing to do with Miriam. I simply thought Christopher too young to be thinking of marriage. He was just twenty-one, you know."

"I know," Nia answered softly, the pain in his voice making her catch her lip between her teeth. Whatever the man's faults, it was obvious he had loved his brother, which made his neglect of Amanda all the more mysterious. Given that affection, she would have thought he'd have moved heaven and earth to provide for his niece.

Wyatt leaned back in the seat, fighting for a composure he was far from feeling. A niece, he thought dazedly. Christopher had left a child behind. The notion was almost overwhelming, but even as joy welled up he fought it down with hard practicality. Until he had the whole truth, he would refrain from committing himself. His eyes narrowed on the woman sitting opposite him. Clearly the first thing he must do would be to learn all he could about her, then he would decide what to do about his alleged "niece."

"May I ask you a question, Miss Pringle?" he queried, idly stretching his long legs out in front of him.

"What is it?" Nia answered warily, not caring for the lazy note in his deep voice.

"I surmise you didn't light the lantern so as to keep your presence a secret, but is it necessary to keep us in shadows?"

Nia was annoyed to feel her cheeks warming with color. "I am afraid I haven't any flint with me, Your Grace," she muttered. "I hadn't thought it would be necessary."

Wyatt's lips quirked at the waspish words. "I will see what I can do," he said, rapping on the roof of the coach to draw his driver's attention. A few minutes later and they were on their way again, the carriage lantern his father had installed as a novelty blazing brightly.

In the flickering golden light Wyatt could clearly see his mysterious visitor's face, and what he saw both amused and intrigued him. Her dark hair was rioting about her small face, and a pair of bright hazel eyes sparkled behind the gold-rimmed spectacles she had just slipped on her face. Her nose was small and somewhat pointed, as was her chin, hinting at the aggressive and determined nature he'd already encountered. High cheekbones and a ripe, full mouth softened the sharp angles of her face, giving her an almost fey beauty. She was, he decided calmly, the perfect caricature of a schoolmistress, and he didn't trust her so much as an inch.

Nia burned under his sharp-eyed scrutiny, her resentment simmering along with her temper. "Well?" she demanded tartly when he seemed satisfied. "Do I pass muster?"

"You'll do," he responded with an indifference that set her teeth on edge. "You spoke of proof earlier. May I see it?"

It took Nia a few seconds to take his meaning. "I thought you said you knew of your brother's marriage," she said, frowning in suspicion.

"I do, but you mentioned a birth record. Because

Miriam and Christopher wed, it doesn't necessarily follow there was a child."

Nia had to grant him that, and dug out the papers she had secretly removed from Mrs. Langston's study earlier that day. "She was born in Bournemouth, as you can see," she said, handing him the papers. "She'll be seven in a little over two months."

Seven, he thought bleakly, studying the papers he had been handed. He'd been an uncle all this time and Christopher had never even written him. He'd known the rift that had parted them was deep, but he'd never thought it ran so deep as this. A fresh wave a pain washed over him as he thought of how much his brother must have hated him.

"I—I have a portrait of her," Nia said hesitantly, seeing the pain darken his eyes. "I painted it myself so it's not very good, but I like to think it's a fair resemblance. Would you like to see it?"

"Please."

Nia dug the miniature out of her reticule, thanking the impulse that had made her bring it with her. At the time she'd thought it might serve to further prove Amanda's identity, but after seeing His Grace she wasn't so certain. She handed it to him, and as he gazed down at the portrait she took the opportunity to study him.

As she'd noted when he'd climbed into the carriage, he was quite tall, with the broad, muscular shoulders of the natural athlete. His tanned features were too harsh to be termed handsome, but it was his hair and eyes, both the color of polished ebony, which most fascinated her. She'd been expecting an older, more masculine version of Amanda, with her wheat-blond hair and violet-blue eyes, and the sight of a man who looked more like a dashing Corsair than an English lord left her somewhat disconcerted. Surely, she thought uneasily, there would be *some* resemblance between an uncle and his niece.

Wyatt stared at the miniature in his hand, a painful lump forming in his throat. My God, he thought, his hand shaking as he brushed his fingers across the child's sweetly smiling face. She was the very image of Christopher, of generations of Perryvales, and to think that until this moment he hadn't even known of her existence. He raised his eyes to find Miss Pringle watching him, a wary expression on her face.

"You said she is a pupil at your academy," he said, his voice sounding strained even to his own ears. "I take it then that Miriam has also died?"

"In a carriage accident," Nia replied carefully. "She had been living with her sister, but the family was unable to continue providing for Amanda, and so she was brought to us."

The thought of the little girl being deposited at an orphanage like an unwanted cat made his lips tighten in displeasure. "And it never occurred to them to notify *me?*" he demanded, his dark eyes flashing. "Whatever the differences between Christopher and me, she is my niece as well."

Nia could only gape at him. "I daresay it did occur to the Jensens to notify you," she retorted, "and doubtlessly they met with the same response I did— haughty indifference and threats of legal action if they persisted in their claims. You are hardly the injured party here, my lord."

"But this is the first I have heard of her!" Wyatt exclaimed, angered by her cutting words. "I have been traveling a great deal since coming into the title. In fact, I was out of the country when word of Christopher's death reached me. I would never have allowed my own niece to languish in an orphanage had I known of her plight. Good God, woman, what sort of man do you take me for?"

"But I—"

"Never mind," Wyatt interrupted with an impatient wave of his hand. "None of that matters now. The important thing at the moment is Amanda."

Although this was a sentiment Nia could readily understand, she wasn't certain she trusted his abrupt change of heart. "What about Amanda?" she asked warily.

"I want you to take me to her," he answered, meeting her suspicious scowl with equanimity. "I am taking her home."

Nia stared at the duke in disbelief. "You wish to take Amanda home?" she echoed, her eyes wide. "*To-night?*"

"Certainly tonight," Wyatt replied, impatient to meet his niece now that he knew of her. After two years of desolate loneliness, he had a family. The thought filled him with joy.

"But, Your Grace, it is after midnight!" Nia protested, feeling rather like a novice rider strapped to a runaway stallion. "Amanda is already in bed, and I hardly feel yanking her from a sound sleep and thrusting her into a stranger's care will prove in the least beneficial to her."

Wyatt frowned at her words. "I hadn't thought of that," he admitted reluctantly. "You're right, it might upset her."

"And you'll need to make arrangements with your household," Nia continued, warming to her theme. "A child isn't a piece of furniture, you know. You can't simply pick her up and cart her home without proper preparations. You will need to hire a maid, and a governess, and—"

"You've made your point, Miss Pringle," he said, coming to an abrupt decision. "Very well, I shall come for her tomorrow morning, then. Kindly have her ready by ten o'clock."

Nia paused, not certain what to say. This was the very thing she'd worked for all these months, but now that the moment was finally here she was aware of an odd urge to cry. She tried telling herself it was all for the best, but that didn't help the burning ache in her throat.

"Ten o'clock, Your Grace," she said, blinking to hold back the tears. "If you will please tell your driver to let me out here, I will be on my way."

Wyatt tore his mind off thoughts of his niece long enough to send her a puzzled look. "Let you out?" he echoed with a frown. "Don't be absurd, Miss Pringle. These streets aren't the safest even in the daylight. I will see you home."

The charge of absurdity brought a martial gleam to Nia's eyes. "I am hardly a society miss who must be cosseted and comforted, Lord Tilton," she said coolly, her chin coming up with pride. "My father was an army physician, and I spent my entire life following the drum. London's teeming streets hold no dangers for me that I cannot handle."

Her argumentative tone brought a speculative gleam to Wyatt's dark eyes. "Ah, yes," he drawled, his gaze straying to the gun she was still holding. "I'd forgotten about the pistol. Armed to the teeth, are you?"

Nia decided now was not the time to tell him the gun was not loaded. "As a matter of fact, yes."

"Mmm," he answered with lazy indifference, and then in a move so fast she could not see it, he leaned forward and snatched the weapon from her hands.

"My lord!" she gasped indignantly, making a desperate grab for the pistol.

He easily held it out of her reach, examining it with obvious expertise. "Just as I thought," he replied, tucking the pistol into the pocket of his greatcoat. "I don't know if I should commend you for your bravery or shake you within an inch of your life, madam. Your audacity appears to know no bounds."

"Well, what else was I to do?" Nia defended her actions with a toss of her head. "I'd done everything I could to get your notice, and I was at my wit's end. The pistol was merely to guarantee you would hear me out. I certainly had no desire to actually shoot you."

"A circumstance for which I am most grateful," Wyatt said, trying not to smile. "Again, Miss Pringle, your audacity appears boundless. Are all the instructors at the academy so dedicated?"

She gave a guilty start, her eyes dropping to her hands. Even though he seemed eager to accept Amanda, there was still a small chance he was furious with her. Furious enough, perhaps, to retaliate against the school. She glanced up, trying to read his expression.

"The staff is devoted to our students," she replied carefully, "but I am the only one who climbed into your coach. If . . . if you are displeased, I would prefer that you retaliate against me rather than the others. They had nothing to do with this."

Her willingness to accept responsibility for her ill-advised actions impressed Wyatt. "Somehow, Miss Pringle, that doesn't surprise me in the least," he said, inclining his head with a smile. "If you will be so good as to give me the direction of the academy, I can inform John Coachman. Unless it is your intention that we continue driving in circles as we've been doing for the past half hour?"

Nia shot him a resentful look, hating him for his sarcasm. The notion of defying him was sweetly tempting, and for a moment she almost gave in to the impulse. But in the end common sense prevailed, and she grudgingly provided him with the address. Other than raising a dark eyebrow, he gave no response, and they were soon making their way from the elegance of Mayfair to St. John's Wood, where the academy was located.

To her relief he seemed disinclined to make idle conversation, and she turned her head toward the window, her expression thoughtful as she gazed out at the darkened streets. Now that the matter of Amanda had been settled, she could turn her attention to other concerns, such as how she was going to explain these events to Mrs. Langston. Something told her the headmistress would be less than pleased with her actions.

Another thing which puzzled her was the duke's insistence he was unaware of Amanda. At first she'd suspected him of prevaricating, but his expression when he'd seen the portrait had disabused her of that notion. He'd looked as if he'd just taken a bullet in the chest, and the pain and stunned disbelief on his face had convinced her that he was innocent. Yet, why had the knowledge been kept from him? What could his staff possibly hope to gain by telling him nothing of her own visits and letters? It made no earthly sense.

Across from her Wyatt was asking himself the same questions. He'd been in London less than a sennight, but that didn't explain his staff's neglect in informing him of Miss Pringle's attempts to contact him. His butler's actions were a little less suspect, as a good major domo seldom bothered his master with every caller who appeared on his doorstep. He was even willing to concede his secretary might have been justified in keeping Miss Pringle's letters from him, especially if he thought she was attempting to dun him for money. But that didn't explain his solicitor's actions.

According to Miss Pringle she'd contacted Mr. Elliott, and he'd responded by threatening her with legal action. That being the case, why hadn't he been informed? He was willing to grant his solicitor a certain degree of leniency, but he could not approve of him taking such steps without his permission. First thing tomorrow he would call upon the man and learn the truth. And his explanation had best be damned good.

They continued the journey in silence, each lost in his own dark thoughts. They reached their destination some time later, and Wyatt surveyed the brick building with interest.

"The household appears to be abed," he said, his eyes narrowing as he gazed up at the darkened windows. "Shall we wait until you manage to rouse someone?"

Nia was annoyed to find she was flushing with

shame. "That won't be necessary, Your Grace," she replied, ducking her head as she dug a key from the depths of her pocket. "I have a key to the servant's door."

"How provident," Wyatt drawled, wondering if the administrator was aware of that particular fact. "I will have the footman escort you to the door. It is doubtlessly quite dark in the rear of the house."

Nia opened her lips to refuse, but a glance at his face changed her mind. "Very well, Your Grace," she said, telling herself she wasn't giving in so much as humoring him. "I shall see you tomorrow, then."

Wyatt thought about tomorrow and the niece he would meet for the first time. A niece he'd never have met had it not been for the woman climbing out of his carriage. "Miss Pringle?"

"Yes, Your Grace?" She sent him a wary glance.

"Thank you for telling me about Amanda," he said quietly, his eyes meeting hers. "I am in your debt."

The sincerity in his deep vice made Nia pause. "You are welcome, my lord," she replied, inclining her head politely. "Good night to you."

The footman not only saw her to the rear door, but also waited until she was safely inside. Shaking her head at the duke's unexpected gallantry, she quietly made her way up the back stairs to the instructor's quarters. She thought of peeking in on Amanda, but since the little girl shared a room with a dozen other girls, she thought it best to wait until tomorrow. Although what she would say to her, Nia did not know.

In her room Nia removed the black cloak and hung it carefully in her wardrobe. She'd borrowed it from one of the other instructors, and with luck she'd return it before the woman discovered it was missing. Normally she'd never have resorted to thievery, but there hadn't been time to ask permission. Her eyes twinkled as she imagined Miss Smythe's reaction were she to learn her cloak—a gift from her father, the rector of Asheford—had been used to fool a footman into thinking its wearer was a common prostitute. Doubtlessly she would swoon with horror and order the thing burned, Nia decided, sliding between her cold sheets with a chuckle.

Despite the excitement of the evening, Nia fell into a deep sleep, rising refreshed and eager to face the morning. After careful consideration she decided to confront Mrs. Langston before talking to Amanda; providing the headmistress didn't order her tossed from the house, she added, grimacing as she tucked her hair beneath her starched cap.

Once downstairs, she hurried to the front of the house where Mrs. Langston's study was located. The door was shut, and Nia drew a deep breath for courage before knocking.

"Come in."

Nia opened the door, a respectful smile pinned to her lips as she stepped inside. "Good morning, ma'am," she said, aware of how hard her heart was pounding in her chest. "I was wondering if I might have a word with you."

"Why, certainly, my dear," Mrs. Langston replied, sending her a surprisingly warm smile. "As a matter of fact, I was just about to send for you. It was all a mistake, you see."

"A mistake?" Nia repeated, frowning as she lowered herself onto the chair set before the desk.

Mrs. Langston gave a vigorous nod. "A terrible mistake, and he was as apologetic as could be. It seems we have both been rather harsh in our assessments, which only proves that the Holy Scriptures are right. 'Judge not, that ye be not judged'."

"I see," Nia repeated faintly, wondering what the other woman was talking about. There were times she feared the headmistress's reasoning skills were not all they should be.

"You could have knocked me over with a feather when the maid came and told me he was here. Why, it wasn't even eight o'clock, and everyone knows quality sleeps until noon! I thought it was a joke at first, but when he showed me his card I knew he was telling me the truth. And there was something so . . . commanding in his aspect, so regal. Not that he was in the least impolite, mind. Indeed he could not have been more charming. He—"

"Mrs. Langston, what on earth are you talking about?" Nia demanded, a terrible suspicion forming in her mind. "Who could not have been more charming?"

"Why, His Grace, of course," Mrs. Langston replied, giving her a confused look. "The duke of Tilton. He called upon me first thing this morning."

"*What?*"

"He's just returned from the country," the headmistress rushed on eagerly. "Apparently his household staff took it upon themselves to write those dreadful letters, and I for one would not wish to be in *their* shoes, he was that furious. But all's well that ends well, for he cannot wait to meet Amanda. He shall be back for her at ten o'clock. Is that not wonderful?"

Nia sifted through the jumble of words, swiftly reaching the only conclusion that mattered—His Grace hadn't betrayed her. When Mrs. Langston began mentioning his visit, her first thought had been that he'd come to demand she be dismissed. Apparently she had misjudged the man . . . again.

"Wonderful," she echoed, slumping back against the chair. And it *was* wonderful, she told herself sternly. In a few hours Amanda would have a real home, with an uncle who seemed determined to do his best for her. The teacher in her rejoiced at her pupil's good fortune, but the woman in her was already missing a special little girl.

"I was hoping you would inform Amanda of her uncle's intentions," Mrs. Langston continued in her brisk manner, relieved at how satisfactorily things had turned out. "She is certain to be anxious, and I'm sure speaking with you will help ease her fears. The two of you are quite close, aren't you?"

"Yes, quite close."

"Good, good, I knew I could rely on you." Mrs. Langston's mind had already turned to other matters. The duke had promised a sizeable donation, and she was plotting how best to spend the unexpected largesse. Perhaps she'd have the academy supplied with the new gaslight everyone was talking about, she mused. Candles were becoming so expensive . . .

Sensing her headmistress's distraction, Nia rose and slipped quietly from the room. It was scarce past eight in the morning, so she knew Amanda would be in the great hall taking breakfast with the other children. A sad smile touched her lips as she thought of how significantly the girl's life was about to change. She doubted Amanda would be dining on porridge and watery tea in His Grace's townhouse.

As she suspected, she found Amanda greedily devouring her second bowl of hot cereal and engaging in a heated argument. "And what is this all about?" Nia asked, her voice stern as she bent beside Amanda's chair. "You know you're not permitted to call another pupil an old silly."

"Well, he is," Amanda grumbled, her violet eyes narrowing as she glared at the boy sitting across from her. "He said Napoleon was French. *Everyone* knows he is a Corsetcan."

"Corsican," Nia corrected, her hand trembling as she brushed a blond curl from Amanda's flushed cheek. "But as he was also emperor of France, I would say Timothy's argument is not without validity. You will apologize, young lady, and then you will come with me. There is something I wish to discuss with you."

Amanda hesitated, torn between the injustice of having to apologize and eagerness for a few minutes privacy with her most favorite person in the world. In the end her desire to be alone with Miss Pringle won, and she heaved a noisy sigh. "Oh, very well," she said, her bottom lip thrusting forward in a mutinous pout. "I am sorry for calling Timothy an old silly ... even if he is one," she added, shooting her nemesis a defiant scowl.

The arrogant pride on her face put Nia in mind of her uncle. Apparently the two were more alike than appearances would indicate, she thought, hiding a smile as she pulled out Amanda's chair. "That is better," she said, helping her down. "Although we might have done without the last part of your apology."

She led the little girl into the parlor set aside for the staff's private use. After making sure the door was closed behind them, she turned to face Amanda, her heart pounding in her chest. Until now she had no idea that doing one's duty could be so painful, and she could feel tears burning in her eyes. The thought of never seeing Amanda again was agony, and for a brief moment her resolution wavered. She thrust the traitorous weakness aside and knelt beside the little girl who was staring up at her with wide, apprehensive eyes.

"I have something to tell you, sweetest," she said quietly, slipping her arms about Amanda and drawing her close. "It is about your uncle. You see, something wonderful has happened ..."

While Nia was breaking the news to Amanda, Wyatt was sitting in his solicitor's office, his face rigid with control as he confronted the other man. "Well, Mr. Elliott?" he demanded, his voice dangerously soft. "I trust you have some explanation for keeping my niece's existence from me?"

Duncan Elliott seemed unperturbed by his employer's cold displeasure. If anything, he appeared amused, his manner condescending as he removed his spectacles and began polishing them with his handkerchief. "It is as I have already explained, Your Grace," he said, slipping his glasses back on his face. "Letters such as the ones this Miss Pringle sent are common occurrences for a man in your position. I simply saw no reason to trouble you over something so trivial."

Wyatt's lips tightened in anger. "I'd hardly call my niece's welfare a *trifle*," he replied coldly. He'd been awake most of the night, and his patience was tenuous at best. The last thing he was in the mood for was his prim solicitor's impertinence.

"To be sure, my lord." Mr. Elliott inclined his head graciously. "Provided, of course, that she *is* your niece. We've only Miss Pringle's word on the matter."

Wyatt remembered the miniature of the little girl with his brother's blond curls and violet eyes. "She is Christopher's child," he said, his voice firm.

Mr. Elliott's thin mouth quirked in a slight smile. "It is good of Your Grace to be so trusting," he said, stroking a lock of graying hair from his forehead. "Unfortunately I am not so naive. Without proof—"

"Amanda is the very image of my brother," Wyatt interrupted, wearying of the other man's incessant protestations. "That is all the proof I require."

To his surprise the solicitor paled, his hand dropping to his sides as he gazed at him. "You ... you have seen the child?"

"A miniature. Miss Pringle showed it to me, as well as a copy of her birth record and my brother's marriage lines."

"But, Your Grace, that is hardly acceptable proof!" Mr. Elliott exclaimed, his expression imploring as he leaned forward. "I'm not certain what this Miss Pringle may be about, but I urge you not to act precipitously. Until we know—"

"Enough!" Wyatt leapt to his feet, pinning the solicitor with a furious glare. "Amanda has my family's blond hair and blue eyes, and I am more than satisfied that she is my niece. That is all that need concern you."

Mr. Elliott opened his mouth as if to protest, then leaned back in his chair, his expression unreadable as he lowered his eyes to his tightly clasped hands.

When he raised them again there was a look of sly cunning shimmering in their ebony depths. "I trust your lordship will forgive me, but I would be failing in my duty if I didn't point out that not all Perryvales are blessed with such"—he paused meaningfully—"distinctive features."

Wyatt flinched as he sat back down. Dark fury rose in him, but much as he longed to deny the unspoken accusations, he did not. How could he? All his life he had suspected he wasn't his father's natural child, and the solicitor was only giving voice to his most secret fear.

"Perhaps not," he agreed, hiding his anguish behind an implacable expression, "but that is not the case here. One has but to look at the child to know she is Christopher's daughter."

"But you've not looked at her, have you?" Mr. Elliott persisted, raising a hand when Wyatt would have spoken. "I know you've seen her portrait, but portraits can be altered to give the desired appearance. Even if no deliberate deception is involved, one must consider the artist's interpretation of his subject. You say the girl resembles your brother because of her coloring, but so must a hundred other children of the same age. Are they all your brother's offspring?"

"Of course not," Wyatt snapped impatiently. "But that—"

"Then you must agree there is some doubt this Amanda is your niece," Mr. Elliott concluded masterfully, his dark eyes burning with triumph. "You have no real proof."

Wyatt glared at him, hating him for his relentless logic. What if he was wrong? he thought running a weary hand over his burning eyes. He'd been bosky last night, and the light in the carriage had been poor at best. What if he'd only seen what he wanted to see in that miniature? Miss Pringle had told him the girl was his niece. Perhaps he'd seen a resemblance that wasn't there. Perhaps . . .

No, he decided, lowering his hand to his side.

Amanda was his niece. He knew it; deep inside of him, he knew it. And it had nothing to do with the way she looked. When he had seen the portrait, when he had brushed his fingers across the painted features, he had suddenly felt less alone in the world. He raised his eyes to meet Elliott's dark gaze.

"I have already told you I have all the proof I require," he said, his voice coldly certain. "Have the necessary papers granting me legal custody drawn up at once."

There was a brief silence before Mr. Elliott gave a slight nod. "As you wish, Your Grace," he said tonelessly. "You will be making her your heiress, I presume?"

"Of course." Wyatt rose to his feet, gathering up the hat and gloves he'd placed on the desk. "Why do you ask?"

Mr. Elliott's lips tightened. "No reason, Lord Tilton. No reason at all."

Wyatt glanced up suspiciously, then shrugged his shoulders. It was almost ten o'clock, and he'd have to hurry if he meant to be at the academy on time. There was just one other matter he must deal with, and he waited until he was almost at the door before turning around.

"Elliott?"

"Yes, Your Grace?"

"At the moment I am willing to accept that you believed you were acting in my best interests in keeping Amanda's existence from me," he said, the threat in his voice unmistakable. "But if I should learn differently, your services will no longer be required. I trust you understand me?"

A nerve ticked in Mr. Elliott's cheek. "Yes, Lord Tilton," he said, executing a stiff bow. "I understand perfectly."

Chapter 3

“Amanda, will you please hold still?” Nia implored, her fingers awkward as she struggled with the stiff satin. “How am I to tie this if you keep hopping about?”

“I am sorry, Miss Pringle.” Amanda complied at once, shooting Nia an apologetic look over her shoulder. “I don’t mean to move, but I think my feet are nervous. They won’t stay still no matter how hard I try.”

Nia hid a smile at the ingenious explanation. “Then you must tell them they have nothing to fear,” she said, concentrating on the bow. “There.” She gave it a final tug and struggled to her feet. “I finally have the wretched thing straight. Mind you don’t untie it again. Your uncle will be here any moment now, and you don’t want him to think you a hoyden.”

The mention of her uncle brought a worried frown to Amanda’s face. Much as she liked the notion of living in a duke’s house, the thought of leaving Miss Pringle and the academy made her stomach feel wobbly, and she gave a loud sniff.

Nia heard the suspicious sound and gently turned Amanda around. “Whatever is wrong, dearest?” she asked, seeing the tears pooling in Amanda’s eyes. “You aren’t frightened, are you?”

In answer Amanda threw herself against Nia. “Oh, Miss Pringle, I don’t want to leave!” she wailed, clinging to the only security and love she knew. “I want to stay with you!”

“Oh, Amanda.” Nia gave in to the tears she herself

had been fighting all morning, and pressed a tender kiss on the girl's forehead. "I want to stay with you, too, but I can't."

"Why?" Amanda drew back to gaze up at Nia. "Won't my uncle adopt you, too?"

Nia gave a half-laugh at the thought of the fastidious duke making so unlikely an offer. "I'm afraid that's not possible, love," she said, brushing a blond curl from Amanda's cheek. "We aren't related, you see, and in any case, I am far too old to be adopted."

"Then could you come and visit me?" Amanda asked hopefully. "We could have tea and cakes like real ladies."

"That would be nice," Nia murmured, although she doubted the duke would permit such a thing once Amanda was in his care.

Amanda gave another sniff, recognizing a prevarication when she heard one. She lowered her eyes to the front of Miss Pringle's dark blue gown. "I'll eat all my food," she promised in a small voice, her fingers playing with the lace fichu laying crookedly on the bodice. "I'll do all my sums and say my prayers every night. Maybe then they'll let you visit me."

"Maybe." Nia could scarce speak for the pain in her heart. "But you must promise to be good regardless, dearest. You must make us proud of you."

"I will," Amanda said, wiping at her tears with a chubby fist. Her eyes met Nia's. "I love you, Miss Pringle."

The childish confession sent pain through Nia's heart. She thought losing her parents was the worst suffering she could endure, but even that paled in comparison to the anguish she was feeling now. It was several seconds before she could trust herself to speak. "I love you, too, Amanda," she said, giving the little girl a fierce hug. "And I always will, no matter what."

They continued holding each other, so lost in their private grief they forgot they were in the drawing room where anyone might enter. They never heard the door open and then quietly close behind them.

Wyatt stood in the hallway, unashamed of the painful lump in his throat. *Blast!* he thought, scowling at the memory of the affecting scene. How could he take his niece away from the woman she adored and who so obviously adored her? He knew what it was like to grow up alone and bereft of love, and he didn't want that for Christopher's child. But, on the other hand, he told himself sternly, he couldn't leave her in an orphanage. There had to be something . . . and then it came to him.

"Ah, Mrs. Langston," he said, hiding his emotions as he turned to the older lady standing beside him, wringing her hands in obvious embarrassment. "I was wondering if you might do something for me."

"Certainly, Your Grace," she replied, vigorously blowing her nose. "What is it?"

"It occurs to me that Amanda will have need of a governess," he said, taking care to keep his voice languidly indifferent. "I know little of such matters myself, and I was hoping you might recommend someone for the position."

Mrs. Langston paused in the act of dabbing her eyes. "A governess?"

Wyatt gave a cool nod. "The females in my family have always been educated at home, and a school is out of the question. She'll need a well-bred lady to give her instruction in deportment, watercolors, that sort of thing."

"Watercolors," Mrs. Langston repeated, a slow smile spreading across her face. "Yes, indeed, I can recommend just such a lady. One of our instructors, a Miss Pringle, is a gifted artist, and I am sure she is more than qualified to teach Amanda."

"What of deportment?" Wyatt asked, remembering the hoyden who had dressed as a doxy and held him at gunpoint. "Is she qualified to teach that as well?"

Mrs. Langston hesitated, reluctant to perjure herself to a peer of the realm. Then she remembered the tearful embrace they had just witnessed. She drew herself upright and met the duke's dark eyes. "There is no one more qualified," she said, praying the Almighty would understand.

Wyatt's eyes lit with rare humor at the less than glowing endorsement. "She sounds a paragon among governesses," he drawled. "May I rely upon you to secure her services for me?"

"It shall be my pleasure, Lord Tilton," she replied, beaming at him in delight. "In fact, I shall see to it while you're making Amanda's acquaintance. And Your Grace?"

"Yes, Mrs. Langston?"

"God bless you."

Twenty minutes later Wyatt stood in the center of Mrs. Langston's private parlor waiting for Amanda to join him. Although he'd never considered himself a coward, he found he was trembling, and the thought of fleeing back to St. James was sweetly tempting. His eyes strayed to the dainty bottle of sherry his hostess had set out, and he considered sampling some Dutch courage. After a moment's consideration, however, he rejected the notion. He didn't want to meet his niece for the first time with the smell of spirits on his breath.

Thinking of Amanda brought a frown to his face. What did he know about children? he asked himself angrily, thrusting an impatient hand through his hair. This was madness; he had to have been jug-bitten even to have considered the matter. Elliott was right; he had no real proof the chit was Christopher's, and even if she was, why should *he* be saddled with her? She seemed content at the school. Wouldn't it make more sense to leave her where she was, and pay her whatever visits custom demanded?

"Are you my uncle?"

The shy question blasted Wyatt out of his dark reverie, and he whirled around to find a small girl staring up at him with solemn violet eyes. In that instant he lost his heart completely and irretrievably. She was the very image of Christopher as a lad, and he knew he'd do whatever it took to keep her with him.

"I am the duke of Tilton," he said, finding his voice with difficulty. "I suppose that would make me your uncle."

The little girl continued to regard him gravely. "Mrs. Langston said I am to call you 'Your Grace,'" she said in a wispy voice. "Must I? It sounds so formal."

An all-but-forgotten memory brought a sad smile to his lips. He remembered a laughing Christopher saying much the same thing prior to his going into the army. "Be damned if I'll 'Your Grace' you, old boy," he'd teased, his violet-blue eyes dancing with mischief. "Though I must admit you've the arrogance to go with the title. You're even more pompous than the pater!"

Wyatt shook off the bittersweet memory with difficulty, his heart aching as he gazed down at his brother's child. "You may call me Uncle, if you like," he said quietly, wishing he dared touch the blond curls surrounding her small face. "In fact, I'd rather prefer it if you would. We are family, after all. What else would you like to know?"

She chewed her lip, another trait she shared with her father. "Am I to have a title?" she asked at last. "I know you are a lord, and I shall be staying with you. Does that make me a lady like when Miss Portham married the earl of Colford?"

"You are already a lady," Wyatt replied, unable to resist the temptation of ruffling her silky hair. "Your grandfather was a duke, and your father held a minor title as well. You are Lady Amanda Perryvale. Do you like that?"

She nodded, her lips curling in a gloating smile. "Oh, yes!" she assured him with a laugh. "Now Timothy Shanks shall have to bow to me. He will, won't he?" She shot him an anxious look.

"A gentleman, regardless of the station he occupies

in life, always bows to a lady," he assured her with a smile. "Now if you've no more questions, I fear we must be on our way. It's almost luncheon, and I'm sure you must be hungry."

Amanda bit her lip again, her gaze dropping to the toes of her slippers. She knew she'd promised Miss Pringle to be brave and go with her uncle without making a scene, but she suddenly felt small and alone. She raised wary eyes to study her uncle's face.

Wyatt sensed her unease, and without a thought for his immaculate trousers, dropped to his knee beside her. "What is it, poppet?" he asked, drawing her toward him. "You may ask me anything you like."

Amanda decided to take him at his word. "Do you have a large house?" she asked, eyeing him hopefully.

Wyatt thought of his huge and elegant home on Berkeley Square. "Large enough, I suppose," he replied, wondering what she was getting at. "Why do you ask?"

Amanda drew a deep breath. "If it is *very* big, as big as this house, then you must have dozens of rooms, mustn't you? And if you have dozens of rooms, then perhaps you wouldn't mind lending one to Miss Pringle."

Wyatt raised his eyebrows at her daring. He'd been about to tell her her beloved schoolteacher would be coming with them, but apparently she'd decided to take matters into her own hands. Perhaps having a forward hoyden like Miss Pringle as her governess wasn't such a good idea, after all, he mused with a whimsical smile. 'Twould seem his niece was already developing some of the minx's managing ways.

"I suppose that could be arranged," he said slowly, pretending to consider the possibility. "Will she eat very much, do you think?"

Amanda shook her head. "Oh no!" she assured him anxiously. "She hardly eats *anything!* And I would be happy to share my food with her. She'll be ever so good. I promise you won't even know she is there!"

Wyatt remembered Miss Pringle's soft breasts and the delicacy of her perfume, and doubted he'd ever be unaware of her presence. Also, the idea of the student vouchsafing the conduct of the teacher struck him as decidedly humorous. It showed him how very close they were, and a faint jealousy stirred in him. He pushed it aside with a flash of shame.

"Very well, Amanda," he said, giving her nose a gentle tweak. "We shall ask Miss Pringle to come with us. Just be sure the two of you are packed and ready to leave within the hour. I haven't all day, you know."

He'd meant the last as a jest, never dreaming Amanda would take him at his word. A look of alarm flashed across her face before she turned and dashed toward the door. Her hands were on the handle when she paused and then ran back to where he was standing.

"Thank you, Uncle Wyatt!" she cried, flinging her small arms about his waist and lifting her head to give him a blinding smile. "You're the best uncle in the whole world, and I know I shall love living with you!"

Wyatt's home was located on the north side of Berkeley Square, its cream-colored bricks and Palladium-styled portico putting even its elegant neighbors to shame. The first time Nia had visited the house she'd been too busy trying to bully her way past the servants to pay her surroundings much mind, but gazing at it now filled her with unease. The thought of living amongst such cool perfection was lowering, and she prayed she wouldn't disgrace herself. How, she wondered glumly, was she ever to fit into this . . . this mausoleum?

Beside her Wyatt noted her expression with annoyance. "Is something wrong, Miss Pringle?" he asked,

unexpectedly stung that she should find fault with
his home.

Nia gave a guilty start, embarrassed she'd allow
her emotions to show. "Certainly not, Your Grace,"
she lied, her chin coming up as she met his midnight-dark gaze. "It is quite lovely, in fact. Isn't it,
dearest?" She turned her attention to the little girl
standing quietly at her side.

"It is a palace," Amanda replied, turning her head
first one way and then another in an effort to take in
everything at once. A sudden thought struck her, and
she transferred her gaze to her uncle.

"Does the prince live here?" she asked, thinking
what great fun it would be to meet an actual prince.

Wyatt smiled at her question. "I'm afraid not, my
angel," he said with a regretful shake of his head.
"He lives in Carlton House when he's in London,
and I'll show it to you someday. Would you like
that?"

If the grin on her face was any indication, his suggestion had clearly found favor in his niece's eyes.
"Oh yes, Uncle Wyatt!" she assured him with a vigorous nod. "That would be ever so wonderful! Timothy Shanks lords it over everyone just because *he*
has seen the Tower of London."

"Well, we shall see the Tower, too," Wyatt told her
with a laugh, delighting in her bellicose tones. He
cocked an eyebrow at Miss Pringle. "I gather she and
Mr. Shanks are not on friendly terms?" he observed
wryly. "This is the second time I've heard her mention his name in less than a complimentary fashion."

"The two scrap like cats and dogs," Nia replied
bluntly, then flushed with shame. Prior to Nia's departure, Mrs. Langston had taken her aside to read
her a stern lecture about the proper behavior for a
governess in so noble a household, mentioning rather
forcefully the need to keep a civil tongue between
her teeth. She'd promised the headmistress not to
disgrace either the academy or herself, and it was a
vow she was determined to keep. At least ... for as

long as possible, she admitted with a flash of wry honesty.

The door to the house was suddenly flung open by a liveried footman, and they were ushered inside by no less a personage than the duke's butler, a distinguished individual whom Wyatt introduced simply as Johns. "He has been with our family since I was your age," he told Amanda in an effort to make her feel at home. "Is that not so, Johns?"

"As you say, Your Grace," Johns replied with a low bow. "And may I say, Lady Amanda, what a pleasure it is to welcome you home? You've the look of your father and grandfather about you, and we are most happy to have you here."

Amanda, delighted at hearing herself addressed as Lady Amanda, gave the butler an angelic smile. "Thank you, Johns," she said, in perfect imitation of her uncle's cultured voice. "That is very kind of you. May I have some tea, please?"

"Of course you may, my dear." A pink-cheeked woman in a spotless white apron bustled forward to beam down at Amanda. "I'm Mrs. Mayton, His Grace's housekeeper, my lady, and I shall be happy to fix you the finest tea you've ever had."

"And cakes, too?" Amanda asked, her eyes shining with eager anticipation.

"And cakes, too," Mrs. Mayton repeated with a chuckle, offering Amanda her hand. "This way, then."

Nia made to follow, but the duke lay a restraining hand on her arm. "One moment, Miss Pringle, if you will," he said, his dark eyes unreadable as he gazed down at her. "There are a few things we need to discuss."

"Certainly, Your Grace," Nia replied calmly, doing her best to hide her sudden nervousness. Aside from a brief discussion with Mrs. Langston present, this was the first time she'd spoken with him since last night, and the memory of what had passed between them on that occasion made her cheeks burn with hectic color. Heaven only knew what he must think of her, she thought, following him down a wide hallway and into a book-lined study.

Memories of that encounter were also in Wyatt's mind as he took his seat on the red leather chair behind his massive desk. Even though she was now wearing a severe gown of uninspiring blue topped by a prim, white apron, he kept remembering how she had looked last night with her dark hair tumbling about her shoulders, and her soft, creamy breasts gleaming in the moonlight. The erotic memory made his body react with unmistakable passion, and he angrily banished the image to the back of his mind.

"Pray be seated, Miss Pringle," he said, his tone clipped as he indicated one of the chairs with an impatient wave of his hand. "I know you are eager to see Amanda settled, but first I feel we should discuss your duties as governess."

"My duties, sir?" Nia repeated in a bid for time to compose herself. When Mrs. Langston told her the duke wished to secure her services as Amanda's governess, she'd been too relieved to question the matter, but now she wondered if she hadn't been a trifle hasty. She had the distinct impression he didn't approve of her, and given her extraordinary behavior of last night she supposed she couldn't blame him. What if he'd only pretended to hire her, and would dismiss her now that she was in his power? The possibility had her nervously fiddling with her spectacles until her pride reasserted itself.

What nonsense, she told herself sternly. The duke might well be her employer, but that didn't mean she was in his power. And who was he to sit in judgement of her actions? *She* wasn't the one who attacked a defenseless woman while in her cups! Just let him attempt to ring a peal over her head, she vowed, her eyes sparkling with temper. She'd soon set the arrogant beast straight.

Wyatt watched her struggle for composure with

cool amusement. He wondered if the minx knew how much her face revealed, and then decided she did not. He doubted she would be so free with her emotions if she was aware how obvious those emotions were to those with the wit to see. The thought was most intriguing, but at the moment there were more immediate concerns to be dealt with. He leaned back in his chair as he met her watchful gaze.

"As you know, I am a bachelor whose experience with children is nonexistent," he began, cutting to the heart of the matter without preamble. "I am relying on you to see that Amanda is well cared for and lacks for nothing. Is that understood?"

Nia, who'd been preparing to mount a spirited defense of her actions, was taken aback. "My lord?"

"I am placing my niece completely in your hands," Wyatt rephrased, pleased to see he had caught her by surprise. "In addition to your duties as her teacher, I wish you to see to her other needs. Wardrobe, toys, that sort of thing. Naturally you'll be compensated for these additional duties," he added when she didn't respond at once.

Nia straightened in her chair, her pride flaring at the hint she should be so avaricious. "Such compensation is unnecessary, Your Grace," she informed him tartly. "I would be delighted to see to all of Amanda's needs."

"I should also like to be kept apprised of Amanda's progress on a weekly basis," he continued, ignoring the temptation of her flashing eyes. "You will report any problems to me at once, and if you wish to take Amanda anywhere you must first have my approval. Agreed?"

These seemed reasonable requests to Nia, and she inclined her head in agreement. "Very well, Your Grace," she replied, matching his cool tones. "Will there be anything further?"

"There is, actually." He studied her over his steepled fingers. "Matters progressed so quickly I fear we've overlooked the matter of your salary. Shall we say fifty pounds per annum?"

Despite her mental vow to appear sanguine, Nia felt her jaw drop. "*Fifty* pounds?"

"If that isn't sufficient, I should be happy to—"

"Oh, no!" Nia interrupted, giddy at the thought of such largess. "It is enough . . . more than enough, in fact. 'Tis far more than I was paid at the academy."

"Then we are agreed." Wyatt gave her a polite smile. "And of course I shall pay for all expenses you may encounter, as is, I believe, customary in these matters?" He raised an eyebrow as if seeking agreement.

"Of course, sir," she replied, not about to reveal her ignorance of such things. Prior to her job at the academy, her positions had all been in far less exalted households, and she was as ignorant as he how such affairs were managed in the *ton*. Not that she intended telling him that, of course.

"Very well, we are in agreement," he said, rising to his feet. "You might have Mrs. Mayton give you a tour of the house once you and Amanda are settled. With the exception of my private rooms, I've arranged for the second floor of the house to be set aside for your use. I hope you will be comfortable here."

"I'm sure we shall, sir. That is most gracious of you," Nia said, surprised at his generosity. In one of her last posts she and her charge had been confined to three drafty rooms in the upper regions of the house.

To her astonishment the duke's expression became closed. "Not at all," he said, his voice cold. "She is Christopher's daughter, and this is her true heritage. I want her to feel welcome. It is the least I can do."

Nia digested that in thoughtful silence, wondering yet again why a man so apparently devoted to his late brother could have allowed his daughter to languish in an orphanage. She considered voicing her questions to His Grace, but the withdrawn look in his eyes made her think better of it. His reasons, whatever they might be, were his affair, not hers. All that mattered was Amanda, and with that conviction uppermost in her mind she excused herself and started toward the door. She almost reached it when the duke called out to her.

"Miss Pringle, wait."

"Yes, Lord Tilton?" She sent him a curious glance over her shoulder.

Wyatt hesitated, hating the necessity for apologizing, but knowing he had no other choice. Whatever the truth of his parentage, he had been raised a gentleman, and no man could behave as he had without begging for forgiveness. He straightened his shoulders and met her curious gaze with equanimity.

"I should like to apologize for my unspeakable behavior last night," he said, his voice quiet but firm. "I admit I was in my cups, but that is no excuse for what I did. I only hope you can find it in your heart to forgive me, although I admit I do not deserve such courtesy."

Nia gaped at him in shock. The last thing she expected was an apology, especially one so obviously heartfelt, and she was at a loss as to how she should respond. The important thing, she supposed, was that he had apologized, and given that, the least she could do was accept it. She swallowed the last of her anger and gave him a cool smile.

"That is quite all right, Your Grace," she began. "I—"

"No," he interrupted with a shake of his head. "It is *not* all right. It is never all right for a man to use his superior strength against a woman. Even if you had been the doxy I took you for, I was wrong to grab you as I did." His lips twisted in a self-deprecatory smile. "I don't blame you for pulling that pistol on me, ma'am. God knows I deserved it."

His candor pleased Nia, and as she was never one to hold a grudge, her smile was genuine. "Easy for you to say, Your Grace, when you know the pistol was unloaded," she said, her eyes sparkling with humor. "Had I thought to put bullets in it, you might not be so sanguine."

He expelled the breath he'd been unconsciously holding, relieved she was accepting his apology with such grace. Things would have been awkward if she'd flown up into the boughs, or worse, gone creeping about the house in terror of what he might do next. He enjoyed women, and the thought one might fear him made him feel less than a man.

"Yes, I'd forgotten about that," he said, easily matching her light tone, "and again, Miss Pringle, your daring leaves me breathless. In future, however, might I suggest that the next time you level a gun at a man you take care to see it is loaded? Another man may not be as forgiving, especially in light of the trick you pulled prior to sticking the gun in my face."

Nia's own face flamed scarlet at his words as she remembered the feel of his hard, strong body against hers. "Well, it's no less than you deserved," she muttered, looking anywhere but at him. "Your actions left me no other choice."

"On that I believe we are agreed," Wyatt replied, inclining his head. "I'm not complaining, mind. Your maneuver was most effective. I would appreciate it if you would also teach it to my niece. It will relieve my mind to know she can handle her over-ardent beaus so"—he paused delicately—"efficaciously. Good day, Miss Pringle, that will be all."

Following tea, Nia and Amanda accompanied Mrs. Mayton on a quick tour of the house. The little girl was greatly taken with the glittering gold and white ballroom, while Nia fell quietly in love with the violet- and cream-colored drawing room which the housekeeper identified as the duchess's room.

"Not that it gets much use these days, mind," the older woman sighed, casting a regretful look about her. "And a terrible waste I think it, too. A room like this cries out for people."

"I quite agree, Mrs. Mayton," Nia said, running an admiring hand across the back of a carved settee. "But what do you mean, the room is seldom used? Does His Grace not entertain?"

"Oh, to be sure, Miss Pringle," Mrs. Mayton replied, using the corner of her apron to wipe a speck of dust from the top of a side table. "But . . . well, this is such a *feminine* room, don't you think? And His Grace, being a man, prefers the front drawing room when he entertains. I don't imagine this room has been used more than half a dozen times since Her Grace passed away, God bless her soul. That is her portrait there." She indicated the painting hanging above the gilded fireplace.

The woman was elegantly attired in a fashion that was all the rage some twenty years earlier. Her hair was a deep chestnut and arranged in a classic knot, with several tendrils falling loose to lay upon her creamy shoulders in a manner that was both demure and wanton. There was a sensuous pout on her rosy lips and a sly, knowing look in her light blue eyes that made Nia stiffen in dislike, and she turned away to give the housekeeper a polite smile.

"She was quite lovely," she said, wondering what it was about the late duchess that had set her teeth on edge. "Have you a portrait of the duke's father? I am sure Amanda would like to see a painting of her grandpapa. Wouldn't you, sweet?"

"Yes, Miss Pringle," Amanda agreed, shifting from one foot to the other. They had been in the pretty room for the longest time, and she was anxious for them to be on their way. The footman who had served her tea had told her there were over twenty rooms in the huge house, and she wanted to explore them all before Miss Pringle remembered it was a school day and made her do lessons.

The housekeeper escorted them to the front drawing room, proudly indicating the painting which was hung above the Egyptian-styled settee. "The fifth duke of Tilton," she said, as if performing a formal introduction. "As you can see, Lady Amanda, you have his hair and eyes, just as your papa did."

While Amanda sighed with appreciation, Nia studied the portrait carefully, searching for some resemblance between the golden-haired, violet-eyed duke and the dark, taciturn man she had left less than an hour ago. "This is His Grace's father?" she asked in surprise, although she thought she recognized the duke's firm mouth and aquiline nose in the painted features.

"Yes, Miss Pringle," Mrs. Mayton replied. And then as if divining Nia's thoughts, she added, "The present duke takes after his maternal grandfather, he does. All black hair and dark eyes, just like a gypsy lad when he was younger. It caused no end of talk, I don't mind telling you. Why, there's some as say . . ." She broke off abruptly, a horrified look stealing over her face.

"Shall I show you and her ladyship to your rooms?" she asked, her eyes sliding away from Nia's as she nervously fingered her chatelaine's keys. "I hate to be hurrying you, but I've my other duties to see to, and the day is getting on."

"Of course, Mrs. Mayton," Nia said, understanding that the housekeeper had said more than was perhaps wise. Ah well, she gave a mental shrug, she had no use for servants' gossip.

The housekeeper rushed them through the rest of the tour, barely giving them time to glance in at one room before bustling them on to another. The whirlwind tour concluded on the second floor, and after showing them their bedrooms and introducing them to Nancy, the young girl who'd been chosen to act as Amanda's nursemaid, the housekeeper dashed off again, leaving a bemused Nia to stare after her.

She had little time to consider the other woman's singular behavior, however, as Amanda soon distracted her with demands that she see her new bedroom.

"Did you ever see anything so pretty?" the excited girl demanded, bouncing up and down on the blue silk counterpane. "It is a princess's room!"

"So it is," Nia agreed, trying not to wince as she studied the delicate Sevres vase on the dressing table. It was obvious that the duke had been entirely truthful when he said he had little experience with children, but he hadn't mentioned that his household shared a similar deficiency. No one with an ounce of sense would have put a six-year-old child in a room filled with costly antiques, and the first thing she meant to do was to move anything breakable out of harm's way.

These next few days would be difficult enough without any avoidable disasters to mar the peace.

Chapter 4

"Tilton! Wait!"

The sound of his name being called made Wyatt look up, and he saw Ambrose Royston waving at him from across St. James Street. He raised his own hand in acknowledgement, waiting impatiently as the other man dashed across the street, avoiding carriages and other obstacles with varying degrees of success.

"Blast," he said, grimacing as he joined Wyatt on the corner, "and these boots were new, too. My man shall doubtlessly give notice when he sees what I've done to them."

"That is why the good Lord invented bootscrapers," Wyatt replied easily, indicating one of the handy objects on the stone steps of the nearest building. "Just mind you do a thorough job of it. I much doubt the major domo at White's will appreciate your tracking that into the club."

Ambrose complied with Wyatt's suggestion, grumbling all the while. "I don't see why these things always happen to me," he complained, shooting Wyatt an accusing look. "You could walk barefoot across a bloody pasture and manage not to step in anything. Unnatural, that's what it is."

"Do you think so?" Wyatt was amused. "I prefer to think of it as luck . . . and ability, of course. One must develop a light step if one means to walk about the streets of London."

"Rot." Ambrose gave a light laugh, his usual sunny spirits restored. "There's not a piece of dirt in

50

the kingdom that would dare adhere itself to the exalted personage of the duke of Tilton. Breeding, old fellow, it always serves one in the end."

Wyatt lost his easy smile. "If you say so."

"I do," Ambrose said, as they made their way up the steps to their club. "Take me, for example; the younger son of a mere baron. Mud and filth feel perfectly free to attach themselves to me whenever they like, and there's naught I can do about it. Rather like that last scandal I was involved with, and the worse thing about scandal is that it is a great deal like mud. Once it is flung, it has the depressing tendency to stick."

Wyatt gave Ambrose a thoughtful frown. "That sounds rather ominous," he said slowly, his eyes meeting his friend's. "Would you care to explain yourself?"

"In a moment," Ambrose said, indicating the liveried servant who had opened the door. "There is some talk being bandied about town, and I thought you should know as it concerns you."

Wyatt raised an eyebrow, his expression guarded as he surrendered his hat and gloves to the waiting servant. Several minutes later they were sitting in the far corner of the red drawing room, ignoring the brandy that had been poured for them.

"Well?" he demanded, leaning his shoulders against the plush leather. "What is this all about? What did you mean by that cryptic remark about mud and scandal?"

Ambrose was too well acquainted with Wyatt's forceful nature to waste time in prevarication. "There is some unpleasant talk in the clubs," he said bluntly, meeting Wyatt's hooded gaze. "They are saying you have a love child, and that you have moved her into your townhouse."

"What?"

"I know, I was shocked when I heard it, but—"

"How the devil could any of this have got out?" Wyatt demanded harshly, controlling the level of his voice with difficulty. "My God, Amanda only moved in this morning!"

Ambrose's blue eyes grew wide. "Good God, do you mean to say it's true?"

"Of course it isn't true!"

"Then who is Amanda? You haven't moved your *cherie amie* into the house, have you? That would cause even greater tattle than taking your bastard child under your wing."

Wyatt's eyes narrowed with rage. "In the first place," he began, his soft tone making Ambrose pale, "I never want to hear you refer to any child in so slighting a manner. In the second, who I have in my home is my concern, and no one else's. I will thank you to remember that. However, if it will relieve your mind, Amanda is neither my mistress nor my child. She is Christopher's daughter, his *legitimate* daughter. I have adopted her."

"Christopher's daughter? Are you quite sure?"

"I am quite sure," Wyatt said, his voice clipped.

"I meant no offense, Wyatt," Ambrose hastened to assure him. "It is just . . . well . . ."

"What?" Wyatt pressed when Royston did not continue. He knew he was behaving outrageously and made an effort to control his temper. "Don't be afraid to speak your mind, Ambrose. I shan't take your head off."

Ambrose's eyebrows arched in sudden amusement. "Have I your word on that?" he teased. "No, what I was about to say is that given the fact you and Christopher were estranged at the time of his death, it is rather difficult for you to be certain about anything . . . isn't it?"

Wyatt picked up his glass, studying its amber contents with a thoughtful frown. "Perhaps," he conceded reluctantly. "My solicitor asked much the same question this morning, and as I told him, Amanda has the Perryvale looks. There is no doubt in my mind that she is Christopher's daughter."

"Well, so long as *you* are convinced, that is all that

matters," Ambrose said, relieved the awkward moment had passed. "How old is . . . Amanda, did you say?"

"Yes, and she is six . . . almost seven," Wyatt said, his harsh expression softening at the thought of his niece. "She is quite the little charmer, and I shall doubtlessly have my hands full when she makes her bows. The beaus will be buzzing about her like bees about a rose."

Ambrose gave another chuckle as he raised his glass in a mock toast. " 'Tis a pity I never paid our Latin tutor any mind, else I daresay I could think of a dozen or so phrases that would be more than appropriate for the occasion. But as I cannot, I shall simply have to resort to plain old Anglo-Saxon." He took a sip of brandy and poked a teasing finger at Wyatt. "You, my friend, have been served up with your own sauce, and only fair, I would call it. Considering all the feminine hearts you broke in your salad days, 'tis only fitting that you should now be thrust into the role of anxious papa. I'll wager you'll scarce let her out of your sight. That's always the way it is with you reformed rakes."

"Who says I am reformed?" Wyatt asked, and then a pained expression darkened his eyes.

"What is it?"

Wyatt did not pretend to misunderstand his friend's concern. "Amanda is six, Ambrose, and until last night I didn't even know she existed. Christopher hated me so much that he kept even the knowledge of her birth from me. If it hadn't been for Miss Pringle, I might never have known I had a niece."

"Miss Pringle?"

"A teacher at the Portham Academy. That is where Amanda has been living for the past few months."

"The Portham Academy!" Ambrose was clearly horrified. "Good Gad! That's an orphanage, isn't it? How the devil did the child end up there?"

Wyatt quickly told him the sad story, or at least as much of it as he knew. "So, you see," he concluded heavily, "my staff and my blasted solicitor kept me completely ignorant as to Amanda's plight. You may rest assured that had I known of the situation, she wouldn't have spent so much as a single day in that place, let alone all this time."

"You needn't tell me that," Ambrose said, giving Wyatt a chiding look. "But what I do not understand is why your solicitor took it upon himself to keep you in such ignorance. Whatever could he have been thinking?"

"Damned if I know," Wyatt replied, frowning at the thought of Elliott's appalling incompetence. "I pinned back his ears for it, however, and told him if he ever took such liberties again I would dismiss him."

"As well you should," Ambrose grumbled with a shake of his head. "That he should not tell you of the child is bad enough, but to threaten the school for attempting to contact you ... well, had it been me, I would have already given him the boot."

"Don't think I wasn't tempted, but if truth were to be told, I really cannot blame him for responding as he did to Miss Pringle's missive. She means well enough, but I have yet to meet a more obstreperous female."

"A dragon, is she?" Ambrose asked with a chuckle. "The name brings to mind a tremendous-bosomed lady with spectacles and a fierce expression."

Wyatt remembered a pair of soft breasts that just filled the cup of his hand, and the seductive scent of roses clinging to pale skin. "You're right about the spectacles and the fierce expression," Wyatt admitted, the corners of his mouth curving in a secretive smile. "But as to the other, I cannot say. She is scarce into her twenties, and hardly any bigger than Amanda. Not that her small size matters, mind. The first time I made her acquaintance she held a gun on me."

"You are joking!"

"I am in dead earnest," Wyatt answered, stunned

to realize the momentous event had happened only last night. "Not that she meant to shoot me, of course. She assures me she only wished to catch my attention."

"That would have caught mine in a thrice," Ambrose said, shaking his head. "Well, what happened to this remarkable creature? Did you demand the school dismiss her?"

"Not at all. In fact, she is Amanda's new governess."

Ambrose regarded him in complete disbelief, then threw back his head and laughed. "I have to give you credit, Tilton, you are truly the most understanding of employers. What will you do if the dragon pulls a pistol on you a second time? Promote her to housekeeper?"

"Turn her over my knee," Wyatt corrected, his eyes sparkling. "It's what I was tempted to do last night, but I managed to curb the impulse. Should she begin to make a habit of it, however, I shall not vouchsafe my behavior."

"Then allow me to wish you the best of luck, Your Grace," Ambrose said with another toast. "Something tells me you shall have need of it over these next few weeks."

Nia and Amanda spent the first evening in their new home dining in solitary splendor. Amanda seemed quite cast down when the duke didn't join them, and Nia made a mental note to speak to him. She knew it was fashionable amongst the *ton* for parents to have as little to do with their children as possible, but as far as she was concerned His Grace would simply have to set a new fashion. Amanda needed the reassurance of her uncle's presence, and Nia meant to see she received it.

After seeing her charge safely settled in her huge bed, Nia retired to her own set of rooms, which for convenience's sake was located across the hall from Amanda's. She'd explored the rooms shortly after her arrival, and she still felt slightly dazed that such elegance was hers. Compared to her room at the academy and the quarters she'd endured in her travels with her father, her new surroundings were positively luxurious, and she was determined to repay the duke for his generosity.

Thinking of Lord Tilton brought a faint frown to her face, and as she sat brushing her hair Nia brooded over the enigmatic man who was now her employer. When she'd first met him she'd thought him impossibly high in the instep, but seeing him with Amanda had altered that perception. He was so gentle with the little girl, and far more patient than she would ever have credited. He seemed genuinely concerned with her welfare, and that more than anything made her willing to overlook his high-handed behavior. Provided, she added with a self-deprecatory grin, he didn't become *too* top-lofty. There were limits to what she was willing to tolerate even for Amanda's sake.

The next morning Nia rose early, eager to begin her new life. At her previous post she had been expected to keep her own rooms clean, and she was in the process of making her bed when there was a light tap on her door and the nursemaid walked in.

"Why, Miss Pringle, what be you doing?" she cried, her hands flying to her cheeks.

"I am making my bed," Nia answered, wondering what ailed the younger woman. Judging from her expression one would have thought she'd been caught pinching the family's silver, she thought sourly, giving her pillow a final fluff before placing it on the counterpane.

"Oh, you needn't bother with that, miss," the nursemaid said, hurrying into the room. "Your maid will see to it."

"My maid?" Nia stared at her in surprise.

"Didn't Mrs. Mayton tell you. His Grace has ordered that you be given your own maid. To see to your things and such so that you'll be free to look after Lady Amanda," she added when Nia continued staring at her. " 'Tis the way things are done in the better households."

Nia bristled at the condescension in the nursemaid's voice. "I see," she said, drawing herself up to her full height. "That is very generous of His Grace. Thank you, Nancy."

"You're welcome, Miss Pringle." Having scored her victory, the nursemaid was eager to make friends. "I just peeked in on her ladyship, and she's still fast asleep. Will you be wanting to get her up for her breakfast?"

Nia considered the matter and then shook her head. "No, I think it will be all right if we let her sleep in just this once. But after today I'll expect her to be up by eight o'clock. Idleness has ruined kings, you know."

"If you say so." Nancy looked as if she wasn't sure how to take such a stricture. "I'll just be getting back to her ladyship's room, then. Will there be anything else?"

"No, that will be fine," Nia said, wondering if she ought to remind the maid that she had come into her room on her own accord. Then she thought of something. "Oh, wait."

"Yes?"

"In my other positions I usually took my meals with my pupils. Is that how it is done in this house?"

"Yes, miss. You and Lady Amanda are to take all your meals in the sitting room. Unless His Grace should say otherwise, I suppose," she added, after giving the matter careful thought.

Nia recalled her decision to request the duke eat with them on occasion, and was about to say something when she suddenly thought better of it. Perhaps it would be best if she waited a few more days, she decided. She needed to set up a schedule for Amanda before she began disrupting it. Once things were running smoothly, she would approach His Grace and arrange something.

After a quick breakfast Nia went to the small parlor she had chosen as their schoolroom. Under her orders several footmen carried down a set of desks and books from the attic, and by the time Amanda came dashing in to greet her, Nia had everything ready for her. They spent the rest of the morning working on Amanda's sums, and were about to begin on her penmanship when something made Nia glance toward the door. The duke was standing there, his dark eyes narrowed as he studied his niece.

"Uncle!" Amanda threw down her pen and raced to his side. "Have you come to visit me?"

"That I have, poppet," Wyatt answered, a reluctant smile softening his features at the delight in her voice. "I thought I would look in and see how you and Miss Pringle are doing. How do you like your new home?"

"It's beautiful!" Amanda assured him anxiously, lest he think her ungrateful and send her packing. "It's the most beautifullest house I've ever seen."

"Most beautiful," Nia corrected, rising to her feet and giving the duke a polite curtsey. "Good morning, Your Grace. I trust you are well?"

Wyatt gave her a cool look. "Quite well, Miss Pringle, thank you," he said. "And you? Have you found all to your liking?"

"Indeed I have," Nia replied, taking her clue from his distant manner. "Your staff is proving most helpful."

"Good, good, you must let Mrs. Mayton know if you lack for anything, and she shall see to it," he said, gently pushing Amanda to one side as he began exploring the new schoolroom. Books he remembered from his childhood were arranged on a shelf, and one title in particular caught his attention. Delighted, he picked it up, running a finger down the cracked spine.

"*Tacitus*," he exclaimed, flipping open the book and thumbing through the pages. "Gad, I can remember how Christopher and I used to spend hours locked in our schoolroom while our tutor tried to drum the finer points of Latin into our unwilling heads. Whatever is it doing here?"

"Because I am attempting to drum the finer points of Latin into Amanda," Nia said, suddenly intrigued by the image of the duke as a rebellious schoolboy. She could imagine he had been a rare handful, and her heart quite went out to the unknown tutor.

Wyatt glanced up at that. "You are teaching my niece Latin?" he asked, faintly surprised. Granted, he was unfamiliar with the curriculum for young ladies, but he doubted it usually included the classic languages.

"Indeed, I am," Nia replied, preparing to defend her choice to him. "It is the basis for all the romance languages, and if Amanda is to fully understand Italian and Spanish, to say nothing of French, then it is imperative that she know Latin."

"I quite agree," Wyatt said, returning the book to its shelf. "But it is required that she speak Italian and Spanish? They hardly seem necessary skills for a lady."

"All knowledge is useful," Nia said, resenting his words, although, in truth, she had encountered them more than once during her years as a teacher. Why men seemed to think a woman's knowledge should be limited to watercolors and frocks she knew not, but it did seem to be the prevailing attitude.

"So it is." Wyatt decided to let the matter drop. He'd already surmised Miss Pringle was a bluestocking, and so long as she didn't expose Amanda to anything too unseemly, he didn't mind what she thought.

"I already know some Latin, Uncle," Amanda piped up, hoping to please him. " *'Magna est veritas'*; truth is mighty."

"Very good, Amanda," he praised, patting her head. "You've inherited your father's talent for languages, it would seem."

Amanda's eyes shone with curiosity. "Did my papa speak Latin?" she asked.

A pained expression crossed Wyatt's face. "He took honors at his forum," he said, recalling the party his father had given when Christopher had returned from Oxford. It was just before his brother went into the army, and it was one of the last times he and Christopher had seen each other before their falling out.

Amanda was too young to note the change in her uncle's mood, but Nia was not so innocent. She saw the bleak agony in the duke's eyes, and wondered what had put it there. Before she could speculate any further there was a knock at the door, and a footman entered.

"I beg your pardon, Your Grace," he said with a low bow, "but Mr. Johns says Mr. Royston has arrived for your ride, and is waiting for you in the front drawing room."

"Thank you, Stephen. Pray tell Mr. Royston I shall be with him in a moment." Wyatt acknowledged the message with a curt nod. When the servant departed, Wyatt turned his attention to Amanda, who had taken his hand in hers and was staring up at him hopefully.

"I am afraid I must be off, Amanda," he said, squeezing her fingers with regret. "But I'll look in on you when I return."

"Promise?" She gave him a melting look.

Wyatt gave a soft chuckle. "I promise," he said, aware he was being shamelessly manipulated. "In the meanwhile mind you obey your governess, hmm?" He met Miss Pringle's hazel gaze.

"Ma'am," he said formally, "I wish you good day. Again, if you lack for anything, you have only to tell a member of the staff. They will fetch it for you."

"Yes, Your Grace," Nia answered, impressed with his kindness. "Enjoy your ride."

That day set the pattern for those that followed, and Wyatt made a point of stopping by the schoolroom each morning. He took tea with them one afternoon, and at Miss Pringle's suggestion agreed to dine with them at least one evening a week. He mentioned this to Ambrose as they were out riding some ten days later, and was annoyed by his friend's amused response.

"Good lord, but you are becoming domesticated," Ambrose accused, his blue eyes teasing as he studied Wyatt's face. "You'll take to powdering your hair and criticizing the prince for his loose living, if you aren't careful."

Wyatt shot him a black look, failing to find any humor in the situation. "I've already criticized the prince for his racketing ways," he informed Ambrose coolly. "And what is wrong with my becoming 'domesticated,' as you put it? I am thirty, you know. It is past time I was settling down and setting up my nursery."

"Yes, but it is generally done using one's own children, rather than usurping those of one's brother," Ambrose quipped. "And I assure you, no criticism of your behavior was intended. I quite approve of your dining with your niece. I have never understood this nonsense of hiding one's children away until they are of age. Why go to the bother of having the little wretches, if you only lock them in the attic like a mad relation?"

Wyatt's anger faded at this wry observation. "I shall have to share that observation with Miss Pringle," he said, his mouth curving as he imagined her response. "I sometimes get the impression she thinks me neglectful in my duties toward Amanda."

"That is the way it is with these governesses," Ambrose said with a solemn nod. "They have but to look at one in that all-knowing way of theirs, and one is left feeling like a guilty schoolboy with jam-stained fingers."

"Perhaps Miss Pringle is not quite so bad as that," Wyatt replied with a low chuckle. "Although I do confess to worrying my cravat may not be tied correctly when I am in her presence. She is a most formidable lady."

"So it would seem," Ambrose agreed, straightening in his saddle with sudden alertness. "And speaking of formidable ladies, look who is coming this way."

Wyatt grew wary at the sight of the approaching group of riders. There were several ladies among them, and he had no trouble identifying the two stunning beauties at the front. There were the twin daughters of his nearest neighbor in the country, and he'd spent the better part of several seasons dodging the attempts of their respective parents to foster a match between himself and one of them.

"Good morning Your Grace, Mr. Royston." Lady Alexandria Declaire, now Lady Geoffrey Covingdale, greeted them with a languid smile, her dark green eyes full of speculation. "I hope the two of you are enjoying the morning?"

"Indeed we are, Lady Geoffrey," Wyatt answered, raising his hat to her and the others. "And what brings you out at such an unfashionable hour? It is scarce eleven o'clock."

"We are here to act as duennas for our Katie's gallop with Captain Addams," replied Lady Anne, the countess of Redvale, edging her bay closer to Wyatt's stallion. "Even though she is twenty she is still unmarried, and so we must keep a watchful eye on her reputation." She turned to the simply dressed blond riding next to her. "Katie, dearest, you do remember the duke of Tilton, do you not? He is papa's neighbor."

"Yes, we have met before," Lady Catherine Declaire replied in a soft voice, lifting blue-gray eyes to meet Wyatt's gaze. "It is nice to see you again, Your Grace."

"Lady Catherine." Wyatt gave her a polite smile, trying to remember when they had met. It must have been during her first season, he decided, for he'd spent most of last year in mourning for his brother.

"May I say how lovely you are looking?" he added, too polite to admit the truth. "I don't believe I've ever seen you on horseback."

"It is good to have you back in London, Your Grace," Lady Geoffrey said before Lady Catherine could acknowledge his compliment. "And do allow me to extend my belated condolences on the loss of your brother. He died in battle, you know." She added this as an aside to the bored young dandy in the uniform of a Fusilier.

"The dangers of a soldier's life," Captain Addams responded with a shrug. "Take Waterloo, for example. We carted 'em off by the wagonload. Is that where your brother fell, Your Grace?" he asked, flicking Wyatt a languid look.

"New Orleans," Wyatt corrected through clenched teeth. The captain's indifference to the appalling suffering of his fellow soldiers infuriated him, and it was all he could do not to knock the other man from his horse. He doubted the useless little dandy had ever seen anything more dangerous than a parade field.

"Ah, the American nonsense." Captain Addams gave a prim sniff. "Waste of men and shot, if you want my opinion. To say nothing of the havoc it raised with our commerce. My father lost two ships to those demmed privateers. Beg pardon, ladies." He dutifully apologized for his rough language.

"Speaking of poor Christopher, what is this I hear about your adopting his daughter?" Lady Anne interposed quickly. "I was unaware that he had any children."

"As was I, my lady." Wyatt turned his shoulder on the captain in a deliberate slight. "I only learned of her existence a sennight ago, but we are fast becoming old friends now that she is with me."

"How old is she?" Lady Geoffrey's eager interest betrayed the real reason they had sought him out. "No one knows a thing about her, and since you keep her locked up in that house of yours, I fear we are left to draw our own conclusions. You would not believe the whispers that were first being spread," she added, tilting her head to one side as she issued a challenging smile.

Wyatt met her smile with a look of stony implacability. "Amanda is six, my lady," he said, his voice as glacial as his eyes. "As for my keeping her locked up, I had no idea I was so cruel. Perhaps I could bring her to your home so she might meet your children? I believe you have a daughter her age?"

Lady Geoffrey's smug smile was replaced by a look of irritation. "My daughter is but five," she snapped, obviously annoyed by this reference to the fact that she was a mother. "And my son is two. Naturally they are in the country with their nurse."

"Naturally." Wyatt allowed himself a faint smile before turning to the countess. "And what of your children, my lady?" he asked with a smooth innocence that fooled no one. "Are they also in the country with their nurse?"

Lady Anne's outraged expression was a perfect mirror of her twin's. "I have but one child, Your Grace," she informed him haughtily, "and neither the earl nor myself would dream of exposing him to the dangers of London air. Now, if you will excuse us, I fear we must be going. Come Alexandria, Katie," and she dug her heels into her horse's side, sending the little animal bolting forward.

"A charming lady," Ambrose observed wryly, his blond eyebrows arching as he watched the small group gallop off. "A family trait, I gather?"

"Apparently," Wyatt replied, already dismissing the countess and her poisonous twin from his mind. "Although Lady Catherine seemed most pleasant."

"How could you tell?" Ambrose asked with a laugh. "The chit had scarce five words to say for herself. Although," he added thoughtfully, "I suppose it would be difficult to get a word in at all in that litter of tabbies."

They continued the rest of the ride in companionable silence, and after promising to meet Ambrose at his club later that afternoon Wyatt returned to his own home. He was handing his gloves and hat to the butler when a girlish laugh echoed in the hall. He turned to look just as Amanda came whooshing down the carved banister, a look of delight and terror on her face. When she saw Wyatt standing in the entryway, she waved in excitement.

"I did it, Uncle Wyatt, I did it!" she crowed. "I slid all the way down, clear from the top!"

The paralysis of fear that had held Wyatt broke, and he dashed across the marble floor to snatch his niece from the railing. "Amanda!" he cried, anxiously searching her for any sign of injury. "Are you all right? You might have been killed!"

"Oh, pooh!" Amanda gave a pretty laugh, her arms resting comfortably about her uncle's broad shoulders. "You must try it, Uncle. It is ever so much fun."

Wyatt imagined the little girl falling from the top of the grand staircase and tried not to shudder. "Where is Miss Pringle?" he asked ominously, only to have his question answered when Miss Pringle also came flying down the banister, her blue skirts tucked about her legs. The starched cap she always wore was askew, as were her wire-rimmed spectacles, but it was the sight of her slender ankles and calves that drew his attention. Her curved backside collided with the newel post, and he took a moment to admire it before raising cold eyes to her flushed face.

The sight of the duke standing there with Amanda in his arms drove the smile of triumph from Nia's lips. "Oh dear!" she said, reaching up to straighten the spectacles.

Wyatt handed Amanda to the butler, who had materialized beside him. He then lifted Miss Pringle from the banister, ignoring her awkward attempts to free herself. When he had her safely on her feet he stepped back, his eyes holding hers. "If you would be so good as to escort Lady Amanda to her rooms, I should like to see you in my study," he said, his voice carefully controlled. "Shall we say in five minutes?"

Rather than flushing with shame or bursting into tears at his haughty tones, Miss Pringle merely nodded. "Five minutes, Your Grace," she said formally. "Come, Amanda." She held out her hand to the little girl and led her up the stairs they had just descended so precipitously.

Wyatt went into his study, crossing the carpeted floor to where the cellaret stood. He poured himself a glass of sherry and downed it in a single gulp, the cloying taste of the pale wine making his face screw up in protest. When he'd finished the second glass, he set the goblet down with a thump and stalked over to stare down at the fire burning in the grate.

Lord, he thought, thrusting a shaking hand through his hair, he had never been so frightened in his life. Each time he thought of Amanda clinging to that narrow piece of wood three floors above a hard marble floor, and what would have happened had she lost her grip, his blood ran cold. She might have been killed, he raged silently, or crippled at the very least. He had no idea what the devil Miss Pringle meant by encouraging such a stunt, but he meant to find out.

He was contemplating what he would say to her when there was a tap on the door and Miss Pringle entered. "You wished to see me, sir?" she asked, her tone defiant as she met his gaze.

All of the cold, succinct comments he had rehearsed fled from Wyatt's mind as he glared at her. "Just what the bloody hell did you think you were doing?" he demanded, his good manners lost with his temper. "Amanda might have been killed!"

Nia's resolve faltered at the note of panic in his voice. Arrogance and temper were things she could have easily fought, but the genuine terror she saw burning in his dark eyes was another matter. She'd come into the room fully prepared to do battle, but now she found herself wanting to comfort him instead.

"I know it must have looked dangerous, Your Grace," she said soothingly, taking a cautious step toward him, "but I promise you the risk to Amanda was minimal at best. You must know I would never allow her to come to any harm."

"And how do you know what the risk was?" he snapped, his jaw clenched with anger.

"Because I tested it myself before letting her try."

Wyatt blinked at her. "You what?"

"I tested it myself before letting her try. I knew she was going to do it anyway," she added when he continued to stare at her in disbelief. "I'd already caught her trying twice before, and I knew it was only a matter of time before she succeeded. I thought that if I went first, showed her how best to do it, the danger wouldn't be so great."

"But Amanda came down first," he protested, his heart lurching at the memory.

Nia cleared her throat, her cheeks pinking with embarrassment. "That was my second time," she admitted, lowering her eyes to the floor.

Wyatt stared at her another moment, and then incredibly, he was laughing. "Miss Pringle, if all governesses are like you, then I am eternally grateful I have yet to meet another one," he said, shaking his head in wonder. "I do not think my nerves could stand the strain."

Nia glanced up, not certain she had heard right. "You aren't angry with me, Your Grace?" she asked, scarce believing her luck. "You won't dismiss me?"

"I am furious with you," Wyatt informed her, although his voice lacked conviction. "But no, I shan't dismiss you. Not unless you try another stunt like that, that is," he added quickly. "No more sliding down banisters for either Amanda or you, ma'am. I mean it."

Nia's shoulders slumped with relief. "Yes, Your

Grace," she promised, her eyes earnest as they met his. "I shall speak to Amanda, and—"

"No," he interrupted, raising his hand. "*I* shall have a word with her. It is about time she and her poor uncle came to an understanding regarding her stay here."

Nia wanted to continue debating, but decided not to press the issue. She was wise enough to know she'd tried her luck enough for one day. Lord Tilton had won the field this day, but next time, perhaps, it would be she who emerged victorious. And there would be a next time, she admitted as she left the study. Given both their stubborn and willful natures, future skirmishes were inevitable, and she knew it was only a matter of time before they crossed swords once more.

The prospect should have alarmed her. Instead she was looking forward to it.

Chapter 5

Over the next few days Wyatt found himself remembering Lady Geoffrey's accusations. Her charge that he kept Amanda locked away stung, all the more so because he feared she was right. In the fortnight since Amanda had been in his care he'd not so much as taken her for a drive, and the realization of his neglect made him squirm. He also recalled he'd promised to show her Carlton House, and decided it was time he kept his word.

The next morning he strode into the schoolroom only to find his niece and her governess had already left for the day. "Did they say where they were going?" he demanded, scowling at the nursemaid who stood in front of him ringing her hands.

"T-to the park, Your Grace," Nancy stammered, her heart pounding at the fearsome look on the duke's face. "They was going to s-study the flowers."

"Which park?" he asked, making an effort to control his impatience. "There are several of them, you know."

Nancy's pale eyes filled with tears. "I don't know, sir," she confessed, certain he would dismiss her on the spot. "M-Miss Pringle didn't say."

Surmising he would get nowhere by terrorizing the hapless maid, he went in search of Johns, hoping his butler would be slightly better informed. He was not disappointed.

"I believe they have gone to Green Park, my lord," Johns said with a low bow. "Miss Pringle inquired where one might find the best selection of flora, and

I recommended the park. Is there some problem?" he added at his employer's look of displeasure.

"Only that she neglected to inform me of her plans," Wyatt replied grimly. "When did they leave?"

"Approximately half an hour ago, Your Grace. I sent William, one of our footmen, with them as I did not feel it proper for Lady Amanda to go out without proper escort. They were," he added with a disapproving sniff, "walking."

Wyatt's jaw clenched in fury, and after thanking Johns for his assistance he went outside where his crested carriage was waiting. Less than five minutes later he was at Green Park, but it was another ten minutes before he succeeded in tracking down his quarry. He found them sitting on a stone bench, studiously examining a dusty and forlorn rose.

"As you can see, Amanda, William, the petals are almost symmetrical," Miss Pringle was saying, indicating the rose's drooping blossom with the tip of her slender finger. "This is but one example of how one might find mathematical precision in nature. Another might be—"

"Uncle!" Amanda was the first to spy Wyatt, and she lost no time in racing to his side. "Have you come to look at the roses, too?" she demanded, tilting her head to gaze up at him.

"Actually, I've come to take you for a ride in my carriage," he replied, brushing back a strand of blond hair that lay on her cheek. "I did promise to show you the prince's house, remember?"

Amanda's eyes widened in delight. "Will I meet the prince?"

"I am afraid not," Wyatt apologized. "But perhaps we might catch a glimpse of him as we drive by."

"Miss Pringle! I am going to see a prince!" Amanda ran back to where Nia was standing.

"So I hear," she said, raising her head to study the duke. He was standing on the stone pathway looking darkly handsome in a blue velvet jacket and tight, buff nankins, his cravat knotted beneath his lean jaw.

That jaw, she noted, was clenched with temper, and she wondered what she'd done to anger him this time. Suppressing a resigned sigh, she gave him a polite nod.

"Good morning, Your Grace," she said, her tone wary but respectful. "I hadn't thought to find you here."

"Nor I you, Miss Pringle," Wyatt returned, capturing her hazel gaze. "You may imagine my surprise when Johns informed me you and Amanda had left the house without my knowledge."

Nia flushed, belatedly recalling she'd promised to keep him apprised of her and Amanda's movements. She was about to offer a stiff apology, but the duke had already turned to William.

"You may return home," he said, slipping a coin into the footman's hand. "And when either Lady Amanda or Miss Pringle leave the house, you are to accompany them. Is that clear?"

"Yes, Your Grace!" William said, blushing with gratitude. "You can count on me, sir. I'll keep my peepers on 'em!"

"I'm sure you shall." Wyatt gave him a warm smile. "Go on now, lad, and tell Mr. Johns we shall be home for luncheon."

After William had rushed off, Wyatt glanced down at Amanda, taking in her appearance with a thoughtful frown. Like her governess his niece was wearing a plain cloak of blue wool, her hair stuffed beneath an even plainer white cap. He thought of the other children he had passed while walking through the park, and realized they'd all been dressed in velvets and furs.

"Where is your other cape, Amanda?" he asked, taking care to keep any hint of censure from his voice. "That one doesn't look very warm."

"Oh, it's warm enough." Amanda dismissed the matter with an indifferent shrug. "And I haven't got another cape."

A sharp pain knifed through Wyatt at this further

proof of his neglect. "I see," he said, striving for calm. "Perhaps we shall buy you one when we are out today. Would you like that?"

Amanda gave another shrug. "All right," she said, not really interested. "But I'd much rather have a doll . . . or a book," she added, her eyes taking on a thoughtful gleam. "One about balloons, if I may."

"Your birthday is at the end of next month," Nia interposed quickly, recognizing the adventurous sparkle in her pupil's eyes. "Perhaps you might receive a book then."

Wyatt gave her a sharp look. "I hardly think purchasing a doll and a book at the same time will put me in dun territory, Miss Pringle," he said coldly. "My pockets are deep enough to bear the expense, I assure you."

Nia's lips tightened at the subtle rebuke. "I didn't mean to imply they weren't, my lord," she said, struggling to control her temper. "I was but making an observation."

Wyatt made no reply, although the look he shot her spoke volumes. He glanced down at Amanda, whose amethyst eyes had lost their shine. "Are you ready to go, poppet?" he asked, giving her an encouraging smile. "I brought my special carriage with me. It has a team of coal-black horses, and my crest is painted on the side. Everyone who sees you in it will know you are riding with a duke, and they shall be green with envy."

Amanda frowned thoughtfully. "Even Timothy Shanks?"

"Especially Timothy Shanks." Wyatt gave her nose a gentle tweak. "Now let us be off. There is a great deal I wish to show you."

As promised, Wyatt had the coachman take them past the elegant stone edifice that was Carlton House. Amanda gave the building a critical stare before dismissing it with a sniff. "I don't see any onions," she said when Wyatt asked what was wrong.

"You said there would be onions," she added, shooting Nia a reproving look.

Nia was puzzled at first, and then she gave a reluctant laugh. "I believe she is talking about the regent's pavilion at Brighton, Your Grace," she explained. "And the dome is not built of onions, Amanda," she added with a smile. "It is merely said to resemble one."

"Well, I do not see why anyone should want to live in a house like that," the little girl responded with a disgruntled pout. "It must be ever so ugly. Yours is much prettier, Uncle."

"Thank you, Amanda. Although you'd best take care not to repeat such things in public. The prince may take offense and clap you in the Tower."

After driving about Carlton House, Wyatt ordered the carriage to proceed down Bond Street, and the sight of all the shops had Amanda's nose glued to the window of the carriage. While she was preoccupied with looking her fill, Wyatt motioned for Miss Pringle to sit beside him.

"I thought it was agreed you would see to her wardrobe," he said in a low voice once she had joined him. "How is it that she has but one cloak to her name?"

Nia felt her cheeks burn in embarrassment. "I have been researching the matter, Your Grace," she said, hating the fact that he should think her failing in her responsibilities. "And I hope to have a modiste selected by the end of next week."

"Researching the matter?" Wyatt's eyebrows arched at the unexpected reply. "You hire a modiste and order up a wardrobe, and that is the end of it. What else is there to consider?"

Such masculine simplicity left Nia gaping at him in annoyance. "There is a great deal more to consider, sir!" she protested, keeping her voice soft with an effort. "One must think of fashion, and practicality, to say nothing of economy!"

"Economy?"

Nia gritted her teeth at the incredulity in his voice. "I'm well aware that you aren't a poor man," she said, pushing her spectacles back on her nose, "but that is no reason to throw good money after bad. If I went to a modiste and gave her carte blanche to sew up whatever she pleased, I'd soon find myself rolled up horse, gun, and blanket. How am I to teach Amanda financial responsibility if I do not practice it myself?"

"Financial responsibility?" Wyatt was so stunned he forgot to keep his voice low. "Good Lord, ma'am, she is six years old!"

"One is never too young to start learning." Nia stuck to her guns with dogged determination. "I would be failing in my duties if I neglected that aspect of her education."

Wyatt could only shake his head, wondering what the devil he had got himself into. "Just see to it." He sighed, reaching up to pinch the bridge of his nose. "Preferably before it is time to research buying her a wedding gown."

Nia lifted her chin at his sarcasm, but when she would have replied Amanda gave a delighted cry. "Uncle Wyatt, what is that place?"

Wyatt glanced at the building she indicated. "That is Ackermann's," he said, his ill humor forgotten at the look on his niece's face. "Would you like to go inside?"

Amanda assured him there was nothing she would like more, and they were soon walking down the wide aisles, gawking at the stunning array of merchandise. Nia was particularly intrigued by the colorful fabrics on display, and stopped to finger an ell of turquoise satin.

"Shopping for Amanda's wedding gown?" Wyatt teased, pausing beside her. "It would certainly set a new fashion."

Nia gave a reluctant smile and dropped the material. "I suppose it would," she agreed, wondering how much the fabric would cost. Perhaps if it wasn't too dear she'd buy enough for a new gown, she thought, giving the bolt a wistful look.

Wyatt noted the pensive expression on her face. "Would you like to buy the material?" he asked politely. "We can have it delivered to the house with the other things."

Strongly tempted, Nia picked up the fabric again. Her one good gown was decidedly shabby, and perhaps it wouldn't be hopelessly frivolous of her to replace it. The material was so beautiful . . .

"I believe I shall," she said decisively, giving the duke a bright smile. "And then I shall take Amanda over to look at the pattern books. Perhaps we can get some ideas for her wardrobe."

The notion of examining fashion illustrations was not at all to Wyatt's liking, and he was quick to cry off. "I shall leave that to you, Miss Pringle," he said with alacrity. "And while you and Amanda are doing that, I will have a look at the books."

"Yes, Your Grace," Nia agreed, amused at the look of horror on his handsome face. "It shouldn't take above an hour."

After agreeing to meet in the shop's public area, Nia dragged a protesting Amanda up to the first floor where the elegant fashion books were kept. It took some doing, but she was finally able to interest the little girl in the delicate watercolors. While Amanda was busy studying the prints, Nia thumbed through another stack of illustrations until she found a suitable pattern for her new gown. She ordered up the necessary needles and threads, and feeling greatly daring, also ordered some velvet ribbon to trim the neck and hemline.

Once that was done she turned her attention to Amanda, who had struck up a conversation with the pretty blond lady sitting beside her.

"My uncle is a duke," she heard her inform the stranger in a smug voice. "He has a crest on his carriage. Do you have a crest on your carriage?"

"Amanda!" Nia exclaimed, her face crimson as she

hurried over. "I beg pardon, ma'am," she said, dropping a polite curtsey. "I am afraid she is still learning that one mustn't approach strangers when in public."

"I quite understand." The blond's gray-blue eyes were bright with laughter. "I have several nieces and nephews near the same age, so I am accustomed to such forthrightness."

"Do you have a crest on your carriage?" Amanda pressed, eager for an answer. "Does it have a dragon?"

"Well, the carriage I am using belongs to my brother-in-law, and as he is an earl it does have a crest," the woman answered obligingly. "But I'm afraid it doesn't have a dragon. It does have a lion, though, and a griffin. Is that all right?"

"Dragons are better than lions," Amanda said in a self-important voice. "But I don't know what a griffin is."

"We shall study that next week," Nia answered, her eyes flicking toward the younger woman. She believed at once her claim to gentility, and it had nothing to do with her exquisite clothes or the maid hovering protectively at her mistress's side. It was in her face, she decided, in the delicacy of her features and the calm control in her eyes. She was wondering if she should introduce herself and Amanda, when Amanda took the matter out of her hands.

"I am Lady Amanda Perryvale," she announced, hopping off the bench to bob an awkward curtsey. "And this is my governess, Miss Pringle. Who are you?"

"I am Lady Catherine Declaire," the woman answered, rising gracefully to return the curtsey. "And I am most pleased to make your acquaintance, Lady Amanda, Miss Pringle." She cocked her head to one side as a sudden thought struck her.

"Perryvale," she repeated, her blond brows puckering. "You are the duke of Tilton's niece?"

Amanda gave a pleased nod. "He is going to buy me a new cape," she said in a confiding manner,

"and a book on ballooning. Do you know about ballooning?"

"Only that it sounds ever so interesting," Lady
Catherine replied, her lips curving in a sweet smile.
"And I think I would very much like to try it some-
day."

They continued chatting for a few more minutes,
and Nia was delighted at the easy way Lady Catherine spoke with Amanda. It had been her experience
that most adults had a devil of a time with children.
They never seemed to know how to behave around
them, and either treated them like brainless dolts, or
else they were stiffly formal. She was wondering if
His Grace would allow her to invite the young lady
to tea, when she suddenly sensed his presence behind her. She turned just as he reached them.

"Lady Catherine, how delightful to see you again,"
he said, bowing with grave politeness. "I see you
have already made the acquaintance of my niece."

"Indeed I have, Your Grace," Lady Catherine answered, her gaze returning to Amanda. "And may I
say she is completely enchanting. You must be very
proud of her."

"I am," Wyatt replied, his eyes softening as he laid
his hand on Amanda's shoulder. "Are you ready to
go, my dear? I fear it is time we were leaving."

"Yes, Uncle Wyatt," Amanda replied, sliding her
hand confidently into his and giving Lady Catherine
a polite nod. "Good-bye, Lady Catherine," she said,
imitating her uncle's cool manner. "It was very nice
meeting you."

"Good-bye, Lady Amanda." Lady Catherine
smiled. "Are you going to be at home for visitors tomorrow? If so, I should enjoy calling upon you."

Amanda dropped her dignified pose to become a
six-year-old again. "Will you come for tea?" she
asked, her blue eyes sparkling with excitement.

Lady Catherine's eyes rose to Wyatt's, and he gave
an imperceptible nod. "I should like that very much,

my lady," she said, turning back to Amanda. "Shall we say three o'clock?"

On the way back to the carriage Amanda could talk of nothing but her newfound friend. "She is a *real* lady, Uncle Wyatt," she assured him solemnly. "Just like Lady Colford. Do you think she will wear her coronet when she comes to call? I should like to see a coronet. May I have one?"

"When you are older," Wyatt promised, accustomed now to the way Amanda's mind jumped from subject to subject. "In the meanwhile, I have something to show you."

"What is it?" Amanda demanded, eager for anything new. "Is it a balloon?"

"Considering that it's in my carriage, I shouldn't think so," Wyatt replied with a chuckle. "You shall have to wait and see."

Amanda pouted, but knew better than to press. Her patience was rewarded a few minutes later when she climbed into the carriage and found a doll sitting on the seat.

"A doll!" she squealed, snatching it up and pressing it to her breast. "Oh, Uncle Wyatt, thank you!"

"You are most welcome," he said, pleased his present had been so well received. He'd purchased the doll on impulse, feeling slightly foolish lest one of his friends see him.

"What will you name her?" Nia asked, dutifully admiring the porcelain doll with its blond ringlets and rosy cheeks.

Amanda wrapped one of the curls around a finger. "Catherine," she said at last. "I shall name her Lady Catherine."

While Amanda was occupied with her new doll, Wyatt turned to Nia. "Were you able to find a pattern?" he asked, leaning back against the seat.

"Yes, Your Grace," she replied, folding her hands in her lap. "I arranged for it to arrive with the material. If that meets with your approval?" She gave him an anxious look, fearing she may have overstepped her bounds.

"That is fine." Wyatt dismissed her fears with a shrug. "I ordered several items, and the clerk assures me they will be delivered no later than tomorrow." He paused, then added, "You will find some items for yourself among them. I hope you will accept them."

Nia straightened in alarm. "Items? What items?"

"A new cloak, some gloves, nothing extravagant," Wyatt replied, his bored manner indicating he considered the matter of little import. "You are my niece's governess, and your appearance is a reflection upon me. I can hardly allow you to go about in a threadbare cloak."

Nia's cheeks flushed with mortification. She'd hoped the worn condition of her cloak hadn't been obvious, but apparently she hadn't reckoned with His Grace's sharp eyes. She shot him a resentful look, wishing she dared refuse his magnanimity. Unfortunately, she didn't have that luxury. As her employer he was well within his rights to dictate what she wore, and the knowledge stung. She took a deep breath, swallowing her pride with difficulty.

"Thank you, Your Grace," she said, her voice stiff with fury. "That is most generous of you."

"You are welcome." Wyatt bit his lip, hiding a quick smile at her ill-disguised temper. She looked as if she'd like nothing better than to throw his gifts back in his face, and he admired her pride. He had no desire to humble her, but neither did he want to see her dressed in rags when he had more than enough money to buy whatever she required. He was all too aware that if it hadn't been for her he would never have met Amanda, and he was determined to repay her. Even, he admitted ruefully, if she didn't desire repayment.

The rest of the trip passed in silence, and they were soon back at Berkeley Square. Amanda wanted to show her doll to Mrs. Mayton and went dashing back to the kitchens, but when Nia would have followed, Wyatt drew her into his study for a private coze.

"If Lady Catherine should call tomorrow, I would like you to use the duchess's room," he said, settling behind his desk. "I will leave word with Mrs. Mayton to prepare something special."

"Very well, my lord," Nia agreed, her pique forgotten at the thought of using the beautiful room. She'd glanced in at it several times in the past few weeks, and she was quite enamored of it. "Will there be anything else?"

Wyatt hesitated, then said, "Miss Pringle, if I were to ask you something, would you answer me honestly? I promise I shan't hold it against you if you speak the truth."

"I should hope I always speak the truth, Your Grace," Nia replied. And then because they were speaking of integrity she added, "Or at least, I try. What is it you wish to know?"

He smiled, and then grew suddenly serious. "Do you think I am ignoring Amanda?" he asked bluntly, his dark eyes grim as they met hers. "The truth, Miss Pringle, if you please."

Nia was taken aback by his straightforward demand. She already knew he was determined to do his duty by Amanda, but what she could now see was that he genuinely cared about her as well. The last of Nia's resentment faded.

"No, Your Grace, I do not," she answered, her voice firm as she pushed her glasses back up her nose. "In the few weeks we have been in your home you have paid Amanda more attention than many of my former employers paid their children in a year. You are obviously interested in her well-being, and when she speaks, you listen to her. I cannot tell you how rare that is. You are an excellent guardian, Your Grace. Amanda could not ask for better."

Wyatt was genuinely touched by her praise.

"Thank you, Miss Pringle," he said huskily. "You have greatly relieved my mind."

"You are welcome, sir," Nia said, pleased. "If that will be all, I will return to my rooms."

Wyatt knew he should dismiss her, but he was oddly reluctant to do so. Since the night they'd met she had been much in his thoughts, and he was suddenly curious to learn more of the woman who had changed his life so irrevocably. "Before you go, Miss Pringle, I was wondering how you are settling in," he said, leaning back in his chair to study her. "I apologize for not speaking with you sooner, but I fear I have been rather busy. Is all to your liking?"

Since she had been anticipating his question, Nia was quick to reply. "Yes, my lord," she answered with a placating smile. "Everything here is delightful, and your staff has been most accommodating. Indeed, they couldn't be more helpful."

He arched an eyebrow at her response. "I wasn't asking for an evaluation of my household's performance, ma'am. I asked if you are happy. Are you?"

For a moment Nia was at a loss how to reply. In all her years in service she couldn't remember the last time anyone had asked her something so personal. *Was* she happy? she wondered, weighing the matter carefully before responding. "Yes, Lord Tilton," she said, her eyes meeting his. "I am."

Wyatt's broad shoulders relaxed, and he realized he'd been holding his breath. "I'm glad to hear that," he confessed, propping his booted feet on his desk. "There aren't any young ladies here for you to converse with, and I feared you might be growing lonely."

"Not at all," she assured him. "Amanda is more than company enough for me, and truth to tell, I am used to being alone. In my other positions I was often left to my own devices, and when I traveled with my father there were times when there were no other women near my age anywhere in sight. Respectable females, that is," she clarified with a grimace, remembering too well the bold campfollowers who had tagged along after the army.

"Yes, I'd heard you spent several years following the drum with your father," he said slowly, recalling one of the few details he'd learned from Mrs. Langston prior to hiring Nia.

"From the time I was five," Nia replied, her expression softening as she thought of her father. "It was an interesting life, and despite the many difficulties, I enjoyed myself immensely. If Papa hadn't died of the flux when I was nineteen, I daresay I'd still be trooping after him."

Wyatt was thinking it was probably the difficulties she enjoyed most, when the rest of her confession brought him upright. "But what of marriage?" he asked curiously, leaning forward to study her face. "Surely your father would have wanted a more settled life for you."

"Perhaps," Nia agreed, recalling the occasional arguments she and her father had had on that very subject. "For all he was devoted to the army, he was terrified I would marry into the regiment. He wanted me to return to England and marry a 'proper sort of gentleman,' or so he used to claim."

"Why didn't you?"

"Probably because marrying a proper sort of gentleman was the worst fate I could imagine," Nia confessed with a rueful laugh, too lost in memory to consider Wyatt might regard her words as inflammatory. "And, of course, there wasn't enough time. When I was the right age to be introduced, we were too busy tending the wounded of Badjoz to give the matter another thought. A year later, he was dead."

"And that was when you returned to England?" Wyatt was intrigued by this unexpected glimpse into her past.

"There were several of us, widows and orphans, who were evacuated along with the wounded," she said, her eyes growing bleak at the memory of the terrible suffering she had seen. "When I reached London I discovered most of my relations were dead, and the small annuity my father left me wasn't enough to support me."

"And so you became a governess," he concluded, touched at the matter-of-fact way she described what must have been a terrifying nightmare. Looking at her now, with her spectacles and prim if somewhat grubby uniform, it was hard to believe she had led such an adventurous life. She looked the perfect governess, he thought, until one noted the shadows in her hazel eyes and the determined set of her full mouth. His eyes lingered on the curve of her lips, and he wondered if they would feel as soft and passionate as they looked.

"And so I became a governess," Nia agreed, her cheeks pinking as she felt the force of his stare. She knew he wasn't *really* gazing at her mouth as if he'd like nothing better than to kiss her, but that didn't keep her heart from racing with an exciting blend of nerves. Telling herself it was time she was returning to her duties, she rose to her feet, her eyes not quite meeting his as she shook out her skirts.

"If Your Grace will excuse me, I believe I shall peek in on Amanda," she said, praying her voice didn't betray her sudden uneasiness. "We are to have our Latin lessons this afternoon."

"Certainly, Miss Pringle." Wyatt inclined his head politely. "Kindly give Virgil my regards."

After she departed, Wyatt leaned back in his chair, his expression pensive as he gazed up at the ceiling. He hadn't meant to frighten her off, he thought, recalling with pleasure the soft flush that had stained her cheeks. She wasn't as beautiful as many of the women he knew, but there was something about her he found undeniably attractive.

Perhaps it was her defiant spirit, or her devotion to Amanda, he mused, or even the way her spectacles never stayed quite straight on her nose. Whatever the cause, he found himself thinking of her more than was proper, and he was determined to put a halt to such preoccupation.

Miss Pringle was his employee, and as such, his responsibility. The last thing he wished was to place her in an awkward position with his attentions. Not only would such actions strip him of any right to call himself a gentleman, but he much doubted she would tolerate such behavior for a second. At worst she would probably out a bullet through him, he decided, grinning as he remembered that delightful interlude in his carriage. At best, she could simply leave. That thought drove the grin from his face.

Over the past fortnight he had come almost to envy the obvious love between his niece and her unusual governess. They were devoted to each other, and he was loathe to endanger that bond in any way. His fascination with Miss Pringle was nothing more than propinquity, and it would pass with time. It had better, he told himself grimly. The last thing he needed in his chaotic life was another complication.

Chapter 6

A s promised, Lady Catherine arrived at precisely three o'clock, nor was she alone. In addition to her maid, she was accompanied by a plain, middle-aged lady whom she introduced simply as Miss Saunders.

"I am her ladyship's companion," the woman informed Nia with a haughty look. "It would not do for an earl's daughter to go calling unless she was *properly* escorted."

"Indeed?" Nia managed, trying not to wince as she recalled the times she and Amanda had gone out walking without so much as a footman to accompany them.

"Oh, yes," Miss Saunders assured her with a superior smile. "Such things are simply not done in *our* world. Why, even a child as young as Lady Amanda is expected to behave in a manner befitting her rank. Should you have any questions regarding the proprieties, Miss Pringle, you have only to apply to me. My father was the third son of a baron, and I am familiar with the ways of the *ton*. I would be more than happy to instruct you."

When the nether regions of Hades freeze over, Nia thought, although she managed a thin smile. "Thank you, Miss Saunders," she managed, resisting the urge to dump the contents of her teacup over the other woman's head. "I will remember that."

"This is a lovely room," Lady Catherine said into the uneasy silence that followed. "I adore violet."

"As do I, your ladyship," Nia said, grateful for the

younger woman's tact. "In fact, this is my favorite room in the house."

"What is your favorite room, dearest?" Lady Catherine asked, leaning down to smile at Amanda.

"The ballroom," Amanda answered at once, her eyes resting hopefully on a cream cake. "It has hundreds of mirrors."

" 'Hundreds of mirrors,' Lady Amanda?" Miss Saunders repeated with a condescending laugh. "I believe you are exaggerating, my dear. Not an attractive feature in a lady."

"Well, it seems as if it has a hundred mirrors," Amanda replied sulkily, deciding she didn't care for the hatchet-faced lady. She reminded her of the nasty man who had come to her house before her mama died. He had made her mama cry, she remembered, and he had called her a naughty name.

"I am sure it does," Miss Saunders replied, her mouth thinning. "Still, it never does to become *too* enthusiastic, my lady. Enthusiasm is for the lower orders. A lady strives always for dignity and decorum. Is that not so, Lady Catherine?"

"One strives, certainly," Lady Catherine agreed with a laugh, "but whether one actually succeeds, I cannot say. Would you like a cream cake, Amanda? They look delicious to me."

Amanda eagerly accepted the treat, and while she was devouring it the adults continued talking amongst themselves. All too soon the hour had flown, and it was time for Lady Catherine to leave. They were making their good-byes when Lady Catherine suddenly asked to see the schoolroom.

"You needn't come with us, Miss Saunders," she added, giving her companion a sweet smile. "I know your lumbago has been paining you, and I see no reason why you should suffer because of my curiosity. I shall only be a moment."

"That is very good of you, my lady." Miss Saunders looked relieved. "I fear my poor hips are already protesting this damp weather."

They left her in the drawing room to enjoy the fire, and as soon as they were out of earshot Lady Catherine turned to Nia. "I hope you did not take offense to Miss Saunders," she said with a look of rueful apology. "She does mean well, and really, life has not been so very easy for her. She was raised a lady and must now make her living as a servant."

"I understand, my lady," Nia replied, accepting the apology with good grace. Her own story was fairly close to Miss Saunders's, although she had been raised following the drum rather than in the safe world of the gentry.

"Another reason I wished to get you alone is so that I might offer you the name of my modiste. She is very talented, and you may rely upon her to fashion Amanda a suitable wardrobe."

Nia turned to her in amazement. "I beg your pardon?" she said, not quite believing her ears.

"Oh dear," Lady Catherine sighed, her blue eyes worried. "Now I have offended you. I didn't mean to, I assure you. It is just . . . well, I do have eyes, and I can see that Amanda's gown isn't exactly in the current mode. And at Ackermann's I noticed you were studying pattern books. Naturally if I am mistaken, I—"

"No, no, you are not mistaken," Nia interrupted weakly, her pride warring with her common sense. "As it happens I have been looking for a modiste for Amanda, and I would appreciate your help. I am afraid I don't know very much about such things," she added with a self-deprecating laugh.

"Thank you." Lady Catherine gave her hand a gentle squeeze. "I wouldn't have mentioned it, but I feared Miss Saunders would say something and insult you beyond all bearing."

Nia smiled reluctantly. "She does seem rather . . . strong-minded," she amended, not wishing to offend her ladyship after all her kindness. "Now, what is the name and direction of your modiste? Is she French?"

"Creole, actually, from New Orleans. Her name is

Madame DuFrense, and her shop is on Dover Street not far from Picadilly. She designed my gown," she added, indicating her stylish gown with a wave of her hand.

"In that case I shall definitely wish to engage her," Nia said, giving the dress an admiring look. "And thank you, Lady Catherine. I am most grateful for your assistance."

When they were finished with the impromptu tour, they returned to the duchess's room, where they found the duke and a stranger talking with Amanda and Miss Saunders. Wyatt introduced the man to Nia as his very good friend, Ambrose Royston.

"I am pleased to make your acquaintance, Miss Pringle," Mr. Royston said, smiling as he bent over her hand. "Lord Tilton has been loud in his praises of your abilities, and having met your charming pupil, I can see he has not lied."

"Thank you, sir," Nia murmured, deciding she rather like Mr. Royston. He had an open, honest face, and there was something about his light brown hair and laughing blue eyes that made him seem approachable. Unlike *some* people, she thought, her gaze flicking toward the duke, who was sitting beside Amanda.

Dressed in a dark green jacket of Bath superfine, his lean calves encased in a pair of shining Hessians, his grace looked as hard and remote as the first time she had seen him. He was wearing his black hair swept back from his forehead, throwing the austere planes of his face into prominence, and his obsidian-flecked eyes were coolly watchful as he sat in silence. Just as Nia wondered if he ever intended to smile, Amanda tugged at his hand, claiming his attention.

"What is it, my dear?" he asked, his expression softening as he bent his head closer.

"May I show Lady Catherine my doll?" Amanda asked, gazing up at her uncle in hopeful expectation.

"I think that would be very nice," Wyatt approved. "Provided her ladyship has no objections?" he added, raising questioning eyes to meet Catherine's gaze.

"I would adore seeing your doll," she told Amanda with a warm smile. "Please do fetch her for us."

Amanda went dashing off. The door had no sooner closed behind her than Miss Saunders turned to Catherine, her face set in pinched lines of disapproval. "I hate to nettle you, my lady," she began in prim tones, "but may I remind you we are expected at Lady Redvale's? It would not do to be late."

"I am sure a matter of a few minutes is of no consequence, Miss Saunders," Catherine replied, accepting her companion's censure with equanimity. "And if know my sister, she won't make her appearance until ten minutes after her last guest has been seated. Anne has always liked making an entrance."

As this was patently true, Miss Saunders could not object, although she did give a loud sniff before turning to Wyatt. "How are you enjoying the season, Your Grace?" she asked with an ingratiating smile. "Lady Geoffrey mentioned you have only just come out of mourning for your brother."

"I am finding the season quite tolerable, ma'am," Wyatt answered politely, hoping his dislike of the encroaching woman did not show. "London is always a fascinating city."

"I remember my first season," Miss Saunders continued with a sigh. "I was just seventeen, and the city was full of French émigrés fleeing that tiresome revolution. When the peasants began guillotining their betters, I recall we all wore red ribbons about our necks. It was most exciting." She turned to Nia, her dark eyes full of malice.

"And what of you, Miss Pringle?" she asked with cloying sweetness. "What do you remember of your first season?"

"As I have never had a season, Miss Saunders, I fear I have no memories," Nia answered, boldly meeting the other woman's stare. "When I was seventeen I was with my father in Portugal. He was an army surgeon, and I traveled with him until he died."

Miss Saunders blinked. "Oh." It was apparently all she could think of to say.

"You must have seen a great deal in your travels, Miss Pringle," Ambrose said, graciously glossing over the awkward moment. "I've always longed to travel, but I fear I have never ventured out of England. Perhaps now that Bony is safely caged, I can change that."

"Travel can be most educational," Nia agreed dryly, trying not to recall some of the horrors she had witnessed. "When I was no more than Amanda's age my father's regiment was posted to Egypt, and despite all the difficulties, he insisted upon taking us with him. It was ..." She searched for the proper words to describe the searing heat and appalling dirt they'd encountered. "Interesting," she concluded with a half-smile. "You've never lived, sir, until you've had a camel spit at you."

"I'm sure I have not, but if it is all the same to you, ma'am, it is an experience I believe I should choose to miss. I have already been bitten, kicked, and trod upon by English horses, and that is lowering enough to my consequence."

The others were still chuckling over Ambrose's droll observation when Amanda returned, the doll clutched lovingly in her arms. "Uncle Wyatt bought her for me," she said, presenting the toy to Catherine. "I named her Lady Catherine, after you. See? She has blond hair, just like you and me."

Catherine stroked the doll's hair, obviously aware of the great honor Amanda had accorded her. "So she does," she agreed with a misty smile. "Thank you, Amanda. She is a lovely doll."

Amanda next offered the doll to Ambrose. "Would you like to hold her? You may, if you promise to be very, very careful."

The look of horror on Ambrose's face was almost

comical. "I ... that is most generous of you, Lady Amanda," he stammered, sending Wyatt an imploring look, "but I am afraid I—" He broke off as the doll was thrust into his hands.

Content that her doll was safe for the moment, Amanda climbed back up on the settee beside her uncle. "Guess what I saw?" she asked of the room at large. "I saw that carriage again."

"What carriage, Amanda?" Nia asked.

"That carriage," Amanda repeated impatiently. "I saw it yesterday when we were in the park, and once when we were walking I saw it, too."

Wyatt shifted in his seat until he could look down at the child. "What did this carriage look like?" he asked, a frisson of alarm making the hair at the back of his neck stand up. He knew it was probably nothing, but in these dangerous times one could never be too careful.

"It was black," Amanda said in dramatic tones. "And the man driving it was wearing a big hat and a coat with lots of capes."

She had just described half the coaches in London, Wyatt realized, and relaxed his shoulders. "I shall have the servants keep watch," he promised, giving her hand a pat.

"I think it was a villain," Amanda continued, unwilling to give up the center of attention. "I'll wager he was going to snatch me up, Miss Pringle, just like Count Divicchio!"

"Who?" Ambrose leaned forward, temporarily forgetting the doll cradled in his arm.

"No one." Nia spoke quickly, her face scarlet with mortification. She'd read Amanda and the others that silly novel months ago. It never occurred to her that the little girl would remember it in such vivid detail.

"He was the duke of Venice," Amanda informed him with obvious relish. "He was a bad, bad man who was gong to wall poor Louella up in the chapel, but he got walled up instead. Do you have anyone walled up in your chapel, Uncle?" She looked up at Wyatt hopefully. "Can I see them?"

Wyatt bit his lip, torn between laughter and annoyance. It was obvious Amanda was describing a scene from a Minervan novel, and he could think of only one person who might have read it to her. "I am afraid I do not," he said apologetically, his eyes resting on Miss Pringle's flushed features. "But we will speak of this later, Amanda. Our guests were just leaving."

Lady Catherine took the gentle hint and rose to her feet, leaving Miss Saunders no choice but to follow. Judging from the self-satisfied smirk on her face, she was doubtlessly delighted at the small scene, and Nia could well imagine what she was thinking.

After the door shut behind them, Ambrose also stood, his glance full of amusement as it darted between Wyatt and Nia. "I am afraid I must also be taking my leave," he said, a dimple flashing in his cheek. "Shall I see you at the Preshtons' on Thursday, Your Grace?"

"That would be fine," Wyatt answered, his eyes dancing as he studied Ambrose. "In the meanwhile, may I ask you a question?"

"Certainly."

"Will you be leaving Lady Catherine?" He indicated the doll still tucked in his friend's arm. "Or is it your intention to start a new fashion?"

"Well, Miss Pringle, what is your explanation?" Wyatt asked some twenty minutes later as he and Miss Pringle stood in his study. "I trust you have one?"

Nia shoved her glasses back up her nose, resenting the duke's haughty tones. Since the moment Amanda had mentioned the count, she'd known His Grace would demand satisfaction, and she'd been carefully preparing her defense.

"Children inevitably desire that which is forbidden them," she began, her eyes fixed on the knot in his exquisitely tied cravat. "Knowing this, I brought some Minervan novels to the academy, and I sold them to my pupils at so much per page."

Wyatt raised a dark eyebrow. "One would have thought orphans would not have had a great deal of money for such fripperies," he observed sardonically.

Nia's glance flicked up to meet his. "The medium of exchange was work, Your Grace," she informed him in a tight voice, "not money. I required so many pages of mathematics and Latin in exchange for a page of the story. It worked remarkably well."

"Yes, I can see that it would," Wyatt conceded, his estimation of his opponent increasing. He only wished some of his tutors had been half so enterprising. "However," he continued in a stern voice, "I still feel you shouldn't have read such things to someone so young as Amanda. You can see the effect it has had upon her. The poor child sees villains and assassins behind every bush."

"I know." Nia had the good grace to flush. "And in truth, I did usually restrict the arrangement to my older students. But Amanda slipped into the classroom one day and heard me reading to the others. She became fascinated and pleaded with me to hear the rest of the story. I know I should have told her no, but ..." She gave an ineffectual shrug.

Wyatt, who had already found himself being wound about his niece's thumb, could well identify with her predicament. "Then I take it this is the end of it?" he queried, folding his arms across his chest. "I needn't worry about Amanda developing a fascination with moldering dungeons and Italian counts?"

Nia fought the urge to smile at his teasing words. "No, Your Grace, you do not."

"Good," Wyatt said, and gave a sudden chuckle.

"What?" she asked curiously, intrigued by the bemused expression on his face. It made him look younger, more relaxed, and, she realized, her heart skipping a beat, more devastatingly handsome than ever.

"I was just thinking that this is the oddest conversation I've ever had with a lady," Wyatt replied, surprising both of them with his candor. "Usually when I am alone with an attractive woman I am singing praises to her glorious hazel eyes, not discussing the affects of Gothic literature on impressionable young minds. What a disappointing flat you must think me."

Nia felt her cheeks glowing with embarrassment. "Nonsense, my lord," she said gruffly, hiding her discomfort behind a scowl. "I am a governess, not an . . . an attractive woman." She stumbled over the last words, praying he wouldn't think she was angling for compliments.

Her answer amused Wyatt. "I was not aware that being a governess precluded being attractive," he drawled, giving her his most provocative grin. "But naturally, as you are the governess, I shall bow to your superior knowledge of the matter."

"Thank you." Nia rose to her feet with as much dignity as she could muster. "With your permission, sir, I will be retiring to my rooms. It has been a long day."

"Of course," Wyatt agreed, a half-smile playing about his lips as he watched her cross the room. He waited until her hand was on the brass handle before calling out to her.

"Miss Pringle?"

"Yes, Your Grace?" She stopped and sent him a suspicious look over her slender shoulder.

His smile became a full-fledged grin. "Your hazel eyes *are* glorious."

The next week passed in relative tranquility. The purchases from Ackermann's were delivered, and Nia began the painstaking task of laying and cutting out her new dress. She was somewhat dismayed when it appeared her things had been added to the duke's bill, but when she mentioned the matter to Mrs. Mayton, the housekeeper dismissed her fears.

"Not to worry, my dear," she said, patting Nia's hand. "His Grace can always deduct it from your salary if need be."

Nia's lessons with Amanda took up most of the mornings, while afternoons were given over to the time consuming task of arranging the girl's new wardrobe. She was delighted at so much attention, and submitted to the endless fittings like one to the manor born. Nia was not so sanguine, and she felt compelled to protest what she regarded as frivolous waste.

"A riding habit, madame?" she asked, examining a length of claret velvet the modiste had set aside. "The child is but six years old, and she doesn't even have a horse!"

"Perhaps not, but one never knows, *n'est ce pas?*" madame replied, giving Nia a wink. "His Grace was most specific in his instructions, and a riding habit was among the things he ordered for both the mademoiselle and you, Miss Pringle."

"For me?" Nia was surprised. "Why should I require a habit?"

"So that you may instruct her ladyship to ride, I am thinking," the Creole woman replied with obvious patience. "She can hardly learn on her own."

"That is so," Nia admitted, then forgot her reluctance at the thought of riding again. Although she counted herself as a good rider, she hadn't been on a horse in years, and the prospect was decidedly pleasing.

She mentioned this the next time the duke took tea with them, and he gave a pleased nod.

"I was hoping you rode," he said, crossing his booted feet in front of him as he settled back in his chair. "Perryvale is best seen from horseback, and I was hoping to show you and Amanda about, once we are settled."

Nia thought that had a rather intimate sound, and was surprised when her heart gave an unexpected lurch. As usual, she hid her vexing emotion behind a display of efficiency. "The modiste Lady Catherine selected is a godsend," she said, fixing her gaze over his right shoulder. "Not only has she talent and style, but she also has little ones of her own, and understands that a child's clothes must be sturdy as well as fashionable."

"A wise consideration," Wyatt commented, remembering the afternoon he'd caught Amanda attempting to scale the shelves in his library. "That reminds me, there are several trees at the estate that are sure to prove a temptation to one with Amanda's adventuresome spirit. I would be forever grateful if you could keep her from killing herself."

"I shall do my best, Your Grace," Nia promised, thinking that at the first opportunity she would instruct Amanda in the proper way to climb a tree. It was either that, she mused, or put the child back in leading strings. She'd already noticed Amanda studying the trees in the park with a speculative gleam in her eyes.

Wyatt saw the thoughtful look on Nia's face and guessed what she was thinking. "Should your best include a demonstration in the fine art of tree-climbing, Miss Pringle, might I suggest you take care not to fall?" he teased, his eyes lingering on hers. "Governesses are rather like horses, you see. In the sad event they should break a limb, we have them shot."

Nia was still chuckling over the remark the following afternoon as she and Amanda were enjoying their stroll in the park. When she'd first made the duke's acquaintance she'd thought him puffed up beyond all bearing, but since then her opinion of him had altered considerably. Oh, he could still be insufferably high in the instep, she conceded, her lips softening in an indulgent smile, but his arrogance was more than balanced by the compassion he showed to those about him. Why, only yesterday he—

"Miss Pringle! Miss Pringle, it's him!"

Amanda's outburst startled Nia out of her reverie,

and she glanced around, half-expecting to see the object of her daydreams standing before her. "There is who, dearest?" she asked, when she couldn't find any sign of the duke.

"The man!" Amanda exclaimed, dancing from one foot to the other. "The man who has been following us!"

Nia's gaze flew in the direction Amanda was indicating with her finger, and she saw a black carriage parked in the street opposite the park. The driver had been turned in their direction, but when he saw her watching him, he turned away and hunched down in his greatcoat.

"You're sure it's the same man?" Nia asked, wondering if she ought to confront the fellow. "It isn't someone who merely looks like him?"

Amanda shook her head. "He has a funny face," she insisted, twisting her own features to demonstrate. "And when he sees me watching him, he always tries to hide. Like now."

He *was* trying to hide, Nia admitted, watching the man as he shifted nervously on the carriage's high seat. She reasoned an innocent man would have no cause to avoid detection, and her anxiety increased. Lord Tilton was a wealthy man, and it was possible they had attracted the attention of some nefarious person. The prospect made her tighten her hold on Amanda's hand.

"You say you've seen this man several times before?" she asked, cursing herself for not listening to Amanda when she first mentioned the villain.

"He waits by the gate until we go by. I wasn't sure if that was him, but when the other man peeked out the carriage window, I *knew* it was."

"What other man?" Nia demanded in alarm. This was the first time Amanda had ever mentioned more than one.

"The other man in the coach," Amanda elaborated, her tone making it obvious she considered her governess a shocking slow top. "He's there sometimes, too."

"And what does he look like?" Nia began looking for the footman who usually accompanied them. She saw him by the rosebushes flirting with a pretty nursemaid and summoned him over with a wave of her hand.

"I've never seen his face," Amanda admitted with a shrug, "but he has spectacles, like yours. I saw them sparkling in the sunlight when he turned his head."

Certain this was a detail the little girl would never have invented on her own, Nia decided it was time to take action. When the footman rejoined them, she turned Amanda over to him.

"Take her ladyship home at once," she ordered, her eyes never leaving the coach. "I'll be along in a few minutes."

"But, Miss Pringle, His Grace said I was to keep my peepers on ye both!" the footman protested, his cheeks paling in distress. "He'll give me the boot if he finds out I left ye alone!"

The carriage was beginning to move, and Nia knew she'd have to hurry if she wanted to get a good look at whoever was inside. "Just do as I say!" she commanded, picking up the skirts of her gown and running toward the street.

"You there, hold!" she called out sharply, her eyes flashing in indignation as she saw the carriage pulling away. "Stop! I would speak with you!"

She dashed into the street, a plan to block the carriage's retreat half-formed in her mind. But rather than pulling up as she expected, the driver brought his whip down on the horse's backs and whistled a sharp command. In a flash Nia realized the foolishness of her actions, but by then it was too late. The carriage was almost on top of her, and there was no time to think.

She turned toward the curb, but before she could move she was tackled, the impact throwing her to one side. A strong pair of arms closed about her waist, holding her protectively as she and her rescuer tumbled to the ground and rolled out of the path of the carriage's wheels.

Nia could hear screams and shouts about her, but her only thought was that her prey had escaped. Angry and frightened, she took out her displeasure on her rescuer. "Curse it, he is getting away!" she snapped, wiping the mud from her face as she struggled to a sitting position. "What the devil do you think you were doing?"

Instead of the stammering protest she expected, she heard a cold, clipped voice that was all too familiar. "How odd you should ask that, Miss Pringle," the duke said, his voice freezing Nia as her gaze flashed up to his hard, implacable features. "I was about to ask you the very same thing."

Chapter 7

ᘓᗋᕼ

"**W**ell, Miss Pringle? I am waiting."

The duke's deep voice was edged with sarcasm as he regarded Nia from his post by the fireplace. He was standing with one arm resting on the mantel, his booted feet crossed at the ankles, but his indolent pose in no way deceived her. It was obvious her employer was in a towering rage, and she knew she'd have to tread lightly if she hoped to retain her position.

As she always did when she was uncertain, Nia retreated behind a wall of belligerence. "I am sure things were not quite so perilous as they appeared, Your Grace," she said, her mouth set in a truculent line as she raised her face. "I was but attempting to detain the coach so that I could see who was inside. I was never in any real danger."

"Were you not?" Wyatt demanded coldly, his hand balling in a fist as he remembered his fear when he'd seen the coach bearing down on her. "You forget, ma'am, I am the one who snatched you from beneath the wheels of that carriage. I am more than aware of the danger you courted with such reckless abandon. It is a miracle you weren't killed."

Nia paled, her stomach lurching at the memory of the huge wheels passing within inches of her head. If the duke hadn't acted as quickly as he had, she could well be lying broken and bleeding on the cobblestone street. She lowered her gaze to her hands, noticing somewhat distractedly that they were still streaked with mud. After they'd arrived home the duke had

hustled her into his study before she'd had a chance
to change, and she was only now realizing what a
fright she must look.

Not him, though, she thought, resentment simmering in her breast. He hadn't so much as a hair out
of place, and his nankins were as smooth as ever, despite that he had taken the brunt of their fall. She
was brooding over the inequity of this as he continued his lecture.

"I can understand your concern for Amanda's
safety," Wyatt said in a tight voice, making, he
thought, a heroic effort to be patient. "But you ought
to have come directly to me rather than tried to handle the matter on your own."

"But I had to stop him!" Nia protested, lifting her
gaze from her morose study of his neat cravat to
send him an indignant glare. "He would have escaped!"

"And what if he had?" Wyatt demanded, infuriated by her continued obstinacy. "At least *then* we
might have had a chance of catching him!"

The defiance went out of Nia. "What do you
mean?"

"I mean while the man . . . whoever he might
be . . . thought himself unobserved, we might have
been able to set a trap for him," Wyatt retorted, seeing no reason to spare her feelings. "But now that he
knows we are aware of him, the Lord above knows
what he might do next."

His words struck Nia crueler than any whip might
have done. She *had* been foolish, she admitted, swallowing a painful lump in her throat, and worse, it
might not be she who paid the price but Amanda.
She shifted uncomfortably in her chair, fighting back
tears of shame.

Wyatt saw her bend her head, and felt his own
contrition. He'd wanted to drive home how impru-
dent she'd been, but he'd never meant to make her
cry. Feeling every inch the villain, he pushed himself

away from the fireplace and crossed the room to kneel beside her.

"Come now, tears?" he chided, slipping his hand beneath her chin and raising her face to his. "Never say the redoubtable Miss Pringle would actually dissolve into a watering pot merely because of a few scolding words? How disillusioning."

His teasing words had the desired effect as Nia gave a reluctant laugh. "I sincerely hope a few tears would not qualify me for such an appellation, Your Grace," she said, blinking as she met his gaze. "And for your information, I wasn't crying because you reprimanded me."

"You weren't?" He stroked his thumb over her cheek.

"No," she replied, trying not to blush at his touch. "I . . . I was upset because you are right. It was wrong of me to act so thoughtlessly. Amanda might have been hurt because of me."

"Perhaps Amanda wasn't my main concern," Wyatt said, and was shocked to realize he was speaking the truth. Astonishing as it sounded, his only thought had been to reach Nia before the oncoming carriage crushed her beneath its wheels. He hadn't even thought of Amanda until he saw her standing next to the horrified footman, her small face streaked with tears.

Nia stared up at him, her heart pounding with a fear that had little to do with her brush with death. For more nights than she dared admit, images of the duke had kept her awake as she longed for things a woman in her position had no right to long for. Fearing he would read her thoughts in her eyes, she turned her head, freeing her chin from his gentle hold.

"Yes, I recall what you said about governnesses who break their limbs," she said with a shaky laugh, her eyes fixed on one of the portraits lining the wall. "I should hate to put you to the trouble of finding a new governess at such short notice."

Wyatt gave her a sharp look, aware of a strong desire to correct her assumption that his interest in her was solely because of her value to Amanda. Only the knowledge that such a confession would shock her kept him from acting on his impulses, and with great effort he swallowed the words. His face was expressionless as he helped her to her feet.

"I want you to spend the rest of the afternoon in bed," he ordered, placing his hands on her shoulders for a moment. "And you will allow the doctor to examine you. I don't think you are hurt, but I prefer not to take any chances."

Nia felt such precautions were unnecessary, but when she saw the concern in the duke's dark eyes, she held back her objections. "As you say, Your Grace," she said instead, her voice cool as she forced herself to meet his gaze.

His lips quirked. "Don't be too docile, my dear," he warned with a soft laugh, "else I shall insist you be bled as well. You must surely be sickening after something if you are going to give in so easily."

The following afternoon Nia was in the schoolroom going over Amanda's penmanship papers when the maid appeared with a message that the duke wished to see her.

"He said you was to wear your cape, Miss Pringle," the maid added, her eyes bright with speculation. "And he has called for his carriage as well."

"Did he say I was to bring Lady Amanda?" Nia asked, wondering if the duke was taking them on a drive, as he occasionally did.

"No, miss, just you."

Other than raising her eyebrow at the maid's smug tone, Nia managed to hide her trepidation. She didn't really think Wyatt (as she privately thought of him) would dismiss her because of yesterday's contretemps, but she couldn't be certain. The thought was depressing, but she was determined to take the news with as much pride as she could muster. She was her father's daughter, she told herself sternly, and she would face the enemy's fire with courage and determination.

Lord Tilton was pacing the hall as she came down the stairs, and when he looked up and saw her, his lips lifted in a smile of welcome. "Good day, Miss Pringle," he said, coming forward to take her hand. "May I say how pleased I am to see you aren't one of those ladies who delights in keeping a fellow waiting while she primps? I own I've little patience for such creatures."

His teasing words brought an annoying rush of color to Nia's cheeks. "A true lady is known for her punctuality, Your Grace," she said, privately vowing to keep a proper distance. "And you may make sure I shall install that belief in Lady Amanda."

Her starchy tone and the cool look of censure on her face had Wyatt biting back a smile. He wondered if she knew how adorable she looked when she was trying so very hard to be prim. "Then I am a most fortunate guardian," he drawled, deciding to press his luck by carrying her hand to his lips for a brief kiss. "Now I shan't have to listen to Amanda's beaus complaining when she keeps them cooling their heels in the parlor."

Short of engaging in an undignified struggle, Nia had no choice but to allow Wyatt to retain possession of her hand. "Nancy said you wished to see me, my lord," she said instead, her back rigid as she fixed her gaze over his right shoulder.

Wyatt took pity on her and released her hand, albeit with a sharp pang of reluctance. "Yes, I wanted to discuss yesterday's incident with you," he said, stepping back. "And I thought it might be pleasant for you to have some air at the same time."

Nia was tempted to inform him that she was in no need of such a commodity, but something stopped her. As her employer, he was within his rights to command her presence anywhere he pleased, within reason, but she doubted this was a mere whim on his part. Something was clearly afoot, and she waited until they were in the privacy of his coach before demanding to know what was going on.

"You don't think one of the staff is involved in all of this, do you?" she demanded, coming to what she felt was the only logical conclusion. "They are devoted to Amanda!"

"Even the most devoted servant has been known to wag his tongue when he would have been better advised holding it," Wyatt answered cryptically, his jaw setting with anger. "I have an uneasy feeling those men, whoever they are, knew precisely who Amanda is, and they had to learn that from someone. I shall not rest until I learn who that someone is."

"But—"

"Enough of that for the moment," Wyatt interrupted, settling back against the seat. "Tell me what you think of London. Will you miss it, should you leave?"

"What has that to do with anything?" Nia demanded, glowering at him in frustration. "We were discussing Amanda!"

"We always discuss Amanda," Wyatt replied, unperturbed by her obvious disapproval. "But if it will help soothe your overly rigid sense of propriety, I am asking because I'm thinking of leaving London for my country estate. I was wondering how you'd feel about it."

"I love the country," Nia assured him, feeling slightly foolish for her outburst. "But even if I loathed it, it wouldn't matter. I'd never leave Amanda."

"Of course." Wyatt wondered what it was like to love someone so much that no sacrifice was too great. Lord knew it wasn't an emotion he'd ever experienced either as a lover or the one loved. Even his parents had seemed indifferent to him most of the time, and given what he suspected of his birth, he supposed he couldn't blame them.

"Are you leaving because of what happened yesterday?" Nia asked, noting the withdrawn look on his face. "Isn't that refining too much on what might be nothing more than a coincidence?"

Wyatt's gaze met hers. "Do *you* think it is a coincidence?"

"No, but—"

"Neither do I. And neither does Bow Street."

His calm pronouncement brought Nia snapping forward. "Bow Street!" she exclaimed, her eyes round with shock. "You've hired a runner?"

"An associate might be a more apt description," Wyatt clarified, thinking of the older man he'd spent the morning interviewing. "Runners have a tendency to attract undue attention, and I don't want to draw any more notice than we already have. Hemsley assured me no one will pay him more mind than they would any other servant."

"Servant? Do you mean he will act as a . . . a . . . spy?" Nia was entranced at the thought.

"I believe he prefers to think of himself as an agent operating deep in enemy territory," Wyatt said with a half-smile. "That was one of the reasons I wished to go for a drive. I don't want any of the servants, even my major domo, to know his true identity."

That made sense to Nia, and she relaxed slightly. "Ah, then your desire to put the roses back in my cheeks was nothing but a hum, eh?" she accused, refusing to be disappointed. "You just wanted to get me off where we wouldn't be overheard."

Wyatt gave her another of those slow smiles that made her heart race. "You wound me, Miss Pringle," he murmured, his eyes full of devilry. "I said my telling you about Mr. Hemsley was *one* of the reasons I wished to get you alone. The roses in your cheeks are of paramount interest to me, I do assure you."

Instead of being flattered or even amused by his witticism, Nia experienced a flash of pain. She drew herself up and glared at him. "False flattery is like false coin, Your Grace," she snapped. "It is easily spent, but of little value."

Her vehemence startled Wyatt. "What makes you so certain it is false?"

"Because it is." Nia was furious to find she was close to tears. Her feelings for Wyatt were new and troubling, and it cut her to the quick that he should treat her like a flirt. "If I learned nothing else in my years with my father, it was to look at life as it is, not as we would wish it to be."

"Then you wish my flattery was true?" he asked, trying to fathom what had upset her.

His conceit enraged Nia even further. "Don't put words in my mouth, sir! I am more than capable of speaking for myself!"

"So I have noticed."

"Oh!" Nia lifted her hands in exasperation, too furious to remember he was her employer. "You make me so angry! When we first met I thought you a cold, puffed-up prude, but you are nothing but a . . . an uncaring dilettante! Amanda might well be in the gravest danger, and you treat it like a lark. Do you care for nothing and no one?"

Wyatt's confusion and indulgence vanished at the accusation. "Why should I?" he retorted before he could stop himself. "Except for Christopher, no one has ever cared a damn for me."

The conviction in his voice shocked Nia out of her anger. She stared at him in horror. "But surely your parents . . ."

"Tolerated me," he finished for her, confessing what he had never confessed to another soul. "My mother especially seemed to have little use for me, but since she treated Christopher the same way, I told myself it did not matter."

His raw admission brought a lump to Nia's throat. It explained so much, she thought, her heart going out to the little boy who had stoically accepted his mother's neglect. No wonder he held himself aloof from the rest of the world. It was the only thing he knew.

"I am sorry," she said softly, wishing she could touch him, even if only to lay her hand on his.

"For my parent's indifference?" He gave a bitter laugh. "Why should you be? It's the truth, and it's the way things are done in my world."

"No." Nia shook her head. "I meant I am sorry for ripping up at you as I did. I know you were only funning me. It is just I was so worried about Amanda that I fear my sense of humor quite deserted me. I do have one, you know," she added when he didn't respond.

"Do you?" Wyatt realized she was trying to tease him out of his brown study, and was grateful. "I was beginning to wonder. At times you seem so ferociously determined to be such a pattern card for the perfect governess.

She gave him a quizzical frown. "But I *am* a governess."

"I know, but somehow I don't see you as one."

She had to ask. "How do you see me?"

He considered the matter for a long moment before replying. "As a friend," he said, his gaze solemn as he met hers. "Someone I can talk to, laugh with." He gave an unexpected chuckle. "I suppose it has to do with the way we first met. It is hard to treat anyone with propriety once they've held a pistol on you."

She covered her face with her hands and groaned. "I wish you would forget about that. I still cannot believe I behaved so outrageously."

"There you go, being the proper Miss Pringle," he chided, reaching out to take her hands in his and gently lowering them. "Come, admit it. You adored having me at such a disadvantage."

"It did have its moments," she said, delighting in his touch even as she warned herself to be prudent. "It isn't often a governess is allowed the upper hand with her employer, you know."

"I don't know about that. It seems to me you have no difficulty keeping me well in line," he drawled, his nostrils flaring as he caught again the faint scent of her perfume. It reminded him of the infamous night when they first met, and the memory of her white shoulders and soft breasts made the breath catch in his throat. He silently uttered a heartfelt curse and forced his thoughts away from the carnal memories.

"Practice, Your Grace, practice." To his relief she seemed unaware of the telling affect her nearness was having upon him. "Another thing I learned at my father's knee is that it never does to show any weakness to an enemy. He will only make use of it, to your grief."

"I would hope you do not see me in quite that light, Nia." Her given name came easily to his lips. "I am not your enemy."

"I know, my lord. I was but teasing," Nia said, deciding it was time to turn the conversation to safer topics. "And speaking of enemies, what does this Hemsley fellow intend to do about the men following Amanda?"

"We are discussing possible strategies." Wyatt followed her lead with relief. "In the meanwhile, what are your plans for Amanda? I know better than to think you will allow either her or yourself to remain safely behind locked doors."

Nia sent him a sharp look, but decided he wasn't serious. "We will exercise whatever caution you deem prudent, Your Grace," she said coolly. "But no, I have no intention of allowing us to become prisoners in our own home. In fact, we were talking of an outing to the Tower tomorrow afternoon. Amanda has been looking forward to it all week, but if you truly feel it is too dangerous, I suppose we could postpone it until these men are caught."

Wyatt considered that and then reluctantly shook his head. "Since I can't guarantee that will never happen, you might as well go ahead with your visit," he said with a sigh. "God above knows how long this could take, and I don't want to deprive you or

Amanda of the sights. But I believe Ambrose and I shall accompany you, just to be safe."

They spent the rest of the ride discussing the visit to the Tower, and by the time they returned home Nia had all but forgotten their earlier altercation. But Wyatt evidently had not, and just as Nia was about to climb down from the carriage, he laid his hand on her arm.

"You are wrong to say I care for nothing and no one," he said quietly, his expression forbidding as he held her gaze with his. "I *do* care, for Amanda ... and for you. I would give my life to keep you safe. Remember that."

"Uncle Wyatt is going to the Tower with us?" Amanda's eyes were bright with pleasure when Nia broke the news to her the following afternoon. "That is wonderful! Do you think he will show us the scaffold where Mary, Queen of Scots lost her head?"

"I shouldn't think it would still be standing," Nia said, accustomed now to the bloodthirstiness of the young. "But if it is, I am sure he could be persuaded to show you a peek."

"And the jewels," Amanda reminded her. "You said the warden would show them to us if we asked politely."

"Provided there aren't a great many people there. Although that shouldn't be a problem," Nia added, casting a worried glance at the rain lashing against the latticed window. "Are you quite sure you want to go out, dearest? I fear you may catch a chill."

"Pooh," Amanda replied with youthful disregard for such practical concerns. "I'll wear the new cape Uncle Wyatt bought me, and I shan't feel a drop."

"I'm sure you won't," Nia agreed wryly, thinking of the fur-lined cape of purple velvet that had arrived yesterday along with several new dresses.

"Will you wear your new cape?" Amanda asked, cocking her head to one side. "It's ever so pretty."

Nia's cheeks grew rosy at the mention of the black

alpaca cape that had been delivered along with Amanda's things. It was elegant and simple, and except for the French braid across the shoulders, devoid of decoration. It was a perfect cape for a governess, she acknowledged, but it stung that Wyatt had bought it for her.

"Yes, I believe I shall," she answered, putting her pride aside with conscious effort. After yesterday she felt she and Wyatt had come to a sort of understanding. His buying her the cloak wasn't meant as an insult. He was only trying to look after her, and his thoughtfulness touched her.

Besides, she added with a private smile, what choice did she have? He'd insist she wear the wretched thing, even going so far as to put it on her himself if she refused. Arrogant devil, she thought, her eyes glowing with emotions better left unexplored.

While Nia and Amanda were adding the finishing touches to their appearances, Wyatt and Ambrose were in the drawing room holding an impromptu council of war.

"Now remember," Wyatt began, "I want you to keep a sharp eye about you. If you suspect we're being followed, inform me at once. I will handle matters from there."

The note of deadly intent in his friend's voice brought Ambrose's brows up in speculation. "As you wish, Tilton," he replied easily, "but I still say you are going about this all wrong. Are you quite sure you won't pack your niece off to the country? At Perryvale Manor, a dark man in a strange coach would be very noticeable."

Wyatt turned away from the fireplace and stalked over to the window. He and Ambrose had been arguing all day, and although he knew his friend's concerns were valid, he couldn't bring himself to send the little girl away. He'd been up half the night wrestling with his decision, and the more he thought

about it the more determined he became to keep
Amanda with him. He'd never forgive himself if she
came to grief and he wasn't there to protect her.

"If I could be there to keep watch over her, it
would be one thing," he said in a grim voice, swinging around to meet Ambrose's gaze. "But you must
know I can't leave town while Parliament is in ses-
sion. Until then, we'll have to be doubly vigilant and
guard her as best as we can."

"Any more ideas as to why she is being followed?"
Ambrose asked. "I must own it makes no sense to
me. I mean," he added before Wyatt could speak, "I
can understand that someone might wish to kidnap
her because she is your niece, but how would they
know she is your niece? You've hardly paraded her
about town in an open cabriolet."

The same thought had occurred to Wyatt, but he
was no closer to an answer. "I can only suppose they
heard the gossip being bandied about," he said,
wishing he knew more. "You did say it was the talk
of the town."

"Mmm," Ambrose replied, rubbing a thoughtful
finger over his lips. "If we could discover how they
learned of her, we might be closer to finding out their
identity. You've questioned the staff, I take it?"

"Both Hemsley and I questioned them at length,
and we are convinced they are innocent of any
wrongdoing."

"Hemsley?" Ambrose gave a slight grin. "That
would be the charming gentleman with the scar on
his face and the manners of a top sergeant? I thought
I saw him skulking about when I arrived."

Wyatt smiled at his friend's telling description.
"Never mind Hemsley's manners," he told Ambrose.
"He comes highly qualified, and that is all that matters to me. Although I'll have to question those qual-
ifications if a dandy like you managed to spot him."

Ambrose took no offense to Wyatt's charge; he
merely smiled enigmatically. "There is more to us
lackadaisical dandies then you may first suppose,"

he drawled, looking smug. "But in defense of Mr. Hemsley's sterling reputation, he was dressed as an ostler and checking the horse's traces when I arrived. He tipped his hat to me and wished me a very cheerful good day."

"Good. I wouldn't—" He broke off as the door opened and Amanda raced inside.

"We're ready, Uncle Wyatt!" she cried, sliding to a halt in front of him and tipping her head back to meet his eyes. "May we go now, please?" She added the last with an enchanting smile.

Wyatt bent to scoop her into his arms. "If you are quite sure you really want to go, poppet," he teased, savoring the feeling of holding her safe. "Wouldn't you rather stay home and do your Latin lessons?"

Amanda's eyes widened in horror. "Oh no!" she denied, shaking her head from side to side. "I really, really want to see the Tower. It's ... it's ..." She struggled for the right word. "It's educational," she said, twisting around to appeal to Miss Pringle, who had entered the room behind her. "Isn't it, Miss Pringle? It will help me understand my kings and queens. You said so."

"So I did," Nia agreed, smiling. "Good afternoon, Your Grace, Mr. Royston," she murmured, curtseying to each man in turn.

"Miss Pringle," Wyatt said, pleased to see she was wearing the cloak he'd ordered. He'd half-expected her to refuse it, and was fully prepared for a fight. Hopefully she'd be as sensible about the other things he'd purchased, he thought, lowering Amanda to her feet with a pat on her head.

They set out for the Tower in the duke's crested carriage. Nia noted the presence of several grooms clinging to the back of the coach. She hated to think of them shivering in the cold rain, but she was grateful for the added security they offered. She wondered if any of them were armed, and decided she would ask Lord Tilton the moment they were alone.

As she suspected, the inclement weather had kept

away all but the hardiest of souls, and they were able to explore the historical buildings in relative solitude. Amanda, of course, was more interested in the dungeons and sites of executions than in the dusty details of history that Nia dutifully offered, and she soon gave up the effort.

"I had no idea children could be so gruesome," Wyatt commented as Amanda dashed over to peer at the Bloody Tower, where the little princes were rumored to have met their fate. "I'd have thought she would be terrified of such a place."

"She is," Nia informed him with a rueful smile. "That's half the attraction for her. It wouldn't be any fun at all if there wasn't the added spice of fear."

"I hadn't thought of it quite like that," Wyatt agreed, a smile tugging at his mouth. "At Perryvale there is an old cottage where a hermit once lived. After he died the villagers wouldn't go near it, claiming it was haunted by the old man's ghost. One summer's night Christopher and I decided we would stay the night there—to show our manly courage, of course," he added, giving her a rueful look.

"And did you?" Nia asked, amused by the idea of the duke as a young boy shaking with fear and excitement as he walked toward the abandoned cottage.

"We made it as far as the front door when an owl screeched and sent us fleeing home," he confessed with a laugh. "We were never able to work up the courage to try a second time."

"Is the building still there?" Nia asked, her eyes straying across the cobblestoned courtyard where Amanda was standing with Mr. Royston.

"I'm not sure. Why?"

"Because if it is, I suggest you have it boarded up. If Amanda should hear the story, I can guarantee she won't rest until she's explored the place."

"I'll write my steward at once and have him see to it," Wyatt promised with alacrity. "Ghosts aside, the place is doubtlessly unstable, and I wouldn't want her to be hurt by falling stones."

They continued walking about, but the rain was causing Nia's spectacles to fog over, and she was finding it more and more difficult to see.

"Blast!"

"What is it?"

"The curse of those who must wear spectacles," Nia grumbled, removing the offending item with a scowl. "I can't see a thing."

She looked so much like a cross owl that Wyatt could not help but chuckle. "Allow me," he said, pulling a kerchief from his pocket and offering it to her with a bow. "I wouldn't want you to walk off a parapet."

"Thank you, Your Grace," she replied, accepting the square of soft cambric with relief. "You have no idea how disorientating the world looks all covered with spots!"

"I'm sure I do not," he agreed, his gaze resting on her face. Without her glasses he could see that her eyes were an enchanting blend of green and gold, and lavishly rimmed with thick, dark lashes. The rain had brought a soft glow to her cheeks, and tendrils of chestnut-colored hair had slipped from beneath her ever-present cap to curl about her forehead. He realized he'd never seen her with her head uncovered, and he found himself wondering what she would look like without the prim covering.

"There," Nia said, returning her spectacles to her nose with a relieved sigh. "That is much better. Now I can actually see what I am looking at." She glanced about her. "Where are Amanda and Mr. Royston?"

"Over there, by the gate," Wyatt answered, indicating the others with a nod. "Amanda has been dragging him from one gruesome venue to another. I'd put an end to it, but he seems to be enjoying himself almost as much as she is."

Nia smiled at the sight of the elegant man bending to read a brass plaque bolted into the stone wall.

"Yes, he does seem rather contented," she said. "I wonder how he will react when we stop at the Egyptian Hall."

"The Egyptian Hall?" Wyatt repeated, his brows lifting. "I don't recall your mentioning this yesterday."

"Didn't I?" She contrived to look innocent. "Oh dear, I thought I had. Napoleon's coach is on display, and—"

"Stop!"

The shout brought Wyatt's head snapping around to see Ambrose struggling with a man in a shabby cape. He started forward at once, his hand closing around the loaded pistol he'd slipped into his pocket that morning. He'd taken less than a step when a second man materialized from a recess near the gate and snatched up a screaming Amanda. The sight of his niece held in the unknown man's arms filled Wyatt with a murderous rage.

"No!" he roared, drawing his pistol and levelling it on the man. "Let her go, you bastard!"

At the threat the man turned, his eyes glittering wildly in his dirty face. At the sight of the pistol, he panicked and began backing toward the wrought iron fence.

"Stands back!" he warned, a knife flashing as he held it high. "Stands back, or I swears I'll cut her throat!"

The words lanced through Wyatt, but he forced himself to remain calm. He could feel Miss Pringle trembling beside him, but couldn't take the time to reassure her. He cautiously lowered the gun, but did not drop it.

"Think, man," he advised softly, his eyes never leaving the villain's face. "You cannot hope to get away. Look about you; you are surrounded."

The man spared a quick glance around him, his eyes growing even more frenzied as they fell on the small crowd that had gathered, drawn by all the shouting. He ran the hand that was holding the knife across the back of his mouth, and Wyatt allowed himself to relax marginally.

"I won't bring charges," he promised, taking a wary step forward. "Just let my niece go, and tell me who hired you to abduct her. He's the man I want, not you."

"Ye says that now, but how does I know ye'll keep yer word?" the man asked, sweat mingling with the rain on his face. "And even if ye does, I'm a dead man. 'E'll kill me sure if I was to tell 'is name."

Wyatt opened his mouth to reassure the man when Miss Pringle suddenly stepped forward, her arms held out in front of her. "Let her go," she implored, advancing step by deliberate step. "You don't have to tell us anything if you don't want to. Just don't hurt her."

The man hesitated, his eyes darting from Nia to Wyatt. The crowd was pressing closer, and in the distance a female voice could be heard shrieking for the guard. The thought of soldiers was evidently more than he could bear, for without warning he threw Amanda roughly to the ground and rushed forward.

"No!" he screamed, the knife still clasped in his upraised hand. "I won't let ye 'ang me!"

Nia remained frozen in place, fear and stunned disbelief holding her fast. She could see the madness in the man's eyes, feel the hatred emanating from him as he dashed toward her, but she could not move. It was like watching a pantomime, she thought dazedly; it wasn't real. It couldn't be real. The knife flashed in the thin, gray light as the man brought his arm down, and Nia closed her eyes, waiting for the hot pain she was sure would follow.

Wyatt saw the man rushing forward and knew what he had to do. Without thinking he shoved her to one side, stepping in front of her and pulling the trigger in the same instant. The pistol roared and the man jerked backwards, the knife flying from his hand. He was dead before he hit the wet pavement.

There was a short charged silence, and then everything started happening at once. Women began screaming, and he could hear the sound of approaching footsteps as several men burst around the corner of the stone Tower. Ambrose was stepping over the still form of the man who had attacked him, moving toward Amanda lying on the ground. Wyatt bent to Miss Pringle.

"Are you all right?" he asked worriedly, his eyes skimming her for any sign of injury. "He didn't hurt you, did he?"

Nia batted his hands away. "Never mind me!" she snapped, straightening her glasses with a shaking hand. "See to Amanda!" When he hesitated, she gave him a none-too-gentle prod. "Go!"

Wyatt needed no further urging, and hurried over to join Ambrose. "Is she alive?" he demanded, his voice harsh with fear as he hunched over the crumpled form lying so still on the ground.

"I think so," Ambrose replied, laying a gentle finger against Amanda's neck. "Her pulse is steady, thank God, and she seems to be breathing without difficulty. Perhaps she has just fainted."

As if in response, Amanda's lashes fluttered, and she peered up at her uncle through eyes that weren't quite focused. "I did not faint!" she denied in a thready voice. "Miss Pringle says only silly chits faint."

"Our apologies then, poppet," Wyatt murmured, his throat painfully tight. "We didn't mean to insult you." He reached out to stroke the hair from her face, then froze at the feel of the wet blood beneath his fingertips. He drew back his hand, staring at the bright blood staining them.

"Are you all right, my darling?" Miss Pringle had joined them.

Amanda's blue eyes filled with tears. "My head hurts," she said fretfully. "And that bad man muddied my new cloak!"

"You may have a new one," Wyatt vowed in a

wooden voice, rising to his feet and staring down at her with eyes that burned like black fire.

His promise brought a speculative smile to Amanda's pale white lips. "And a kitty?" she pressed, her eyelids beginning to droop. "May I have a kitty as well?"

Wyatt had been unaware she wanted a cat, but he was ready to give her anything if only she would be all right. He opened his mouth, but before he could speak, Amanda's eyes drifted closed. She was unconscious.

Chapter 8

"Please, Your Grace, you must get some rest," Dr. Carlysle's voice was filled with concern as he peered at Wyatt over the rims of his spectacles. "You'll do the wee lass no good if you fret yourself like this. Get on with you, now," he added.

Wyatt gave the little girl lying on the bed an anguished look, torn between the desire to stay and the knowledge that two men were waiting for him in his study. Here there was little he could do to help Amanda, but downstairs . . .

"You'll send for me the moment she awakens?" he asked, laying a trembling hand on Amanda's cheek.

"The very moment," the physician promised solemnly. "But I warn you, it may not be until very late tonight. That was a bad knock she took to her head."

Wyatt closed his eyes, knowing he would never forget the sight of Amanda being hurled to the ground. Nothing had ever frightened him more—unless it was the sight of the madman rushing at Nia with the knife still in his hand, he added, his eyes flicking toward the white-faced woman sitting on the other side of the bed.

"Very well, Doctor," he said, straightening to his full height, his eyes still resting on Nia. "Should you require anything, you have only to notify one of the servants and they will fetch it for you. Also, if there is any change at all, I wish to be informed at once."

"Of course, Your Grace." Dr. Carlysle inclined his head.

Wyatt held out a commanding hand to Miss Pringle. "Ma'am, if you would be so good as to step out into the hall for a moment, there are some things I need to discuss with you."

Nia opened her lips to protest, but quickly closed them at the weariness and pain evident in the harsh lines of his face. She gave Amanda's hand a reassuring squeeze, then followed him out into the hall. The door had scarcely closed behind them than he took her hands in his.

"I know you won't leave Amanda," he said, his thumbs drawing small circles on her knuckles, "but if I send up a tray, do you promise you will eat?"

That he could think of her comfort when she knew he was worried to distraction over Amanda touched Nia's heart. "That would be very considerate, Your Grace," she said, lowering her eyes to hide their suspicious brightness. "Thank you."

Wyatt stared at her bent head, fighting the sudden urge to draw her into his arms. She'd been so brave, he thought, his fingers tightening on hers. How many women would have possessed the courage to face an armed man like that? he wondered. How many men? She'd kept the man distracted long enough not to use his knife on Amanda, and he knew he would never be able to repay her. She had restored his niece to him not once, but twice.

"You still haven't given me your word," he teased, his voice light to hide the emotion burgeoning in him. "You see? I am becoming familiar with your ways. It is only when I have your most solemn vow that I know you'll do as you are ordered."

That made Nia laugh, and she raised her head to meet his eyes. "Ordered, Your Grace?"

"Earnestly implored," he amended, his smile softening. "You haven't eaten since luncheon, and I know you must be hungry."

She wasn't, but she supposed she could manage a few mouthfuls if it would please him. Suddenly she was aware that he was still holding both of her hands. She could only imagine the eyebrows that would be raised should anyone see them, but she didn't care. Instead she allowed herself the luxury of his touch, revelling in the feel of his hard, warm flesh pressed to hers. It made her feel safe and cherished, and she held the sensation close to her chest, like a miser hoarding gold.

"I promise I shall do my best, Your Grace," she said, knowing it was time to end this foolishness. "Now, if you will excuse me, I would like to get back before Amanda awakens."

He felt her attempts to free her hand, and knew he should release her. It was the wise thing to do, he told himself, but suddenly he had had his fill of doing the wise thing. Without pausing to consider the consequences, he raised both of her hands to his lips.

"Thank you," he said, his voice deep as their eyes met and held. "You've given me more than I can tell you, more than I deserve, and I thank you. With all that I am, I thank you."

The earnest light shining in the ebony depths of his eyes unnerved Nia almost as much as the touch of his mouth against her flesh. All coherent thought fled and she could only stare up at him, lost in a maze of emotion. She nervously wet her lips. "Your Grace, that is very good of you, but—"

"No," he interrupted, his fingers tightening on hers, "don't do that. Don't brush aside my gratitude as if you had no right to it. Accept my thanks as I offer them, simply but with all my heart."

His quiet eloquence melted her reluctance, and feeling greatly daring, she freed her hand and reached up to touch his cheek.

"In that case, I accept," she said softly, her hand trembling as she traced the hard planes of his face with her fingertips. Then, as if abruptly aware of what she was doing, she blushed brightly and took a hasty step backwards.

"I . . . I really must be getting back to Amanda," she stammered, her hand dropping awkwardly to her side. "Good day, my lord." And she hurried away, conscious of his dark gaze following her.

Ambrose and Hemsley were waiting when Wyatt walked into his study, and he wasted no time in getting to the matter at hand. "Well? What have you learned?" he demanded, seating himself behind his desk. "Who hired the men to attack my niece?"

Hemsley spoke first, his rough voice filled with disgust. "What we have learned, Your Grace, is that the man you shot was named Quiggs, and he hired Trulow, the man Mr. Royston here knocked to the ground. But that is all we know."

"But how can that be?" Wyatt exclaimed furiously. "This man tried to kidnap my niece! He must know something!"

"Why?"

The calm question made Wyatt frown. "Why?" he repeated in rising agitation. "Because he is facing the gibbet! He must know who hired him, if not why!"

Hemsley gave him a pitying look. "You don't understand this world, my lord," he said bluntly. "Names and reasons don't matter to men like these. Quiggs offered Trulow fifty quid to help him snatch Lady Amanda, and that's all he cared to know. He didn't even know who you were until we told him, and he was right put out about it. Said he'd have held out for one hundred if he'd known you were a duke."

Wyatt's jaw clenched in frustration. "I want to see this Trulow," he said, his words clipped. "There are several questions I want to ask him."

"As you like." Hemsley inclined his head, his pale eyes fixing Wyatt with a measuring stare. "And now, sir, there are some questions I would be asking of *you*."

Ambrose stirred uneasily in his seat, shooting Wyatt a worried look. "Hemsley, I do not think—"

"No." Wyatt held up his hand to still Ambrose's protest. "Let him ask what he pleases. I am willing to do whatever it takes, if it will put an end to this madness." He met Hemsley's gaze. "What is it you want to know?"

"Have you made Lady Amanda your heiress?" Hemsley asked, folding his arms across his massive chest.

The question took Wyatt by surprise. "I have ordered my solicitor to draw up papers to that effect," he confessed carefully, wondering what the runner was thinking. "But I haven't yet signed anything."

"And who will suffer most by this new arrangement?"

Wyatt gave the question thorough consideration before answering. "The title is entailed," he began, "and in the event I should die without male issue, it would then pass to my cousin, Lord Amberstroke. But that won't change because of Amanda. If she was a boy it would be different, but as a female she cannot hope to inherit."

Hemsley merely grunted. "But what of your personal fortune? Tilton by itself is a sweet enough morsel, I'll grant you, but you are also quite wealthy in your own right. How much of your blunt do you intend leaving the little girl?"

"All of it," Wyatt told him. "Or at least, the greater part of it. I have no children of my own, and I want to be sure Amanda will be provided for in the event of my death. God knows this family hasn't done its best by her until now," he added, his lips twisting in a bitter smile.

"Aye, there is that, isn't there?" Hemsley scratched his cheek thoughtfully. "But back to your money. Who knows you have changed your will?"

"Well, my solicitor, of course." Wyatt's brows met in thought. "And I did inform Amberstroke I was adopting Amanda as a matter of formality, but I . . ." His voice trailed off as understanding dawned.

"My God, you don't think *he* is behind this, do you?" he demanded, pushing to his feet. "The bastard! I will kill him!"

"Mayhap." The threat of violence did not seem to perturb the other man unduly. "But you'll have to be proving it first, and that may not be easy, as the only possible link is now dead."

Wyatt lowered himself back onto his chair. "Quiggs, you mean," he said, running a hand through his thick hair.

"You mustn't blame yourself, Wyatt," Ambrose said, quick to leap to his defense. "The blackguard was attacking Miss Pringle! What other choice did you have?"

"None, but that doesn't make things easier," Wyatt said with a heavy sigh. He glanced up to find Hemsley watching him. "What do we do now?" he asked wearily.

"Get Lady Amanda out of London," Hemsley replied at once. "I'll send some men down with you, but it will be up to you to keep a sharp eye on her."

"I won't let her out of my sight," Wyatt promised. "What of Amberstroke? How will you proceed against him?"

"Cautiously, Your Grace, cautiously. And in any case, there's no saying he *is* the man we're after. It could be someone else entirely."

"Who?" Ambrose asked.

Hemsley shrugged his beefy shoulders. "No way of knowing, sir. But 'tis my experience that these things are caused by one of two things, greed or revenge. Greed is our best possibility, so that is where we shall start. But if greed isn't behind all of this, then everything changes, including our suspect."

An uneasy silence filled the room as the three men considered the implications. Greed would be easy to pin down, they knew, but revenge was a different matter. Wyatt and Ambrose exchanged a long look before Wyatt rose slowly to his feet.

"Thank you for your assistance, Mr. Hemsley," he said, offering him his hand. "Will you be returning to Bow Street now?"

"For now, my lord." Hemsley accepted his dismissal with good grace. "I'll need to check my prisoner, and arrange for you to see him. He is being transferred to the Bailey tomorrow, so we'd best be quick about it."

After Hemsley had taken his leave, Wyatt swung around to face Ambrose. "What do you think?" he demanded. "Do you believe Amberstroke is after Amanda?"

Ambrose shook his head. "I know he is the most likely suspect at this point," he said, his expression troubled, "but there is something about the notion that simply will not wash. He's not even in London, for one thing, and for another he is so timid, he wouldn't say boo to a goose. You heard Quiggs. He was terrified of whoever had hired him."

"That is so," Wyatt agreed, remembering the wild glitter in the ruffian's eyes when he'd spoken of his mysterious master. "But that doesn't mean Amberstroke didn't use an intermediary, someone who would have no difficulty terrorizing a rat like Quiggs. It's done all the time."

"But can you see Harold having such foresight?" Ambrose pressed, warming to his theme. "I know the man is your heir, Wyatt, and I've no wish to be cruel, but there is no denying he is the biggest cloth-head in England! Even if he wanted to dispose of Amanda, he'd only make a cake of it."

A reluctant smile softened the grim lines bracketing Wyatt's mouth. "Undoubtedly," he agreed. "But damn it, Ambrose, if it's not Harold, then who the devil is it? Who else would benefit from Amanda's death?"

"I don't know," Ambrose replied. "But we had best find out, and soon. Next time we may not be so lucky."

Amanda slept through the rest of the afternoon, awakening shortly before dinner. She was subdued and inclined to be fretful, but Nia soon jollied her into better spirits. She even managed to get the little girl to look upon the whole event as a sort of grand adventure. Amanda was regaling Nancy with her version of the attack when the door opened and the duke, hastily summoned by Nia, strode into the room.

"Uncle Wyatt!" Amanda exclaimed, holding both arms out for her uncle. "Where have you been? I have been waiting and waiting for you!"

The sight of Amanda, alive and well, was almost Wyatt's undoing. He felt his eyes burning as he crossed the rug to join her. "Hello, little one," he murmured, bending to accept her exuberant hug. At the feel of her slight arms closing around his neck, he shut his eyes and sent a heartfelt prayer winging toward heaven.

"Miss Pringle said you shot that bad man," Amanda said, drawing back to give her uncle an admiring look. "Is he dead?"

Worried that she might be afraid, Wyatt took her hand in his and lowered himself onto the bed beside her. "Yes, Amanda, the man is dead," he said quietly, "and the other man is in prison. You needn't be afraid of either of them ever again."

"Good." Amanda gave a satisfied nod. "You were very brave, Uncle Wyatt. Just like the hero who stabbed Count Divicchio. Isn't that right, Miss Pringle?" she added, casting Nia an imploring look over her shoulder.

"Very brave," Nia agreed, her heart pounding as she sent the duke a quick smile.

How lovely she looked, Wyatt mused. Even with her spectacles and that blasted cap sitting slightly askew on her dark hair, she was enchanting, and he longed to take her into his arms. He pushed the tempting thought aside and turned his attention to his niece.

"I thought the count was walled up," he drawled, giving her nose a playful tweak.

"He escaped. Villains are nothing if not inventive," Nia answered for Amanda, wondering if she ought to leave. She'd done her best to calm the child, but it was really her uncle she needed most. Nia reached her decision and rose to her feet.

"I'm sure you would prefer to speak with Amanda privately, Your Grace," she said briskly, including both in her low curtsey. "I'll be in my rooms should you have need of me."

"Just one moment, Miss Pringle." Wyatt also stood. "I have something to say to you . . . to both of you," he added, sending Amanda a reassuring look.

"Yes, Uncle?" Amanda folded her hands in her lap and gazed solemnly up at him.

"I have decided it would be best if we returned to the country at once," he said. "I know it is hardly your duty, but can you have everything packed and ready to go for the day after tomorrow?"

Nia thought of the visit to the menagerie she had been planning and gave a silent sigh. "Certainly, sir," she replied, her shoulders straightening with determination. "Is there anything else I can do to help?"

"You might speak with Mrs. Mayton," he said, grateful for her offer. "I am sure she would appreciate any help you could give her. There is a great deal to be done, I am afraid."

"I shall see to it at once," she said, welcoming the chance to lose herself in hard work. She excused herself, and slipped quietly from the room.

After she left, Wyatt and Amanda discussed what her new life would be like at Perryvale Manor. To his relief she seemed eager for the move, her eyes bright as she quizzed him on every detail.

"And I shall have a pony?" she pressed, head tilted to one side. "A *real* one?"

"A real one," he assured her, unable to resist the urge to press a kiss to her cheek. The cold terror he'd felt when he'd seen her helpless in Quiggs's arms remained with him, and it was only by touching her that he was able to hold it at bay.

"What is its name?" Amanda demanded with delight. "Is it pretty?"

"I do not know since I haven't seen it," he answered patiently. "As to the pony's name, that is for you to decide. It is the owner's responsibility to name her mount."

"Then I shall call her Pegasus," Amanda announced with a decisive nod. "What is your horse called, Uncle?"

"Mahdi," he answered, smiling at the memory of his hot-tempered Arabian bay. "It is an Arabic word meaning 'one who is rightly guided.' It is not, I fear, a fitting name for such a stubborn and willful beast. Mind you don't go near him unless I am with you," he warned, well acquainted now with her penchant for mischief. "He's dangerous."

"Yes, sir," Amanda agreed, playing with the folds of his cravat. "Uncle Wyatt, may I ask you a question?"

He tensed, sensing the conversation was about to change, and in a direction he might not like. Amanda wouldn't look him in the eyes, and that alarmed him more than anything. He slipped a gentle hand beneath her chin and tilted her face up to his.

"You may ask me anything you want, Amanda, whenever you wish," he said quietly, his eyes meeting hers. "I promise I will always answer. All right?"

She nodded solemnly. "All right."

"What is it, poppet?"

"Why did you hate my mama?"

He stared at her in shock. "What?"

She gave an uncomfortable shrug. "My aunt said you did," she insisted, her bottom lip quivering. "She said you didn't want us, and that we mustn't bother you. The man who visited us said it, too."

"What man?" Wyatt demanded, feeling as if he'd just walked into the middle of a play in which the performers were speaking some unknown tongue he was expected to decipher.

"That man," Amanda repeated with marked patience. "He came to our house before Mama died, and he said bad things to her and made her cry. I hate him." She added this last with a fierce scowl that was a perfect imitation of Wyatt's own.

"If he made your mama cry, I do not blame you," Wyatt said, giving her a distracted pat. "What did this man look like? Can you describe him to me?"

Amanda frowned, squeezing her eyes shut. "He was tall," she said thoughtfully, "and he had funny hair. It was black like yours, but it had white in it, too. And he wore spectacles," she added, her eyes opening. "He kept polishing them when he was talking to Mama and my aunt."

A cold fist of rage slammed into Wyatt's stomach at Amanda's artless description. "I see," he said at last, his voice tight with the effort of maintaining control. "When did this happen, Amanda? Do you remember?"

"It was after Papa died. I heard Aunt telling my mama it was because his fence was broken."

"His fence was broken?" Wyatt repeated, wondering if he had missed something.

Amanda nodded. "Uh-huh."

Wyatt continued to try to fathom what she meant. "*Mend* his fence?" he asked, her meaning finally becoming clear. "Your aunt said the man came to see you so that he could mend his fences?"

"Yes, I heard her say it was time his nibs got off his high horse and mended his fences, and that blood was thicker than water." Her face clouded over as a sudden though occurred to her. "Is his nibs that man's name? It sounds dreadfully silly to me."

"No, Amanda," Wyatt told her, his cold voice giving no indication of the white-hot fury simmering within him. "That is not the man's name."

"Oh." She considered his reply. "Do you know who he is, then?"

Wyatt's answering smile was chilling. "Yes, poppet. It appears that I know *exactly* who he is."

"If Your Grace would but wait one moment, I can explain everything," Duncan Elliott said, his cultured voice smooth as he studied Wyatt over the rims of his spectacles. "This is nothing more than an unfortunate misunderstanding, I assure you."

"There's been a misunderstanding, all right, and you're the one who made it!" Wyatt snapped, his eyes filled with contempt as he paced the elegant confines of the office.

He'd come to Elliott's rooms directly from the Portham Academy, where he'd spent the morning questioning Mrs. Langston. The knowledge of how badly he'd been betrayed by a man he trusted had left him reeling. In addition to the messages from the academy which Elliott had kept from him, there had been several letters from Amanda's mother informing him of her situation. He had still been recovering from that shock when the schoolmistress had let slip one final bit of information.

According to Amanda's aunt, Christopher had written him shortly before being posted to America, apparently hoping to mend the breach between them. From the dates Mrs. Langston gave, Wyatt realized he'd either been in the country or at his lodge in Scotland at the times the letters were mailed, and that they had been forwarded to Elliott with the rest of his correspondence.

"I realize you are upset, Lord Tilton." Mr. Elliott had removed his spectacles and was wiping them with his handkerchief. "But you must understand that I was acting only in your best interests. I don't know what this foolish schoolteacher told you, but—"

"She told me Christopher tried to contact me!" Wyatt roared, the pain of it almost more than he could bear. "He wrote me, damn you, and you kept his letters from me!"

"I was protecting you from his importuning!" For the first time a note of panic was evident in the solicitor's demeanor. "He had squandered his inheritance and was demanding more!"

"My God, do you think a few pounds mattered to

me?" Wyatt balled his hands into fists. "He was my brother, and had he asked it of me, I'd have signed the entire estate over to him without a word of protest."

"Perhaps he had better claim to it."

Wyatt's head jerked back at the poisonous words. "What the devil do you mean by that?"

A look of cold cunning flickered across Elliott's harsh features and was gone. "Why nothing, Your Grace," he replied, his dark eyes enigmatic. "I was but observing that second sons often want more than is good for them."

Wyatt gave the solicitor a sharp look, suspecting he was lying. It was there in his smooth voice, and in the calculating smile that played about the corners of his mouth. It was as if he was privy to the black secret that had haunted Wyatt through most of his life, and for a moment he was strongly tempted to shake the truth from Elliott. He even took a menacing step forward before his common sense reasserted itself.

Don't be an idiot, he told himself harshly, slowly unclenching his hands. Of course Elliott didn't know the truth. How could he? Even he didn't know what the truth of his parentage was. But the man had lied to him, and because of that Wyatt fixed him with a cold look.

"You may consider our association at an end," he told the solicitor, turning his back on him as he crossed the room to gather up his hat and gloves from a chair. "I will have my man of business pay you whatever sums you may still be owed."

Elliott's face lost its fatuous smile. "Your Grace?"

Wyatt settled his hat on his head. "I told you once what I would do if I discovered you had deceived me," he said, pulling on his gloves. "Be grateful I don't do worse."

The chair clattered to the floor as Elliott pushed himself to his feet. "Curse you, you can't do this!" he raged.

Elliott's audacity brought a dangerous look to

Wyatt's eyes. "I am warning you, Elliott, you had best mind your tongue," he said, his voice soft with menace. "I've no desire to strike a man so many years my senior, but I won't be spoken to in such a fashion."

"*You* won't be spoken to in such a fashion?" Elliott repeated, his lips twisting in a sneer. "And who are you to be demanding anything of me?"

Wyatt's heart began hammering. "I am the duke of Tilton," he said coldly, wondering again just what Elliott knew. He felt as if he was on the edge of a dangerous precipice, and the worst part was not knowing if he should step back . . . or forward.

"Are you? Are you really so sure of that, Your Grace?" Elliott turned the term of respect into the vilest of insults.

Abruptly Wyatt tired of the cat-and-mouse game Elliott was playing. He moved forward without warning, grabbing the other man by the front of his jacket. Everything, even his grief and fury over Christopher, was forgotten in his determination to know, at last, the truth he had been seeking all his life.

"Tell me the truth, blast you!" he demanded, shaking the solicitor as a terrier would shake a rat. "Am I a Perryvale?"

Duncan gazed into Wyatt's face, his eyes full of hatred and triumph as he slowly smiled. "No," he said softly, "you are not."

Chapter 9

Wyatt stared at him, his hands falling useless at his side as the solicitor's taunting words rang in his head. A crude oath formed on his lips and he whirled away, stalking over to the row of arched windows that dominated the far wall. He stood looking down at the noisy street with unseeing eyes, his chest rising and falling in uneven breaths while he sought to control the emotional storm raging inside him. Now that he'd heard what he'd always suspected, it was as if he'd been laid open by a broad sword, and the pain and vulnerability were almost unbearable.

When had he first suspected? he wondered bleakly. Had it been the first time he'd looked down at his infant brother's face and heard the whispered comments about "true" Perryvales? Or had it been when he was six and he'd heard his mother taunting his father with her many affairs? He'd been too young then to fully comprehend her meaning, but he'd known a hurt and a dread that had never left him. He had always wondered, always feared, and now he knew. He knew ...

He turned to face Elliott, his expression carefully controlled. "How long have you known?" he asked, his voice devoid of emotion.

Elliott's eyes were filled with malicious pleasure. "Longer than you may suspect," he said smugly.

"And how did you come by this knowledge?" Wyatt demanded, fighting the urge to plant his fist in Elliott's face. "Did my father tell you?"

Elliott gave a harsh laugh. "Hardly," he said, and Wyatt wondered at the enmity in his voice. "I never had the privilege of meeting the duke. But I assure you, my information comes from an impeccable source."

"Who?"

There was a long silence as Elliott studied him. "I don't believe I shall tell you," he said at last, venom dripping from his voice. "At least, not until I am ready."

Such blatant insolence made Wyatt take a step forward. "I am warning you, Elliott," he began in a harsh voice, "you had best tell me what I want to know, or—"

"Or what?" Elliott interrupted with a mocking laugh. "You're hardly in any position to utter threats ... *Your Grace*. Only think what will happen to your safe, secure little world if I decide to tell the truth."

Wyatt stopped, his face paling not with fright, but with fury. Whether he was a Perryvale or not, he still had his pride, and he was damned if he'd let an overweening mushroom like Elliott bully him. He drew himself up to his considerable height, fixing the solicitor with a contemptuous look.

"You may tell the world what you please, for all the good it will do you," he said coldly. "Without proof there is nothing you can do. I, on the other hand, can do *you* a great deal of harm, and with very little effort. Something you would do well to remember, Mr. Elliott."

Elliott's face flushed a dark, angry red. "Bastard!" He spat out the word like a challenge.

Wyatt smiled coldly. "Apparently," he said, masking his pain behind a show of indifference, "but I am a bastard the world accepts as the duke of Tilton. Cross me again, and I will destroy you."

After leaving the solicitor's office, Wyatt returned to his home on Berkeley Square. As he expected, the

house was in chaos, and he was able to slip unobserved into his study. Once inside he poured himself
a glass of brandy and swallowed it in a gulp before
pouring another. The liquor burned its way down his
throat, bringing a warm glow to his stomach. He was
raising the glass to his lips for another sip when he
remembered the gentle admonishment Ambrose had
given him the night he had learned of Amanda's existence.

*"I know you miss Christopher, but you'll not find him
in the bottom of a brandy bottle however hard you may
try."*

He closed his eyes as pain exploded in him, and he
hurled the glass against the wall. It shattered into a
hundred shards, and he took comfort in the small act
of destruction. When he opened his eyes again, they
were dark with despair.

He remembered what Mrs. Langston had told him,
and his chest squeezed tight with pain. Christopher
had not hated him; the thought was almost as sweet
as it was agonizing. His brother had tried to end
their quarrel prior to sailing for America, but due to
Elliott's machinations the letters had been kept from
him.

Why? he wondered bleakly. Why should Elliott
hate him so? And the solicitor *did* hate him, he acknowledged with a heavy sigh. It had shone in his
dark eyes, and in the contempt dripping from his
voice as he'd taunted him about his irregular birth.
What could he have done to earn such enmity?

He was still wrestling with these questions and
what he should do when there was a tap at the door.
At his command, Nia entered.

"Good afternoon, Your Grace," she said, hurrying
forward to greet him, a list clasped in her hand. "I
was wondering if I might have a word with you."

"Certainly, ma'am," he said, hiding his emotions as
he indicated one of the many chairs. "Pray, will you
not be seated?"

Nia accepted the chair, her gaze flying to Wyatt's

face. He sounded as composed as ever, but her instincts told her something was amiss. "Is everything all right, my lord?" she asked, studying him anxiously. "You haven't learned anything else about the men who attacked Lady Amanda, have you?"

"No more than we already knew," he answered, wishing he could tell her about the confrontation with Elliott. He longed to share his pain and confusion with someone, but everything was still too fresh, and in any case, it wasn't really her concern. To keep himself from blurting everything out, he turned the conversation to what he considered a safe topic.

"Speaking of Amanda, how is she?" he asked, leaning back in his chair. "She hasn't had a relapse or some such thing?"

"Amanda is fine," Nia assured him, wondering what he was hiding from her. "She is quite recovered, and driving us all mad with her demands to be let out of bed. The move has her beside herself with anticipation. Something about a pony, I believe?" She arched an eyebrow at him in a teasing manner.

"I had my steward purchase her a suitable mount," Wyatt explained, narrowing his eyes as he studied her. He thought she looked tired, and regretted asking her to assist with the move. He might have known she would take on more than was good for her.

"That would explain it, then." Nia accepted his statement with a light laugh. "She says she has named it Pegasus."

"A fitting name for a horse," Wyatt agreed. "It will be interesting to see what you will name the mount I have decided to purchase for you," he added, then settled back to watch her reaction. She did not disappoint him.

"*My* mount?" Nia jerked her head up. "You bought me a horse?"

He inclined his head. "Since my mother died a number of years ago, there were no mounts at Perryvale suitable for a lady. I instructed Ferguson to purchase a mare for you so that you could accompany Amanda on her rides."

Nia glared at him, knowing she had been neatly outmaneuvered. By telling her the horse was being provided so that she could ride with Amanda, he had made refusing the animal impossible, and if the complacent gleam in his ebony eyes was any indication, the wretch knew it. For a moment she toyed with the idea of refusing anyway, but she dismissed the notion with a sigh of regret. Given yesterday's events, such behavior would be juvenile at best, and she forced a grateful smile to her lips.

"That is very good of you, Your Grace," she said, her teeth clenching with the effort. "I have missed riding very much, and I shall look forward to a nice gallop."

Wyatt was well-bred enough not to gloat. "You must let me ride with you," he said, wisely hiding a smile. "Perryvale is lovely in late spring, and I would like to show you about."

"I shall look forward to it, my lord," Nia answered, wondering if he would look as handsome in riding clothes as he did in morning dress. The thought was most disconcerting, and she hastily lowered her eyes to the forgotten list in her hand.

"I have all of Amanda's things packed," she began with brisk efficiency, "and both Mrs. Mayton and I are certain we shall have all in readiness by tomorrow. Will you be traveling to Perryvale with us, or separately?"

The question made Wyatt frown. "With you, of course," he said coolly. "Do you think that after yesterday I would allow either you or Amanda out of my sight?"

Nia was disconcerted to hear herself included in his vow of protection. "Certainly I knew you would be making the journey with us," she replied, hiding her confusion behind a hasty smile. "I was merely wondering if you would be riding in the carriage with us. Mrs. Mayton mentioned you usually take several coaches with you when you travel."

"I will ride with you for the most of the journey," he said, accepting her explanation without argument. "I'm bringing my stallion back with me, and I'll ride him part of the way. Traveling in coaches doesn't always agree with me, and I don't wish to disgrace myself," he added with a self-conscious shrug.

Nia was intrigued by his wry comment. Most men of her acquaintance would die sooner than admit to such a weakness, and she admired him for his honesty. "What time do you wish to set out?" she asked, turning her attention to her list. "According to Mrs. Mayton, Perryvale is a good six hours' drive from London, and we will need to leave early if we wish to arrive by dinner. Unless you prefer to spend the night on the road?"

"We will leave directly after breakfast," he said firmly. "I detest public inns, and I've no desire to expose Amanda to their dangers at her tender age."

They spent the next quarter hour going over the other items on the list. At last everything was arranged to Nia's satisfaction. There was only one more matter left to discuss, and much as she hated upsetting the duke, Nia knew she had no choice. Setting the list aside, she folded her hands in her lap and drew a steady breath.

"You Grace, might I ask you something?"

Her quiet solemnity made Wyatt stiffen in awareness. Whatever she was about to ask, he knew it had little to do with travel arrangements. "Certainly, Miss Pringle," he replied, mentally steeling himself. "What is it?"

Nia shifted uneasily on her chair. She'd spent a greater part of last night and this morning brooding over the attack on Amanda, and the more she considered it, the more troubled she became.

"It is about yesterday," she began. "If kidnapping Amanda had been those men's intent, then why did they not strike while we were alone and unguarded but for a footman? Why did they wait until you were with us? It is almost as if ... as if ..."

"As if?" he prodded gently.

"As if they wanted you there to witness it," she concluded. "And yet that makes no sense. Surely they must have known you would do everything possible to stop them?"

"It is interesting that you should ask," he said slowly, thinking about Elliott. "I've been sitting here asking myself the same thing."

"And?" Nia said when he did not continue.

"And I have concluded that while I have a very good idea *who* may be behind the attack, I do not know *why*."

The enigmatic response brought a scowl to Nia's face. "If you know who, why should the motive matter?" she demanded, thoroughly irritated with him.

"Oh, it matters, Miss Pringle," he replied, something cold and dangerous shimmering in his eyes. "It matters a great deal."

"I do not see why," she grumbled, crossing her arms over her chest and fixing him with a disgruntled glare. "You ought to have the beast arrested before he can strike again."

"Perhaps."

"Perhaps?" Nia could not believe her ears. "What the devil sort of reply is that? Amanda might have been killed because of him! How can you just sit there and do nothing? I insist you turn this villain over to the authorities at once!"

"Without a single shred of evidence?" he asked, forcing himself to consider the matter logically. "I think not. The authorities are an odd lot, ma'am, and they require a modicum of proof before hanging a man."

"But you just said you knew who it was!" Nia protested, furious he could be so sanguine. "Surely that is enough!"

Her naivete brought a bitter smile to his lips. "What one knows and what one can prove are two separate things," he told her coldly. "This isn't France, where I can have someone imprisoned with nothing more than a *lettre de cachet*. Until I have something more definite than suspicions, the authorities can do nothing to help us."

Although she knew he was right, his calm pragmatism enraged Nia. She'd been raised to believe that action was the only sensible response to a provocation of this magnitude, and she couldn't believe he intended doing nothing when someone was threatening his niece. She tossed her head back and gave him a challenging look. "Then you intend letting him go unpunished?" she demanded, her voice ripe with contempt.

"I didn't say that."

"But—"

"I said there was no sense in going to the authorities," Wyatt corrected, finding her bellicose attitude amusing, despite the seriousness of the situation. "I thoroughly intend that the person responsible for hurting you and Amanda pays, and pays most dearly. When I am done with him, he will wish himself dead."

The lethal intent in his voice and ebony-colored eyes convinced her of his sincerity, and she felt a flash of shame at doubting him. She should have known he could be trusted to protect Amanda, she told herself, dropping her eyes to her clenched hands. Had he not proven time and again that he was a man of impeccable honor? Then something he had said struck her, and she glanced up to find him watching her.

"What did you mean, the man who hurt me?" she asked, puzzled. "I wasn't harmed."

"Only because I killed Quiggs before he could strike," Wyatt said, his jaw clenching as he remembered the look in the assailant's eyes as he attacked. "And don't forget they did their damnedest to run you down in the street. The man who hired Quiggs and his repellent friend is to blame for everything, and I intend holding him responsible."

Nia supposed she should be horrified at the thought of the duke exacting whatever bloody revenge he could, but she wasn't. Amanda might have died, and it was only right the man who gave the orders be held accountable for his actions. Her only concern was that Wyatt himself would be harmed. He'd already admitted he had a deadly enemy, and she didn't want him taking any senseless chances. She pushed her glasses back up her nose and gave him a worried look.

"You will be careful, won't you?" she asked, feeling more than a little foolish. "This man . . . whoever he is, is obviously dangerous. Perhaps you should let Bow Street see to him."

A slow smile spread across Wyatt's austere features. "Why, Miss Pringle," he drawled in a mocking voice, "never say you are worried about my well-being. I am honored by such concern."

Nia felt her cheeks grow pink, and could have cheerfully bitten her own tongue. "I am concerned for Amanda's well-being!" she retorted, her expression fierce. "The poor child has few enough relations as it is. She can hardly afford to lose another through carelessness."

"Of course," he agreed, the twinkle in his eyes at odds with his solemn tone. "A most pragmatic attitude, ma'am, and one I might have expected from such a logical lady as yourself. Naturally you aren't personally concerned for my welfare."

Nia's lips twitched as she fought back a smile. "You are doing it a shade too brown, Your Grace," she warned. "And I suppose I am a *trifle* concerned for you . . ."

Wyatt was more touched than he cared to admit by her gruff admission. He couldn't recall when anyone other than Ambrose had expressed real care for him. Oh, his servants cared after a fashion, and he supposed any of his current mistresses might be counted

upon to shed a pretty tear or two before finding a
new protector, but that was all. The realization was
deeply disturbing.

"Are you going to tell me who he is?"

The unexpected question brought Wyatt out of his
black reverie, and he gave her a confused look. "Who
who is?"

"Your mysterious malefactor," Nia clarified. "Are
you going to tell me his name, or is it some dark secret?"

Wyatt considered the matter carefully before answering. "Until I decide upon a course of action, I
don't believe I shall tell you. I know you too well,
and I don't want you stealing a march on me." When
she would have protested, he held up a hand.

"I am serious, Nia," he said. "I do not wish for you
to become involved in any of this. I will handle the
man in my own time, and in my own manner, but
that is all you need to know. This is my concern, not
yours, and the less you are involved, the better."

Two hours later, Nia was still fuming over the
high-handed command. She had tried arguing her
point, but when he refused to be swayed she'd
stormed out of his study in high dudgeon. The front
door had shut a few minutes later, and she knew
he'd gone off to pursue his own vague revenge. The
knowledge added to her fury, and she refused to recognize the fear that lay beneath her simmering anger.

How dare he pat her on the head and then send
her on her way as if she was some delicate society
miss who needed guarding from every ill wind, she
brooded, restlessly pacing her elegant sitting room.
She was made of sterner stuff than that, and he
should know that by now. Apparently she'd given
the arrogant devil more credit than he deserved, she
decided with a snort, but she'd soon show him the
errors of his ways. If it was the last thing she did,
she would prove to him that she was worthy of his
trust.

She was contemplating some means of pursuing these nebulous goals when Nancy tapped on her door.

"I am sorry for disturbing you, Miss Pringle," the maid said with a curtsey, "but Lady Catherine Declaire has called and is asking to see you."

"To see me?" Nia asked, her eyebrows arching in surprise. "You're certain she didn't ask for Lady Amanda or His Grace?"

Nancy gave her a horrified look. "An unmarried lady would never call upon a gentleman!" she said, clearly scandalized by the thought. "And I am certain she asked for you. Mr. Johns told me himself."

If the ever-so-efficient butler had given Nancy the message, Nia knew there was no mistake. Wondering what the younger woman might have to discuss with her, she rose to go down to greet her. Instead of moving aside, Nancy remained firmly in place, regarding her with a frown.

"You don't mean to be going down like *that*?" she asked, pointing an accusing finger at Nia's rumpled apron.

Nia was about to say yes when she caught sight of her reflection. Nancy was right, she admitted with a rueful grimace. There was no way she could greet her guest looking like an untidy scullery maid.

"Please tell her ladyship I will be with her shortly," she said, glancing at her wardrobe and praying she could find one suitable gown that hadn't yet been packed.

After Nancy left, Nia rushed through her toilet before donning one of her newer gowns of heather-colored merino. She was debating whether she should wear her cap when the door opened and an excited Amanda dashed in.

"Amanda!" Nia exclaimed, turning from her cheval glass to give the little girl a frown. "What are you doing out of bed?"

"I heard Nancy telling the footman that Lady Catherine is here," Amanda said, fairly dancing from one foot to the other in excitement. "May I see her, Miss Pringle? May I?"

Nia's resolve wavered at the hopeful look in the child's deep blue eyes. The doctor had ordered bed rest for her shock, but perhaps the distraction of company might prove a better cure, Nia decided, reaching out to twine one of Amanda's blond curls around her finger.

"Oh, very well, you shameless baggage," she capitulated, bending to give her a swift hug. "I will bring her ladyship up to see you once we have finished speaking. All right?"

Amanda pouted slightly. "Couldn't I come down with you?" she wheedled, peeking up at Nia through her lashes. "I promise I'll be ever so good."

"I am sure you shall," Nia replied, giving her small nose a playful tweak. "But you will remain abovestairs nonetheless. You had a bad fall, and you need your rest."

Amanda left the room, her small shoulders slumped in dejection. Nia watched her go, biting her lip in fond exasperation. If she hadn't been so familiar with Amanda's tricks, she'd have relented on the spot. As it was, it took all of her willpower to keep from melting.

Lady Catherine was nervously pacing when Nia entered the drawing room. The door had scarce closed behind her than the pretty blond dashed over, her blue eyes filled with concern. "I hope you'll forgive me for barging in like this," she apologized, taking Nia's hand in hers, "but when I heard what happened yesterday, I was so upset that I rushed right over!"

"You know about the attack?" Nia asked in amazement. Given the duke's taciturn nature, she'd have thought he'd have done everything within his power to keep the matter private.

"It is all anyone is talking about," Catherine responded with a shudder. "How awful things have become when a man can't even take his family to so public a place as the Tower without being attacked by ruffians!" She gave Nia an anxious look. "How is Amanda? She wasn't hurt, was she?"

Nia softened at the anxious note in Lady Catherine's voice. "She's bruised and a little frightened, but otherwise she is fine," she said, giving her hand a reassuring squeeze. "She was excited to hear you had called, and I promised her you would go up for a visit when we finished speaking."

Tears showed in Lady Catherine's soft blue eyes before she blinked them away. "I would like that very much," she said, allowing herself to be guided over to the settee. "I have a doll for her. I meant to bring it, but I am afraid I hurried out so quickly, I left it behind."

"Some other time." Nia brushed the matter aside with an understanding smile. She glanced around the drawing room, noting for the first time that they were alone. "Where is Miss Saunders? Did she not accompany you?"

Catherine blushed prettily, and lowered her eyes to her hands. "I am afraid she was also left behind," she admitted with a laugh. "I was so anxious I wouldn't wait for her, but went tearing out of the house. No doubt I shall get a dreadful scold when I return home."

"No doubt." Nia tried not to grin as she imagined the older woman's outraged response. She could almost see her pursing her lips together as she reminded Lady Catherine that daughters of earls did not pay sympathy calls unless they were *properly* chaperoned.

They continued visiting comfortably, enjoying the tea Mrs. Mayton brought them. Lady Catherine's natural charm and kindness greatly impressed Nia, and she couldn't help but admire the lovely picture the other woman made as she gracefully poured out more tea. She would make a perfect duchess, Nia decided, and then frowned at the sudden twinge of pain the admission brought to her heart.

"Is something wrong, Miss Pringle?" Catherine asked, eyeing Nia with concern. "Did I put in too much sugar?"

"What?" Nia blinked at her, then gazed down at the delicate cup in her hand. "Oh! No, my lady, my tea is fine. I was only thinking of the packing. We are leaving for the country tomorrow, and there is still a great deal left to be done."

"And I am keeping you from it." Catherine set her cup down at once. "I am sorry, Miss Pringle. What a rude person you must think me to intrude like this when you must have so much on your mind. I shall go at once."

"I didn't mean that, my lady!" Nia exclaimed, fearing she had given offense. "Indeed, I am enjoying your company. Please don't feel you need to leave on *my* account."

"Well, if you are certain," Catherine said, allowing herself to be persuaded. "But you must promise me you will send me away the moment I become a bother."

"I shall toss you out on your ear," Nia promised solemnly, her eyes dancing.

"Good, I am glad that is settled." Catherine picked up her teacup and gave Nia a bright smile. "And I must say I am relieved, for I am enjoying our little coze. It seems forever since I've had an intelligent conversation with another female, and I am starved for rational discourse. Most of the other ladies I meet are only interested in their gowns and their beaus, or the latest *on-dit*. I can't wait until I see Portia again."

"Portia?" The name was unfamiliar to Nia.

"Miss Portia Haverall. She and her father live in the village nearest our estate and that of His Grace's. Her father is a retired don from Cambridge, and he and Portia are forever squabbling. You will like her, I think, for you are much alike."

"Oh?"

Catherine was pleased with the interest in Nia's voice. "She is intelligent, and very well educated for a lady," she explained, smiling at the thought of her willful friend. "She reads Greek and Latin, and can quote Shakespeare at the drop of a hat. She is also one of the most stubborn and strong-minded ladies I have ever met, which is why I feel the two of you will get along so well. I don't believe either of you has a liking for the complacent and the common-place."

The intuitive observation took Nia by surprise. She had already observed that Lady Catherine was both beautiful and kind; now it appeared she was also perceptive. Precisely the sort of bride a man like Wyatt ... the duke, she corrected hastily ... would require. This time she was prepared for the stab of pain the observation caused.

"You're right, my lady, Miss Haverall does sound most interesting," Nia said, firmly putting all thoughts of the duke from her mind. "If you would be so kind as to give me her direction, I should like to write her and invite her to tea. With the duke's permission, of course," she added, although she was certain Wyatt would have no objections.

"Oh, I am sure His Grace shan't mind," Catherine assured her. "I believe he is acquainted with her father. However, to expedite matters I will write her and let her know she is free to call upon you. I only wish I might be there to introduce you."

Nia noted the slight wistfulness in her voice. "Will you be returning to the country, my lady?"

"Not until the season is over," Lady Catherine said, her lips curving down in a slight frown. "I should like to come sooner, but my sister believes Lord Barstowe is on the verge of offering for me, and she would never let me leave."

"Oh." Nia was uncertain how she should respond to the shy confession. She knew felicitations were clearly in order, but it was equally clear that Catherine was less than pleased at the prospect. In the end she decided it would be safer to go with good manners, and quietly offered her congratulations.

"Thank you." Catherine inclined her head. "Lord Barstowe is a very worthy gentleman, or so I am told, and I am sure we shall be quite happy together. It is only . . ."

"Only what, my lady?"

Catherine's cheeks pinked with embarrassment as she met Nia's eyes. "It is only that I do not love him," she confessed. "Oh, I know it is not the way such things are done in our world," she rushed on at Nia's incredulous expression, "but I have always longed for a marriage based on real love rather than expediency. I see my sisters' lives, and that is not what I want for myself. I suppose that is unforgivably selfish of me, but—"

"It isn't in the least bit selfish!" Nia interrupted, laying a gentle hand on Catherine's arm. "We all of us want happiness. I see nothing so terrible in that."

"Perhaps." Catherine's smile was one of sad acceptance. "But that is because you aren't the daughter of an earl. If you were, you'd know how silly and self-indulgent I am being. Ladies of my class do not choose the men they marry on the basis of something so foolish as love."

"How do they choose them?" Nia asked, although she was fairly certain she knew.

"Oh, by his position, his breeding, that sort of thing," Catherine replied with an uncomfortable shrug. "It sounds so mercenary, I know, but that is how it is done. And usually it is for the best. Marriage is difficult enough, but unless both partners are equals in such things, it can be impossible."

Nia felt as if she had been stabbed. She thought of Wyatt and the huge chasm that separated them, and for a moment she feared she would disgrace herself by bursting into tears. Logically she knew nothing could ever come of her foolish infatuation, but in her heart she had spun foolish dreams of what might be. Hearing the truth so blatantly spoken shattered those dreams beyond all repair, and left Nia with a numbing sense of loss.

"I see," she said, swallowing uncomfortably, staring down at the tea cooling in her cup. "Lady Catherine, might I ask you something?"

"Of course."

"If you were free to marry any man you desired, what sort of man would you chose?"

The question seemed to take Catherine by surprise, but she hesitated only briefly before responding. "One I could respect," she said, her firm reply making it obvious this was a question she had considered more than once. "Lord Barstowe is very nice, but he is so vain and shallow at times, caring only for his appearance and his racehorses. And there is something about him I do not trust. I would much prefer a man of honor and courage. A man I could trust to protect me always. Do you know what I mean?" She gave Nia an anxious look.

Nia swallowed again, her eyes closing against the onslaught of pain. "Yes, Lady Catherine," she said, her voice bleak as she met her inquisitive gaze. "I know precisely what you mean."

Chapter 10

ᘒᘒᘒᘒ

They set out for the country the following morning beneath leaden skies that were heavy with the threat of rain. Nia thought Wyatt would postpone their departure, but he wouldn't hear of it, and after all that had happened she couldn't blame him. She, too, would rest easier once Amanda was far away from London and the danger stalking her.

Amanda started out in her customary high spirits, but as they continued northward she grew increasingly fretful and cross until Wyatt was forced to speak sharply to her. To his dismay she burst into tears and flung herself into the governess's arms, sobbing as if her heart would break. She fell asleep soon afterward. As she slept, he gave Nia a rueful look.

"What an ogre you must think me to make a little girl cry," he said, leaning forward to tuck the traveling robe more securely about Amanda. "I never meant to upset her."

He sounded so contrite that Nia's heart went out to him. "If you hadn't reprimanded her, I would have done so myself," she assured him gently. "Despite everything she has been through, there are still certain rules that must be followed, and Amanda mustn't be allowed to think she can behave so poorly without facing the consequences. She'll recover, don't worry, but I wonder if the same might be said of you." She added this last with a teasing smile.

The smile had its desired effect, and Wyatt settled back against the cushions. "As I have already observed, Miss Pringle, this guardian business is the very devil. I cannot remember a time when I have felt so bewildered." He gave the sleeping girl a loving glance. "I shudder to think what I shall go through once she makes her bows."

Nia's expression softened as she imagined an anxious and overprotective Wyatt watching a grown-up Amanda taking her place in society. "I am sure you will do quite well, Your Grace," she said, the sparkle in her eyes at odds with her prim tones. "After all, how difficult can it be? You'll only have to contend with rakes, fortune hunters, and ne'er do wells all trying to court Amanda for her money. To say nothing of beaus and fops and, of course, the man she will eventually marry."

Wyatt shot a genuinely horrified look at the little girl sleeping in Nia's arms. "If your intention was to terrify me, ma'am, you have succeeded," he said with a shudder. "I am turning Catholic at once, and sending her into a nunnery."

Nia gave a merry laugh, and then lowered her voice when Amanda stirred restlessly. "Hoisted with your own petard, sir," she said, gently laying her charge on the bench beside her. "I daresay you have given more than one father a nervous moment or two in your day. It seems only fair that you should suffer a similar fate."

The amusement died abruptly in Wyatt's eyes. "Ambrose once said the very same thing," he said quietly, turning to gaze out the window. "And I recall feeling quite smug about it. Now I find myself praying that fending off her beaus will be the greatest of my concerns."

Without thinking of the impropriety of her actions, Nia leaned forward to cover his clenched hand with her own. "You're talking about the attack, aren't you?" she asked, her voice gentle.

He gave a bleak nod, but did not look at her. "She could have been killed," he said, his jaw tense with suppressed fury. "I can't forget that. I won't. And when I find proof of the man's villainy, I shall see he pays for his folly with his life."

The brutal words would have made a lesser woman swoon, but Nia was a soldier's daughter. She may not have approved of his plans for deadly vengeance, but she understood his need to exact it. He blamed himself for what happened, and she knew that blame could only be assuaged through action. She only hoped he was prepared for the repercussions. Whatever he might think now, killing another man was never easy. She prayed the guilt wouldn't be too much for him to bear.

The sun was setting when they arrived at Perryvale Manor. Despite having been warned by Mrs. Mayton that the house was "A grand place, miss, with a hundred rooms or more," Nia was unprepared for the sheer size of the elegant estate. Built out of red bricks that had faded to a soft, creamy rose, the house glowed in the dying rays of sun. Mullioned windows winked in the golden light, and wide, stone terraces overlooked gardens that were alive with color.

Gazing up at it, Nia thought she'd never seen anything more beautiful or, she admitted with a heavy sigh, more intimidating. She turned to take Amanda's hand, only to find her in the duke's arms, her eyes wide as she gazed about her.

"Is this really your house, Uncle Wyatt?" she asked, her voice filled with awe.

"It is the home of the Perryvales," Wyatt replied, feeling a raw emptiness as he lifted his eyes to the house that had never seemed truly his. "And now it is your home as well."

"May we go inside now?" she asked the moment she was set on her feet. "I would like to see my room . . . and my pony. I most especially want to see my pony."

Wyatt smiled at her eagerness. "I am afraid you'll have to wait until tomorrow to meet Pegasus," he apologized. "But I think a tour of the house can be arranged."

The household staff was lined up on either side of the great hall to meet them, and after a quick round of introductions that left Nia's head spinning, the duke drew her off to one side. "I know you will want to see Amanda settled," he said, his dark gaze resting on her face. "But I would be most grateful if you would meet me in the receiving room. Shall we say in an hour?"

"Certainly, Your Grace," Nia replied, knowing the polite request was really an order. She'd been hoping to lie down for a bit, but she supposed it could wait.

The rooms that had been set aside for her and Amanda were the most luxurious Nia had ever seen, and it took all of her control not to gawk at them like a country bumpkin. She managed to control herself until Annie, the young maid who was assigned to help Nancy, escorted her into a large bedroom located across the hall from the schoolroom.

"This is *my* room?" she asked, standing on the threshold and glancing around the violet- and cream-colored room with disbelieving eyes. "Are you certain?"

"Yes, Miss Pringle," Annie replied, bustling over to the French windows and throwing them open. "His Grace was most precise in his instructions when he ordered the room redone. Do you like it?"

Nia's dazed eyes moved from the tent bed draped in amethyst silk to the cheval glass set in a gilded frame, before coming to rest on the pair of needle-point chairs angled in front of the tiled fireplace. "It is perfect," she said, her voice soft as she walked over to the bed. She reached out to stroke the shimmering material, wondering why something so beautiful could make her so sad.

"Will you be having a lie down, miss?" the maid asked politely. "You're looking a wee bit whey-faced, if you don't mind my saying so."

"His Grace is waiting for me in the receiving

room," Nia said, turning from the bed. "I'll change, and then go down. It wouldn't do to keep him waiting."

To her surprise Annie insisted upon helping her with her toilet. It was the first time she'd had a maid attend to her so personally, and she found the experience disconcerting. She soon learned that Annie, for all her youth and shy smiles, was a gentle despot, and that it was easier to submit to her ministrations than to argue. It was only when Annie insisted that Nia leave off her starched cap that she felt compelled to protest.

"But, Annie, I am a governess," she said, staring at her reflection with a mixture of disbelief and delight. "It wouldn't be proper for me to go about with my hair uncovered."

"Nonsense." Annie gathered up the rich mahogany tresses she had just brushed and began arranging them in a smooth chignon. "You're a young lady, miss, and there's years yet before you need to be bothering with such things. And you've such pretty hair, it seems a shame to hide it."

Nia was human enough to be pleased by the compliment, and settled back to let Annie work her magic. When her hair was arranged to the maid's exacting demands, Nia was bustled into one of her new gowns of emerald georgette trimmed with black braid. Annie added a fringed shawl of gold and green wool, and Nia knew she had never looked better. She said as much to Annie, and was rewarded with a brilliant smile.

"Thank you, miss," the young maid said, dropping a modest curtsey. " 'Tis my hope to be a lady's abigail someday, and if you don't mind, I thought mayhap I could practice on you. I'll be ever so careful," she added, when Nia didn't answer at once.

"I'm sure you shall," Nia capitulated. She'd helped train enough young girls for service to know that a lady's maid was as high as someone in Annie's position could hope to aspire. "And I would be delighted with your assistance. I'll soon be the best-dressed governess in all the Cotswolds, I'll wager," she added with a teasing smile.

The maid drew herself up, her chin set with pride. "You will be if *I* have aught to do with it," she declared.

Nia was still smiling several minutes later when she walked into the receiving room. Her fear that she would lose her way proved fruitless, as there were footmen everywhere who were more than eager to assist her. The duke was waiting for her, and as she entered he swung around to greet her.

"I am sorry to interrupt your rest when I know you must be exhausted," he began, his expression serious. "But there is something I . . ." His voice trailed off as he took in her appearance for the first time.

"Is something wrong, my lord?" Nia asked, puzzled by the odd look in his eyes.

"You aren't wearing your cap."

Nia blushed scarlet, feeling more mortified than she ever had in her life. "I will go up and fetch one at once, Your Grace," she mumbled, silently cursing herself for allowing her vanity to overcome her good sense. "I apologize if I have offended—"

"No," Wyatt interrupted, stepping forward to offer her a penitent smile. "It is I who ought to apologize to you for having made such a personal remark. It is just that I was taken aback." His eyes lingered on her before he added, "You have beautiful hair."

Nia didn't know what to say. "Thank you, Your Grace," she said at last, deciding it was probably wisest to accept the compliment and be done with it.

Wyatt continued gazing at her, feeling as awkward as a school lad. He'd always thought her lovely, but looking as she did now, she was the most exquisite creature he had ever seen. Oh, he had met women who were more beautiful, but they seemed pale and insignificant when compared to Nia.

Afraid of revealing his thoughts, he turned toward the opened French windows that overlooked the gardens. "There is something of great import I wish to discuss with you, and I thought it best that we get to it at once," he said, his hands clenched behind his back as he stared out at the garden. "It is about the man responsible for the attack on Amanda."

Nia brightened at this bit of news, her uneasiness with the awkward situation vanishing. "Are you going to tell me his name?" she asked, pleased that he had finally decided to take her into his confidence.

Her eagerness for the truth made him flinch, but he knew the time was not right. "Not just yet," he said regretfully, wishing he could be more forthcoming with her. "I still have little in the way of proof, and until such time as I do, I prefer keeping my suspicions to myself."

As if she intended going about shouting the man's name from the rooftop, Nia thought sourly, controlling her disappointment with difficulty. "What is it you wished to discuss, then?" she asked, piqued by his continued obstinacy on the subject.

Wyatt heard the sharpness in her voice and tried not to smile. "I've set some runners to watching him," he told her, recalling the meeting he had held with Ambrose and Mr. Hemsley prior to leaving London. "I don't think he'll attempt to follow us here, but I can't be sure. Because of that I am afraid you and Amanda must be restricted to the estate. If you need to go into the village, either one of the senior servants or I will accompany you. And of course you are forbidden to ride about on your own," he added, wisely anticipating her.

Nia glowered at his back. If the situation hadn't been so desperate, nothing would have given her greater pleasure than to hurl his odious commands back at him. But since she knew he was right she managed to contain her annoyance. "Yes, Your Grace."

Her stilted tones brought him swinging around to face her. "I know these restrictions chafe, Nia," he said, meeting her gaze, "but I assure you they are for the best. I would not have you harmed because of me."

The torment in his husky voice touched something deep in Nia, and she longed to offer him some comfort. She took a hesitant step forward before she managed to regain control of her errant emotions. "Then you agree that it is enmity toward you that is responsible for the incident?" she asked, forcing herself to be as cool and logical as she could.

He nodded slowly. "I spoke with the ruffian who was taken into custody," he replied, sharing with her what he could. "Although he knew next to nothing about who hired him, he did admit that he was told the attack was to occur when I was there to witness it."

"Good God, why?"

"He didn't think to ask, but I would hazard a guess it was because I was meant to suffer. And believe me, if anything had happened to Amanda, I *would* have suffered."

A wave of protective fury welled up in Nia, this time on Wyatt's behalf. The thought that anyone would try to hurt him in such a vicious manner aroused feelings in her that were as powerful as they were confusing. She remembered her vow to protect Amanda, and silently amended it. Not only would she do everything within her power to keep her charge safe, she pledged, but she would also shield Wyatt from any harm. Whoever was after him would have to get past her to reach him.

The first weeks at Perryvale flashed by in an idyllic haze for Nia and her delighted charge. They spent sun-filled mornings exploring the elegant old house, and flower-scented afternoons roaming over the estate on their horses. Wyatt usually accompanied them on their rides, but on those rare days when he was occupied elsewhere, his steward, a Mr. Lohman, rode with them, answering Amanda's ceaseless questions with a stilted dignity that Nia found vastly diverting.

They had been at Perryvale almost a fortnight when Amanda came dashing into the schoolroom, her blue eyes alight with wonder as she skittered to a halt in front of Nia's desk. "Oh, Miss Pringle, you must come quickly! Mr. Sanderfore has a broken knight in his armory!"

Nia's eyebrows climbed as she attempted to decipher this startling pronouncement. One of the things that had captured Amanda's mercurial interest was the estate's extensive collection of medieval armor, and she was always clamoring for a peek inside the ancient suits. Mr. Sanderfore had recently been hired to restore the collection, and although he indulged Amanda to a point, he'd never allowed her to handle the armor, explaining it was too valuable. He had, however, promised that the next time he restored a piece he would let her examine it.

"Ah, you mean he has taken one of the suits apart," Nia said, setting aside the book she had been reading with a laugh. "That does sound interesting. Have you peeked inside?"

Amanda solemnly shook her head. "I only looked in for a moment to wish Mr. Sanderfore a good day, and when I saw the bits of knight lying on the table, I came to fetch you. I thought you'd like to see them, too," she added with the air of one bestowing a rare treat.

"I see." Nia wasn't fooled by such generosity. The armory, with its dangerous collection of swords, maces, and battles axes, was strictly forbidden to Amanda, and she was only allowed to visit it when she was with an adult. She'd already broken that rule and Nia knew she should reprimand her for the infraction, but she didn't have the heart. What could it hurt? she asked herself, adjusting her spectacles as she rose to her feet.

"Very well," she said, offering Amanda her hand. "Let's meet your disassembled knight."

The armory was located in the north wing of the house, in the ancient place the servants called the "keep." The rough walls of damp gray stones were hung with exquisite tapestries and faded battle flags, and the flagstones beneath their feet were worn uneven by centuries of use. Nia could feel the weight of history about the place, and it captivated her as much as the more sumptuous portions of the house left her dazzled.

Perryvale was much like its owner in that respect, she mused, pausing to admire the sunlight streaming through a stained-glass window. It was refined and elegant on the surface, but hard and deadly at its core. The oddest part was that she found it was the cold, stone core she preferred to the polished perfection. The fanciful admission brought a pensive look to her eyes.

The young curator was seated at a table and hard at work polishing an arm piece when they entered. "Good afternoon, sir," she said, greeting him with a polite smile. "I hope we aren't interrupting you?"

Mr. Sanderfore set aside his rubbing cloth and stumbled to his feet. "Not at all, Miss Pringle," he assured her, his pale cheeks flushing a deep brick-red. "You must know I am always happy to receive visitors. Lady Amanda." He patted her on the head. "I thought I saw you peeking in here earlier."

"We have come to see the knight," Amanda said hastily. She inched closer to the long table and studied the pieces of gleaming silver metal scattered on its surface. "Where is the rest of him?" she asked.

"This is all there is, I fear," Mr. Sanderfore said. "This is one of our smaller suits, worn more for ornamentation than for protection. Unlike this piece." He moved to another table that held a confusing array of polished metal.

"Do you see this?" he held up a metallic sleeve fitted at the shoulder with supple pieces of leather. "Most of these joints were of hinged metal or mesh, but this has been made with leather for flexibility.

The elbow is similarly jointed, and would have allowed its wearer greater freedom of movement. An important consideration when one is swinging a sword in battle."

Amanda stroked an admiring finger over the smooth surface. "Is it comfortable?"

"To be honest, I don't know, my lady. I have never had occasion to wear one."

"Will you wear it now?" Amanda asked, her eyes lighting at the thought. "Please? I should like ever so much to see a *real* knight. Wouldn't you, Miss Pringle?"

Nia was examining the helmet. It looked like an epergne to her, and she couldn't imagine how anyone could see anything through the narrow eye slits. "I suppose I am curious," she admitted, slanting Mr. Sanderfore an apologetic look.

His flush deepened and his pale gray eyes began to blink with increasing anxiety. "I . . . that is to say . . . I should like to oblige you, ladies," he stammered, "but I fear I cannot. It would be too confining, and I have a horror of narrow places."

"Oh." Nia, who shared a similar distaste for heights, sympathized with him. "Well, perhaps one of the footmen . . ."

"Miss Pringle!" He snatched the helmet from her hands and clutched it protectively to his chest. "This is a complete set of sixteenth-century battle armor! I am not about to risk it on some silly sprig of a lad who might damage it! Whatever would His Grace say?"

Nothing kind, that much was certain, Nia thought, imagining Wyatt's response should he learn of such desecration. Of course, she mused, picking up one of the heavy gauntlets and slipping it on her own hand, there was no reason he *should* learn of it. Not if they were very, very careful. She glanced up to find Mr. Sanderfore watching her.

"I quite agree with you that we shouldn't risk something so valuable with a footman," she said, her lips curving in a smile that made the curator take a step backwards. "But as it happens I have another idea ..."

Wyatt was reviewing the last of his correspondence when the door to his library was flung open and Amanda ran inside, tears streaming down her face.

"Uncle Wyatt! Uncle Wyatt, oh, do come quickly!"

Wyatt leapt to his feet so fast that his chair clattered to the floor. "What is it?" he demanded, rushing around his desk to kneel beside the sobbing girl.

"M ... Miss P ... Pringle!" Amanda wailed, casting herself in his arms. "In th ... the armory! I think it has eaten her!"

Wyatt caught the words "Miss Pringle" and "armory," and then he was on his feet, his heart pounding as he ran up the narrow, stone steps leading to the keep. Not knowing what he might encounter, he envisioned everything from armed intruders to an accident involving any of the keep's deadly weapons. The last thing he expected was to find one of the suits of armor being held up in the center of the room as several people swarmed around it, all in clear distress. No one seemed to note his arrival, and he watched the unfolding drama with disbelieving eyes.

"If everyone would just remain calm," he heard Nia's muffled voice coming from the armor, "I am sure everything will be fine."

"I knew something like this was going to happen," one of the housemaids moaned, wringing her hands. "They'll sack us all for this, you mark my words."

"Perhaps a hammer and some tongs might work," the hapless curator suggested, eyeing Nia speculatively. "I've repaired suits before, and if one is very careful, it is possible to cut the armor open, and—"

"What the devil is going on here?" Wyatt roared, deciding he'd seen more than enough of this farce.

The maid and the curator emitted startled shrieks and whirled around, their faces wearing identical ex-

pressions of horror. The sudden loss of support as
their arms left her sent Nia tumbling forward, and
she would have clattered to the ground had Wyatt
not leapt forward in time to catch her. The curator
rushed to assist him, and they soon had her balanced
again.

"Are you all right?" Wyatt asked anxiously, peering through the visor of the helmet. "Can you
breathe?"

If it was possible to die from embarrassment, Nia
was certain she would have expired on the spot. Perhaps that might solve the problem, she thought, a trifle hysterical; then they wouldn't need to pry her out
of this blasted contraption. They could simply prop
her up in the hallway with the rest of the relics. She
gave a strangled laugh.

"Nia!" Wyatt panicked at the choked sound emanating from inside the helmet. His hands flew to the
clasp that fastened the visor to the body. "Help me
get this thing off of her!" he ordered Mr. Sanderfore.
"She's suffocating!"

"No! I . . . I can breathe, Your Grace," Nia said
quickly, lifting her hands and fumbling awkwardly
with the helmet. "It is just that this wretched thing is
stuck, and we can't seem to get it off of me."

He brushed her hands aside, his fingers finding the
recalcitrant piece of metal that was responsible for
their woes. "It's bent," he said, examining it carefully.
"Perhaps I can work it back into shape . . ."

"Er, Your Grace,"—Mr. Sanderfore fluttered his
hands nervously—"if I may remind you, that armor
was worn by one of your ancestors while fighting the
Spaniards in the Lowlands. It would be a shame if it
were to be . . . damaged."

"And it would be a greater shame if Miss Pringle
were to die while we stand here debating the matter!" Wyatt snapped, pushing on the hasp of metal
with his thumb. "Although once we do manage to
get her out of this thing, I will be very interested to
learn how she got into it in the first . . . got it!"

The metal snapped beneath his fingers and he raised the visor, peering anxiously at Nia's flushed features. "Miss Pringle," he said, his lips curving in a smile composed of equal parts of relief and mischief, "I trust you are well?"

Nia glared up into his blurred features. She'd removed her spectacles so that the visor would fit over her face, but she didn't need to see Wyatt's face to know he was grinning at her. "Very well, my lord," she answered, marshalling as much dignity as was possible. "But do you think you might hurry in getting me out of this . . . this tin?"

"As you wish." Wyatt had to fight to hold back a chuckle as, assisted by an obviously distressed Mr. Sanderfore, he began removing the bits of armor. The helmet slipped off with only a few tugs, and the gauntlets provided no challenge whatsoever. The breastplate was fastened at the side, and Wyatt hesitated a moment as he studied her.

"I trust you are wearing something beneath this, ma'am?" he asked, his eyes filled with teasing speculation. "I should hate to disrobe a lady by accident rather than design."

Nia, who had donned her spectacles, now saw the smile on his face, and was strongly tempted to kick him. Unfortunately her kid slippers were covered with pointed metal shoes, and she could scarcely lift her foot. She had to content herself with a glare. "I borrowed an old set of footman's livery from your housekeeper, Your Grace," she said, emphasizing his title with cool irony. "I assure you, I am properly covered."

"Pity." He gave her a cheeky grin, and then proceeded to remove the breastplate and back piece. When it came time to remove the leggings, however, an indignant Annie intervened.

"I can see to the rest of it, Your Grace," she said, folding her arms across her chest and fixing Wyatt with a stern stare. "There's no need to trouble yourself further."

Wyatt lifted an eyebrow at the maid's effrontery. He'd been about to suggest the same thing, for much as he longed for a glimpse of Nia's legs, he knew it was not at all proper. "Very well . . . Annie, is it not?"

"Yes, Your Grace." The maid resolutely stood her ground.

"Very well, Annie, I shall bow to your practical suggestion." He was grateful Nia had such a staunch champion, and made a mental note to mention Annie's sterling performance to the housekeeper at the first opportunity.

"Come, Sanderfore." He turned to the curator who was standing beside him, the armor cradled in his arms. "We shall leave the ladies to their privacy."

"As you say, Your Grace." The young curator gave a heavy sigh, his expression one of glum resignation as he followed Wyatt out of the keep.

Chapter 11

〰〰〰

"**I** wish you would stop chuckling, my lord,"
Nia grumbled less than an hour later as she
sat in the duke's private drawing room nursing a restorative cup of tea. "It's not that funny."

Wyatt regarded her over the rim of his cup, his lips
twitching as he took in her mussed hair and embarrassed flush. "If you say so, ma'am," he drawled.
"Naturally a gentleman would never contradict a
lady."

Nia glowered at him, strongly suspecting he was
mocking her. Her fingers tightened around her cup,
and she forced herself to relax them. "I am glad you
didn't dismiss Mr. Sanderfore for assisting me," she
continued, struggling to keep her voice cool and
aloof. "It would have been most unfair to sack him
for something that was entirely my fault."

"So you said," Wyatt replied, remembering her
heated insistence that it was she, and she alone, who
was responsible for the afternoon's contretemps.

Nia saw the laughter lurking in his dark eyes, and
hastened to change the subject. "I was wondering,
sir, if you would escort Amanda and me into the village tomorrow. I am in need of some necessities, and
I know Amanda could do with the diversion."

Wyatt arched his eyebrows at her request. "I
would have thought this afternoon's activities would
be diverting enough for even the most jaded of pal-
ates," he observed laconically, raising his cup to his
lips.

She flushed at the hit. "Yes, well, you must remember Amanda spent several months in an orphanage," she said, her eyes darting away from his. "She is used to the company of other children, and I fear she has grown bored and lonely on her own. Naturally, if you cannot spare the time, I could ask your steward to—"

"I didn't say I wouldn't do it," he interrupted. "If you want to go into town, I would be more than happy to take you. In fact," he added, warming to the thought, "we might even stop to take our luncheon at the Pampered Dove. As I recall, the innkeeper always set a respectable table."

"That sounds an excellent suggestion," Nia approved, relieved he seemed so agreeable. "And perhaps while the two of you are lingering over your sweets I can slip out and buy Amanda her gift. I noted a book shop on the square as we drove by, and I thought I would start there. She loves books."

"A gift?"

"For her birthday. She turns seven in a fortnight."

"Good Gad!" Wyatt sat forward, spilling his tea over the saucer as he placed it on the table. "I'd forgotten all about that! Her birthday is in June, isn't it?"

"On the eighteenth," Nia provided, setting her cup on the table and fixing him with a hopeful look. "With your permission I thought we might have a small party for her. Just the servants and ourselves, and Lady Catherine, if she is back from London."

Wyatt nodded his approval. "A party sounds just the thing," he said, feeling a faint stab of guilt for having allowed the matter to slip his mind. "You might wish to consult with Cook as to the menu, but I'm sure whatever you choose will be fine."

An imp of mischief danced in Nia's eyes as she slanted him a teasing grin. "Granting me unlimited power, my lord?" she asked, pushing her spectacles back up her nose. "That might prove dangerous."

He folded his arms across his chest and met her grin with a look of masculine superiority. "Only to you," he drawled, enjoying their verbal sparring. "And only if you are so foolish as to serve stewed turnips or carrots in any form. Either of those, Nia, my sweet, and I'll have you locked into that suit of armor ... permanently." When he saw her color deepen, he settled back against his chair and gave her his most innocent look.

"Now that the matter of the menu has been settled, what do you think I should buy Amanda for her birthday?"

The village of Chipping Campden was much larger than Nia expected, and far more prosperous. The broad high street was lined with a variety of elegant structures, but it was the huge gabled building at the center of the square that most captivated her. She asked if it was the inn, and was surprised when Wyatt told her no.

"It's the Market Hall, and it was built for the sheep trade," he said, easily shifting Amanda from one arm to the other. "You might have noticed wool is an important commodity in this area. We have several flocks of sheep."

"Lambs," Amanda said, her expression growing hopeful. She snuggled closer to her uncle's broad chest and raised wide blue eyes to his face. "I think a lamb would make a most wonderful pet, don't you, Uncle Wyatt?"

He tweaked her nose with his gloved hand. "I do, poppet, but I fear my housekeeper might disagree. The only lambs you'll find in Mrs. Allison's house are in the stew pot."

Nia winced, anticipating what Amanda's reaction would be.

"She *cooks* baby lambs?" Amanda demanded, clearly horrified. "Our baby lambs?"

Wyatt evidently realized his error too late, and hastily began to mend his fences. "That is why we raise them, Amanda," he said. "Ours is a working farm, and every animal must contribute to ..." His voice trailed off as her bottom lip began to tremble, and he sent Nia a desperate look. "Help."

Laughing, Nia took Amanda out of his arms and set her on the paved street. "We shall discuss this later, Amanda," she said, giving the little girl's hand a gentle squeeze. "In the meanwhile your uncle has promised us lunch at a real inn. Won't that be fun?"

"I suppose." Amanda reluctantly allowed herself to be distracted. "But I won't eat any lamb," she warned, her brows meeting in a scowl that was a perfect imitation of her uncle's formidable expression.

Despite the inauspicious beginning, the rest of the afternoon went just as Nia had planned. While Wyatt and Amanda remained at the inn, she slipped out to return to the book shop they'd visited earlier in the morning. She'd seen Amanda lingering over a volume on wildflowers, and decided it would make the perfect gift. Hoping the book would still be on the shelf, she pushed open the door and stepped inside, accompanied by the rather large footman Wyatt had insisted she take with her to "help carry parcels."

The shop was busy, and Nia had to wind her way around several people before she was able to reach the shelves. The book was still there, and she was reaching to pick it up when another hand suddenly shot past hers to pluck it from the shelf. Nia whirled around, fully prepared to do battle, when she found herself confronting an elegant woman dressed in a stylish cape of blue velvet; a bonnet was set coquettishly on her dark curls.

"Oh, I beg your pardon!" the woman said, her gray eyes full of apology as she met Nia's gaze. "Were you reaching for this?"

Nia's ire vanished at the repentant note in the other woman's voice. "As a matter of fact, I was," she said. "I was here earlier with my charge, and noticed her admiring it. Her birthday is in a fortnight, and—"

"Say no more." The book was surrendered with

alacrity. "I was merely going to peek at the drawings, and I wouldn't wish to deprive Miriam of a sale. You're new in town, aren't you?"

The abrupt shift in conversation took Nia aback for a moment. "In a manner of speaking," she began carefully. "I am Miss Thomasina Pringle, the—"

"The duke's new governess," the woman finished for her, nodding. "That is, the governess to his little niece. The duke is far too old and set in his ways to benefit from instruction. I am Miss Portia Haverall." She offered Nia her hand. "Lady Catherine Declaire has written me of you, and I was hoping we would meet. You do look like a bluestocking. Good. I feared Kate's powers of observation might be dimmed by the dazzling lights of London."

"She did seem intelligent," Nia replied, warming at once to Miss Haverall's somewhat abrupt manner. She might have added that Miss Haverall herself looked nothing like any bluestocking she had ever encountered. She was quite beautiful, in fact, with delicate features and a slender, dainty build that put one in mind of a fairy. Nia would have taken her for a sweet widgeon had it not been for the sparkle in her remarkable eyes.

"Sharp as a tack, that's Kate," Miss Haverall continued in her light, musical voice, not seeming to notice Nia's perusal. "Although I daresay few people in London would take the time to note it. Society is usually too content with appearances to wonder about what might dwell beneath the surface. Have you found it so?"

"I am afraid I'm not familiar with the *ton* or their habits, ma'am," Nia apologized as she waited in line to pay for her purchase. "But I suppose you are right. Most of us do tend to take things as we see them."

"Of course I am right," Miss Haverall replied with no evidence of either pride or modesty. "I consider myself a true scientist, an observer of human nature, and I have oft noted that people will blithely agree with whatever they are told, so long as it is convenient for them. Truth, like appearances, must be comfortable to be acceptable."

"That is an interesting observation," Nia said, much impressed.

"Yes, isn't it? Although I suppose my father would accuse me of paraphrasing Shakespeare. He's why I am here, you know."

"Your father?"

"Shakespeare." She held up a slim volume of sonnets. "Father and I aren't speaking. In fact, he has cut me out of his will."

Nia remembered Lady Catherine mentioning the two weren't getting along, and her heart went out to the other woman. "Oh dear, I am so sorry ..."

"Oh, it's all right!" Miss Haverall gave a pretty laugh. "This is the third time this year he has disinherited me. He'll put me back in his will once I have proven my theory."

"Oh." Nia was tempted to ask what that theory might be, but she was aware that time was running out and the duke might grow anxious if she didn't return at once. She paid for her purchase and surrendered it to the footman, who had remained stoically at her side during her exchange.

She waited until they were outside before offering her hand to Miss Haverall and a guarded invitation to Perryvale Manor. "Of course I must see if His Grace will allow me visitors," she cautioned, since she'd yet to discuss the subject with Wyatt. "But I shall look forward to seeing you again."

"And I you," Miss Haverall replied with a bright smile. "I'm also looking forward to meeting your little charge. Catherine says she is a perfect love."

"She is," Nia said softly.

"Catherine told me what happened," Miss Haverall admitted, her face taking on a somber expression. "We were all of us shocked. The villagers have been keeping a sharp eye out for strangers, and any man who wanders into town may soon find himself the focus of some unpleasant attention."

"Indeed?" Nia was touched that the villagers should be so protective.

"Certainly. Only yesterday a man took some rooms at the inn, and the only thing that saved him from being plagued to death was that old Travlock, the innkeeper's father, recognized him as having once been employed by the late duchess as her secretary. I gather he is thinking of retiring here."

"I hope the poor man wasn't hurt," Nia murmured, envisioning an elderly gentleman being hounded by a suspicious mob.

"Oh, nothing like that," Miss Haverall hastened to reassure her. "People just stared and whispered behind their hands. You know how it is in these villages. Any stranger is considered fair fodder for the gossips to dine upon. And according to Janet, our kitchen maid, the man in question seemed to be above it all. Rather high in the instep for one who was nothing more than a mere secretary, or so rumor would have it."

Nia was amused that the man's former station was still a well-known fact after so long. She wondered if years in the future when she returned to Chipping Campden she'd still be known as Lady Amanda's governess. The thought brought an unexpected pang, and she banished it from her mind. She bid Miss Haverall a hasty good-bye and scurried back to the Pampered Dove, the stone-faced footman trailing at her heels.

It was late afternoon when they returned to Perryvale. The butler met them at the door with the information that they had visitors, and the identity of their guests brought a grim look to Wyatt's face. He turned to Nia, who was standing at his side, her expression mirroring his.

"I must go and see what is wrong," he said, drawing her away from Amanda. "It must be important or Ambrose and Mr. Hemsley wouldn't have left London."

"I understand," she said, her eyes meeting his as

she fought the urge to touch him, to reassure him that whatever was wrong, he wasn't alone. "Will . . . will they be staying the night?"

"I don't know," Wyatt admitted, revelling in the concern he saw in her eyes. "It will probably depend on whatever news they have brought. In the meanwhile, I don't want you to let Amanda out of your sight for a moment."

"Of course." Her chin firmed in that way he was coming to recognize. "You may rely on me, Your Grace."

He smiled, and then, unable to resist the temptation, he reached out and straightened her glasses, which were sitting askew on her nose. "I do rely on you, Nia," he said huskily, his breath feathering over her lips. "More than you may realize. More than I have any right to."

Nia's heart slammed into her chest, and she could feel her pulse racing as his fingers trailed over her cheek. Everything faded away, and there was only the two of them standing in a golden pool of light. The illusion was shattered by the sound of the butler discreetly clearing his throat.

"I have ordered tea served to Mr. Royston and the other gentleman," he told Wyatt, his wooden manner betraying nothing of his thoughts. "Will Your Grace be requiring anything else?"

Wyatt's hand dropped to his side as he stepped back from Nia. "No, that will be all, Chapman, thank you," he said, drawing a steadying breath. He could feel the excitement rising in him, and it amazed him that just touching Nia's cheek could have brought him such pleasure. If merely touching her conjured up such emotions, what would kissing her be like? He found the notion so sweetly tempting that he hurried off to his study before he could give in to it.

Twenty minutes later, all thoughts of kissing were the last thing on Wyatt's mind as he sat glaring at the two men facing him across his desk. He held a silver letter opener in his hand, his thumb idly tracing the intricate design carved into its handle as he listened to Hemsley conclude his report.

"So what you're saying, in essence, is that you have nothing new to tell me," he said when the other man finished speaking. "You're sure Elliott is behind the assault on Amanda, but you don't know how or why."

"We're working on it, Your Grace," Mr. Hemsley replied, taking Wyatt's cold fury in stride. "In the meanwhile we thought you should know that the bleater's disappeared. He managed to give our man the slip two days ago, and it's as if he's sunk into the earth. Don't worry, though. We'll find him soon enough."

"You shouldn't have lost him in the first place," Wyatt muttered, nailing the other man with a dangerous scowl. "Well, since you haven't any more information as to why he might be behind any of this, perhaps it isn't Elliott after all. It could be Amberstroke."

"It's not." Ambrose spoke for the first time. "I'm certain of that, if nothing else. His lordship seems content with the status quo, and almost swooned when I questioned him on the matter. He denies any ill feelings toward either you or Amanda, and I'm damned if I don't believe him."

Wyatt's eyes widened at this bit of intelligence. "*You* questioned Amberstroke?" he asked incredulously.

Ambrose's lips curved in a mocking smile. "I told you we dandies have our uses," he drawled. "Now, returning to the matter of your esteemed solicitor, there is one thing I have found most remarkable, even if Mr. Hemsley does not share my curiosity."

"And what is that?"

"We can establish his movements since he came to London some twenty or so years ago, but before that, were you aware that he was employed by your family?"

"*What?*"

"Nothing in that, Your Grace." Hemsley shrugged his beefy shoulders. "It was more'n thirty years ago. Elliott couldn't have been much out of the schoolroom—twenty-one, twenty-two, if he was a day."

"There *is* something to it since the man never mentioned the matter to me himself," Wyatt snapped, wondering if his faith in Hemsley had been misplaced. "Also, I'd be curious as to how you learned of this." He directed the remark to Ambrose.

"Your housekeeper, Mrs. Mayton, told me," he replied, meeting Wyatt's gaze with equanimity. "She remembered him from the early days, as she called them, and she added that she'd never cared for him above half. Something about his eyes, if I understood her correctly."

"Good God, why didn't she say anything?" Wyatt leapt to his feet and began pacing. "The man was my solicitor for over seven years! One would think she might have mentioned it to me, if only in passing!"

"You have no idea of the awe in which your servants hold you, old boy," Ambrose said with a laugh. "Mrs. Mayton would no more gossip with you than she would the prince! Fortunately for us she still regards me as an overgrown schoolboy in need of a bit of mothering, and thought nothing of spilling the family secrets in my ear."

Wyatt stiffened in alarm. "What family secrets?"

"Nothing scandalous, I assure you." Ambrose grew serious at the expression on Wyatt's face. "Just various gossip about old servants, and so on. I happened to mention Elliott's name, and you could have tipped me over with a feather when she told me he'd once worked for your mother. I—"

Wyatt's head snapped up at that. "Did she say what his position was?"

"He was her secretary," Ambrose said, his brow furrowing at Wyatt's rather abrupt response. "Mrs. Mayton said he was employed for only one summer, and that he was dismissed rather abruptly before your father returned from one of his diplomatic missions."

"I see," Wyatt said, his eyes closing as the pain in his chest grew deeper. He remembered Elliott claiming that his information had come from an "impeccable source," and he wondered if his harlot of a mother had confided her infidelities to her secretary. God knew she'd bragged of them to everyone else, he thought, bitterly recalling that long ago afternoon when he'd listened to his parents quarreling over her latest lover.

"Wyatt?" Ambrose was regarding him with concern. "Is everything all right? You'll forgive me for saying so, but you look like bloody hell."

Wyatt opened his eyes, his mouth curving in a humorless smile at Ambrose's blunt observation. He could see no reason why he shouldn't be equally blunt. The sordid tale was bound to come out once Elliott was apprehended, and he tried telling himself it was for the best. His whole life was founded on a lie, and the time for the truth was long since past. He blew out a pent-up breath and met his friend's worried gaze.

"No," he said with a heavy sigh, "everything is not all right. There is something I have to tell you, both of you, and I want your word that you won't repeat it to another soul."

"My word, Your Grace." Hemsley inclined his head.

"Of course you may rely on me!" Ambrose retorted, obviously stung that Wyatt should doubt him. "What is it?"

"I am not a Perryvale."

"*What*?"

Wyatt told them of his confrontation with Elliott, admitting everything, even his solicitor's accusation that he was not his father's true son. By the time he finished, Ambrose and Mr. Hemsley were staring at him in disbelief.

"My God! It can't be true!" Ambrose said, clearly shaken.

"Can it not?" Wyatt's laugh was bleak. "Look at me, Ambrose. Look at them." He indicated the many portraits adorning the walls. "Do I resemble any damned Perryvale you've ever seen?"

Ambrose reluctantly did as he was commanded. "I'll admit you looks don't run to theirs," he confessed at last, "but dash it, Wyatt, there's more to family resemblance than hair and eyes! Look at me, the sole blond in a family of red-headed giants. Yet you don't see anyone casting doubts on *my* parentage!"

"Perhaps, but then your sainted mother never enjoyed the rather unenviable reputation mine gloried in," Wyatt said, the truth bitter on his lips. " 'The Perryvale whore.' I've heard tales of her liaisons since I was in leading strings, so please don't tell me it's not possible. It *is* possible, damn it, and I've always known it. Always," he added, his eyes flashing with the pain he'd suffered for so long.

"And you say Elliott was triumphant when he told you of this?" Mr. Hemsley spoke for the first time, his expression thoughtful.

"He all but threw it in my face," Wyatt answered, his hands doubling into fists as he recalled the exultant gleam in Elliott's eyes as he'd confirmed his worst suspicions.

"Mmm." Hemsley stroked his chin. "Rather an odd reaction, that. Almost personal, one might think. But why should it be personal to the gent, eh? Unless . . . ." His voice trailed off as he stared off into space.

"What did you know of your mother's other lovers?" he asked unexpectedly. "Did she keep to her own class, or was she more . . . democratic, shall we say?"

Wyatt took his meaning at once. "Are you hinting he was my mother's lover?" he demanded, outraged.

"Was he?"

"How the devil am I to know?" Wyatt retorted. "I wasn't there! And I fail to see why you should be so concerned about it now. A few minutes ago you said there was nothing in the fact that Elliott once worked for my mother. It's rather late to start speculating on it now, isn't it?"

"Never too late to give things a good think through, Your Grace. And if I'd known you was keeping something like this beneath your hat, I might have taken a bit more interest in the solicitor's past. But no harm done," he added before Wyatt could speak. "Now that I know what's what, I'll soon have it set to rights."

"How?" Wyatt demanded with a dark scowl.

Mr. Hemsley took a pipe from his pocket and lit it with almost exquisite care. "If I was to know the answer to that, I'd know the answer to it all," he said calmly, meeting Wyatt's eyes through the fragrant blue smoke. "But it'll come to me, sir, never fear that. It'll come to me."

Nia half-expected that she and Amanda would dine in their rooms that night, and was surprised when Annie came up to help her dress for dinner.

"Are you sure His Grace is expecting us?" she asked as Annie arranged her hair in an elegant style. "I thought he would wish to dine privately with his guests."

"Oh no, miss," Annie said, frowning in concentration as she coaxed a curl to lie flat on Nia's neck. "I heard him telling Cook to be sure and prepare that lemon tart you and her ladyship favor. He'd not have done that if he'd planned to eat without you, now would he?"

Nia had to concede that was so, and silently submitted to Annie's ministrations. The young maid was growing increasingly proficient in her skills, and by the time she was finished Nia scarcely recognized herself. Dressed in a stylish gown of midnight-blue silk, the bodice and tiny puff sleeves decorated with faux pearls, she looked nothing like her former self. A set of pearl teardrops that had once belonged to her grandmother hung from her ears, and a pearl necklace was draped about her throat. She touched the necklace wistfully, and wondered if she would ever be content to don her drab governess togs again.

"A pity we don't have one of them feather things for your hair," Annie said, stepping back to examine her creation with a critical eye. "You'd be as pretty as could be, then."

"An aigrette, I think you mean," Nia replied, turning away from her reflection with a sigh. "And my feathers are fine enough for a mere governess." She shook off her troubling thoughts and managed a bright smile. "Thank you, Annie. Once again you have wrought a miracle."

Annie folded her hands in front of her and beamed with pride. "You're welcome, miss," she said, bobbing a respectful curtsey. "And now you'd best be hurrying. His lordship and Mr. Royston will be expecting you to join them in the parlor for sherry."

Nia hid her surprise at this bit of intelligence, for she knew enough of society to realize governesses seldom took sherry with a duke. Of course, she mused as she drifted down the wide, curving staircase, she and Wyatt hardly shared the common master and servant connection. They were . . . what? she wondered, her heart racing with emotions. Friends? He'd once said he considered her a friend, and it was obvious he respected her. She knew that should content her; indeed, it was far more than a woman in her station could hope for. But it wasn't enough, she admitted unhappily. It wasn't nearly enough. The thought weighed heavily on her mind as she entered the parlor.

Except for Amanda's bright chatter and Mr. Royston's boyish flirting, dinner was a rather subdued affair. Wyatt was withdrawn and aloof, and even Amanda had to work to win a smile from him. Nia worried that perhaps he didn't really want them there, but when he and Royston opted to join her and Amanda in the drawing room rather than linger over their brandy, she quickly discarded that notion. Still, it was obvious *something* was troubling him, and while Amanda was busy trying to teach Mr. Royston the intricacies of Puss in the Garden, she screwed up the courage to ask him what was wrong.

"Does this concern Amanda?" she asked, laying a gentle hand on his arm. "She's not in any danger, is she?"

Wyatt saw the fear in her hazel eyes and laid his hand over hers. "Not directly," he said, wishing he could tell her more, tell her everything. "The man the runners were watching has managed to slip the net, but it's doubtful he'll come here. More than likely he's left the country, but to be safe we'll post guards, and of course, there won't be any more trips into the village for awhile. I hope you don't mind?"

"Not at all," she assured him, sensing there was more to his silence than that. She toyed with the idea of telling him how the villagers were also keeping watch, hoping it would cheer him. In the end she rejected the idea, deciding it might be better to wait until later before telling him. He was such a private person; she doubted he would like the idea that everyone in the village was aware of all that was going on.

Much too soon it was time for Amanda to retire to her rooms. She protested vociferously, but when her uncle gave her a warning look she accepted the unspoken command with a martyred sigh. "Will you go with me, Uncle Wyatt?" she pleaded, apparently hoping to postpone the inevitable a few minutes more. "Please?"

Wyatt looked down into her dark blue eyes, his lips twitching at the tears gathering there. "Oh, very well, you shameless wheedler," he murmured, sweeping her up into his arms and depositing a quick kiss on her cheek. "I'll take you . . . this time.

But don't think I can be this easily manipulated again."

"Don't believe a word of what he says, Lady Amanda." Ambrose was laughing as he joined them. "Where the ladies are concerned, your uncle, like most poor men, is aught but putty."

"What's putty?" Amanda's brow wrinkled.

"Never mind, poppet." Wyatt shot Ambrose an annoyed scowl. "I'll be down in a few minutes, Royston. I trust you won't shock Miss Pringle with your forward ways while I am gone."

Ambrose gave Nia a sly wink. "Miss Pringle strikes me as more than capable of keeping me in my place should I be so bold as to forget it," he drawled. "But to avoid temptation, I believe I shall also retire. It was a long ride up from London, and it will be an even longer ride back." He turned to Nia and bowed with the grace of a skilled courtier.

"Miss Pringle, it was a delight seeing you again. May I hope to see more of you when this sorry fellow brings you and Lady Amanda back to the city?"

"You may hope whatever you please, Mr. Royston," Nia replied, enjoying his lighthearted teasing. "In the meanwhile, allow me to wish you a good night. Amanda, dearest, I shall peek in on you in a little bit. All right?"

Amanda gave a happy nod, and the three of them departed. Nia supposed she should go up to her own rooms, but she was loathe for the evening to end. The French windows were standing open, and she caught the sweet smell of roses wafting on the soft breeze. On an impulse she stepped out onto the balcony, leaning against the stone balustrade as she looked out over the gardens.

How beautiful it was, she thought, her eyes taking in the moonlit flowers and dark, shadowy walks. It was like something out of a dream, and for a moment she imagined herself there, with Wyatt at her side. He would stop to pick a rose, she decided, her lips curving at the romantic fancy. He'd raise it to his lips, pressing a soft kiss to the closed petals before offering it to her. His dark eyes would meet hers as her fingers closed around the stem. And then . . .

The sound of a footstep behind her shattered the tantalizing image, and she whirled to see the tall shape of a man standing in the shadows. It took her a few seconds to recognize Wyatt's broad shoulders, and when she did her breath escaped with a relieved sigh.

"Oh! Your Grace, you startled me," she said, resting her gloved hand against her galloping heart. "I didn't recognize you standing there."

Wyatt stepped out into the silvery moonlight, his eyes resting on Nia's face. "I'm sorry," he apologized in a deep voice. "I should have made my presence known sooner, but you looked so lost in thought I hated to disturb you." He was standing before her, so close he was almost touching her. Almost.

"What were you thinking of to have brought such a pensive look to your face?" he asked, raising a hand to brush back an errant curl from her cheek.

Nia flushed at the intimacy of his touch. "I . . . I was thinking how lovely the garden looks, and how peaceful," she stammered, gathering the strength to turn away from him. "Gardens are so wonderful, you know," she continued in a voice that strained to be light. "Even when everything else fails, you can count on them. No matter what, they keep blooming, filling the world with their fragile beauty."

"Those sound rather profound thoughts," Wyatt said, moving to stand at her side. He'd debated whether or not he should come back downstairs, knowing he shouldn't be alone with Nia. In the end he was unable to resist, although he was hoping to keep his distance. Then he had seen her in the moonlight, and no power on earth could have kept him away.

Nia could feel the warmth and strength emanating from him, and it took all of her control to keep from responding to it. She forced herself to concentrate on something else instead, and drew up an old, forgotten memory.

"There was a garden in Portugal," she began, closing her eyes as she lost herself in the past. "That is, it *had* been a garden. We turned it into a field hospital after a rather bloody skirmish with the French. I can remember walking past the rows of bobbing white jasmine as I helped my father tend the wounded. It sounds odd, but even over the stench of the blood, I swear I could smell the sweetness of that jasmine . . ." Her voice trailed off and she opened her eyes, appalled at what she had said.

"I'm sorry," she apologized, her emotions suddenly raw and vulnerable. "I don't know what made me say that. I hadn't meant to grow melancholy, I assure you." She turned to leave, terrified that in a moment she would reveal something even more personal.

"I really ought to be going," she said, knowing she was babbling, but unable to stop. "It is grown quite late and . . ."

"No," Wyatt caught her by the arms, drawing her slowly against him. "Don't go. And don't apologize either." He bent his head, laying his cheek against her forehead as he held her in a comforting embrace.

"I'm sorry you had to witness such things, Nia," he whispered, forgetting his own pain at the thought of what she must have seen and how it must have hurt her. He'd never been allowed to serve in the army, but he knew no woman should have been exposed to such horror. If it was possible, he would have taken that pain onto himself. But he could only hold her, murmuring comforting words as he tangled his hands in her hair.

Nia's eyes closed as she surrendered to the need to be held. Her arms crept up around his neck and she pressed herself closer, silently accepting the succor he offered.

"It's all right," he soothed. "It's over now. You're safe. I hate it that you should have known such ugliness, but I'm glad, so very glad that you had the jasmine to comfort you."

Nia's arms tightened. That he understood so perfectly touched her beyond expression, and she finally admitted the truth, a truth as bitter as it was sweet. She was in love with Wyatt.

He continued holding her, his hands and voice gentle as he gave her what sustenance he could. She felt so good in his arms, he thought, the blood pounding in his veins as the desire to give comfort gave way to older, more powerful desires. He struggled against the tide of passion rising in him, telling himself sternly that this was neither the time nor the place for such errant foolishness. He might have succeeded in convincing himself had she not chosen that particular moment to raise her head, her hazel eyes sweetly enticing as she looked up at him.

Nia met Wyatt's heated gaze, too dazed by her own feelings to think coherently. She could see the desire burning in his eyes, and it sparked an answering flame deep inside her. She knew she should excuse herself and go back into the house, but somehow she couldn't form the words. All her life she'd fought to do what was right and honorable, but now she didn't care. She loved Wyatt, and even though it meant risking more than she could afford to lose, she would stay where she was.

Wyatt saw the turbulent emotions cross her expressive face; saw the doubts, the determination, but above all the desire. The wonder of it overwhelmed him. Closing his mind to the pain of the past and the dangers of the present, he slowly raised his hands to cradle her face between his palms.

"Do you know, my sweet, that you are rather like that jasmine yourself?" he murmured, burying his fingers in the thick hair coiled at the base of her neck.

"I am?" Nia closed her eyes, biting her lips to hold back a sigh of pleasure at his touch.

"Mmm." Wyatt noted her reaction with satisfaction. "You are soft and delicate, but like the jasmine you are sturdy enough to withstand anything, even the horrors of war." He plucked the spectacles from her face and folded them closed before laying them on the ledge beside her.

Her eyes flew open at the intimacy of his actions. "What—what are you . . ."

"Shh . . ." His hands slipped back up into her hair, removing the pins until the soft waves tumbled into his hands.

"There's another way you are like jasmine," he continued, bending to press a moist kiss on her neck. "You fill a man's head with your sweetness." His lips nibbled on the curve of her chin. "You intoxicate him with your fragrance until he trembles with desire."

"Wyatt . . ." Nia sighed, turning her head to seek his searching lips. "This is madness . . ."

Her soft words made him laugh, his voice rife with sensual promise as he touched the tip of his tongue to the corners of her mouth. "The moon is full, my sweet," he told her in a husky voice, his body throbbing with pleasure as he drew her into an intimate embrace. "What better time for madness?" And he took her lips in a kiss that sent both of them shooting straight into heaven.

Chapter 12

‿⁂⁀

The feel of Nia's lips beneath his own filled Wyatt with exquisite desire. He couldn't remember the last time he'd wanted a woman so desperately, and he gave himself up to the sweet pleasure of holding her. "Nia," he whispered hoarsely, his arms shaking as he drew her against his throbbing body, "say this is what you want, what you need . . ."

Nia trembled at the naked yearning in his voice. She knew he was as caught up in the embrace as she, and it touched her that he would put her feelings above his own. All she had to say was no, and he would let her go. She met his gaze shamelessly.

"This is what I want," she said, a lifetime of reticence cast aside as she stood on tiptoe to brush her mouth over his. "You are what I want."

Her words filled Wyatt with wild hunger and he bent his head, returning her shy kiss with a blazing ardor that bordered on desperation. He'd never felt like this with any woman, and he knew he never would again. He loved Nia, and the admission tore his soul from him. Closing his mind to the pain, he concentrated on the sweetness of her mouth, his tongue flicking teasingly against her lips until they parted.

"You are so sweet, so sweet." He groaned, nipping at her chin as he pressed her to his burgeoning hardness. "You make me burn . . ."

His hoarse voice thrilled Nia almost as much as the intoxicating feel of his hands brushing over her breasts with breathtaking mastery. Her heart was beating so fast it felt as if it would burst, and her legs

186

trembled so that if he hadn't been holding her, she was certain she would have fallen. She tilted her head back, her arms tight around his neck as she wantonly offered herself to him.

Wyatt took what she gave, emotion and desire making him blind to everything but the need to love her. He slipped the bodice of her gown lower, baring her soft breasts to the pale silver moonlight. Unable to resist their temptation, he took one of the rosy nipples in his mouth.

"Wyatt!"

The sound of his name being cried out in pleasure had the odd effect of bringing him out of the sensual mists swirling in his head. He realized that if he did not stop now, he and Nia would be making love in full view of anyone who perchanced to look out the window. Cursing himself, his belated sense of duty, and the situation, he stepped back from the brink of passion, gently covering Nia's breasts with her gown.

"I was wrong, my love," he whispered in a husky voice, resting his forehead against hers as he fought to regain control of his senses. "It's not jasmine you resemble, but brandy. Rich, potent brandy that warms a man's blood and makes him forget everything but the moment."

The admission thrilled Nia, even as his sudden withdrawal left her aching and confused. Her emotions overcame her natural modesty, and she raised her hands to smooth back the hair that had tumbled across his forehead. "Then why are you stopping?" she asked, searching his flushed face with anxious eyes.

Wyatt's lips twisted in a bitter smile. "Mayhap because I've never had a head for strong spirits," he quipped. "And mayhap because in spite of all that's happened I still count myself a gentleman. I care for you, Nia, far too much to take everything when I can offer you nothing in return."

"But Wyatt—"

"No." He silenced her with a firm kiss. "Now, are you taking Amanda for a ride tomorrow morning?"

The unexpected question and the calm tone in which it was asked left Nia gaping at him in mortification. "I—I'd planned on it," she replied, flushing to hear herself stammering like a lovesick school girl. That he could be so cool and disinterested after their heated embrace infuriated her, and for a moment she was tempted to slap his arrogant face. Instead she pushed herself out of his arms, her chin coming up as he fixed him with her haughtiest look.

"Have you any objections, my lord?" she challenged, determined to keep the truth from him at all costs.

The sharpness in her voice made Wyatt grin. "Now you are an English rose, bristling with thorns," he teased, picking up her spectacles from the ledge and sliding them on her nose.

She glowered up at him, her hands shaking as she tried to restore some semblance of order to her hair. "Well?" she demanded, abandoning her hair and concentrating her efforts on her clothing. "Do you mind if I take Amanda out, or don't you? But I warn you, if you do have any objections, *you* may be the one to tell her so. She has been looking forward to seeing the lambs again."

"I've no objections, so long as you take a groom with you," he told her with that same maddening smile on his face. "In fact, I'll be out showing Ambrose some of the improvements I've made since he was last here. Perhaps we'll encounter each other."

"Perhaps," she replied, praying none of her emotions were discernible to his sharp eyes.

He gave a soft laugh at her stiff reply, then, unable to resist, bent his head for a final kiss. "Good night, sweet jasmine," he whispered, his tone as provocative as his kiss. "Sleep well, and mind you guard your sweet petals."

"Are you awake, Miss Pringle, are you awake?"

The bright voice shattered Nia's fitful sleep, and she opened a bleary eye to find Amanda standing next to the bed, wearing a new riding habit and an eager expression. When she saw Nia watching her, she broke into a wide grin.

"Annie said I wasn't to wake you," she said, hiking up her sapphire velvet skirts and scrambling onto the bed beside Nia. "But I knew you wouldn't want to sleep forever."

"Wouldn't I?" Nia mumbled, hiding a yawn behind her hand. "What time is it?"

"It's very late," Amanda replied solemnly, shyly stroking Nia's golden-brown hair laying across the pillow. "Uncle Wyatt and Mr. Royston have already ridden out. They wouldn't take me." She added this last with a sigh that indicated she considered herself to have been sadly mistreated.

"Very late" was not so precise a time as Nia would like, but she supposed it would have to suffice. Besides, she decided ruefully, given the fact that it had to be well after two in the morning before she finally managed to drift off, she was probably better off not knowing the exact hour. Patting back another yawn, she gave Amanda's nose an affectionate tweak.

"Poor poppet," she teased. "I suppose I shall have to take you myself. Give me an hour to breakfast and dress, and I'll meet you at the stable. How is that?"

That was fine with Amanda, and after pausing to deposit a kiss on Nia's cheek, she dashed off to show her new habit to the parlor maids. Nia stared after her, her smile of affection fading as memories of last night washed over her.

What was she going to do? she wondered bleakly, her mind drifting toward thoughts of Wyatt. They'd come very close to making love, and she was honest enough to admit that if she remained at Perryvale, chances were they *would* make love. The thought should have shamed her, but it did not. She loved Wyatt, and nothing would have given her greater pleasure than to love him completely, the way a woman loves a man. His touch filled her with forbidden longings she now blushed to recall, and the thought of yielding to those longings was sweetly tempting.

Yet despite those temptations and the love she bore him, she knew she could never forfeit her honor and become his mistress. And that's all she would ever be, she reminded herself sternly. She was a penniless governess, and even if by some miracle Wyatt did return her love, he would never marry her. His position required that he should wed a lady of equal rank and fortune, and one of the things she most admired about him as his unwavering devotion to duty. The last thing she wanted was to force him to choose between responsibility and desire.

These unhappy thoughts were much on her mind as she and Amanda rode out into the soft sunlight that June morning. The groom Wyatt had selected rode at their side, and Nia was grateful for his taciturn presence, not only for the protection he offered, but because with him there to answer Amanda's many questions her own silence was less remarkable. She was free to brood over her situation, and the more she considered the matter the more she realized there was but one answer. She would have to leave Perryvale.

"Oh look, Miss Pringle, there's Uncle Wyatt!"

Amanda's excited exclamation brought Nia out of her brown study, and she glanced up just as Wyatt and Mr. Royston appeared over the edge of a low hill. They must have spotted them at the same time because Wyatt suddenly changed direction, whirling the bay Arabian he was riding around and sending him thundering down the hill. Suddenly a shot rang out and Wyatt went flying from his horse, tumbling and rolling down the hill until he came to rest in an ominously still heap.

At first shock and horror held Nia immobile, and then she was galloping toward him, terror blanking out every thought. By the time she managed to kick her stirrups free and dismount, Mr. Royston was already kneeling over Wyatt, and she shoved him roughly aside without the slightest compunction.

The first thing she noticed was that Wyatt was breathing. After sending a fervent prayer heavenward, she concentrated on searching for serious injury. The skills she had learned at her father's side stood her in good stead as she swiftly completed her examination. It didn't take her long to find the blood seeping through the shoulder of his torn jacket.

"Is he all right?" Ambrose's voice was grim as he stared down at Wyatt's white face.

"I don't know." Nia forced the words past her frozen lips as she continued to examine Wyatt. "His heartbeat is strong, but he'll need a doctor and a stretcher." She glanced up as Amanda and the groom galloped up to join them.

"Amanda, stop that crying at once!" she instructed in clipped tones, taking charge as she had seen her father do in the past. "You"—her fierce gaze flew to the groom—"I want you to take Lady Amanda and return to the house. Have them send someone into town for the doctor, and then I want you to return with some blankets and a stretcher." She didn't wait to see if her commands were being followed before she turned her attention back to Wyatt.

"What of me, Miss Pringle?" Ambrose asked as the others raced off in opposite directions. "Have you any orders?"

Nia shot him a sharp glance, the hard edge of her fury softening at the worry in his blue eyes. "I want you to help me hold him still," she said. "I don't believe he has broken any bones, but I don't want him thrashing about and perhaps doing himself a greater injury."

Ambrose obligingly bent over his friend, resting his hands gently but firmly on Wyatt's shoulders. He'd no sooner done this than Wyatt's lashes flickered, and a moment later his eyes fluttered open.

"What the bloody hell . . ." he began in a slurred voice.

"Now, now Wyatt, you must watch your tongue," Ambrose remonstrated, increasing the pressure of his hands as Wyatt struggled to rise. "There is a lady present."

"Who . . . ?" His gaze flicked to Nia and he blinked groggily. "Nia?"

"I am here." She was aware of the tears wending down her cheeks, but she didn't bother wiping them away. "How are you feeling? What about your vision? Is it blurred?"

Despite his aching head and the burning pain in his shoulder, Wyatt managed a weak grin. "I might have known you would start firing questions at me," he said, laying his head on the grass and closing his eyes. When he was certain he could open them without disgracing himself, he met Ambrose's anxious gaze.

"I take it I was shot?" he asked without preamble.

"The bullet came from the woods," Ambrose answered in the same controlled manner. "A pistol, I'm thinking."

"It was a rifle, probably a Brown Bess," Nia corrected, deciding if they could be so calm, then so could she. At their suspicious scowls she managed a cool smile. "You forget I spent most of my life following the drum. It was a rifle shot, and judging from the angle of the wound, I would say you're dashed lucky. If you hadn't turned when you did, the bullet would have struck you square in the center of your back instead of grazing your shoulder."

There was an uneasy silence as the two men exchanged grim looks. "I think we had best send word to London," Ambrose said with a heavy sigh. "It appears we may have located Elliott."

"Who is Elliott?" Nia demanded, sitting back on her heels and eyeing both men with marked impatience. She'd already determined the injury to Wyatt's shoulder wasn't overly serious, but she was still anxious to get him home so that she could tend the wound under more agreeable conditions.

"My solicitor," Wyatt answered. "He is the one I believe is behind our difficulties."

"Your *solicitor?*" Nia was temporarily diverted by the news. "Ha, I knew he was a villain the moment I clapped eyes on him!" she exclaimed, her own eyes gleaming with satisfaction. "A more pompous and calculating creature I've yet to meet, and I hope he swings from Tyburn Tree for this!" Then her expression of triumph faded, replaced by a look of confusion.

"But why would your solicitor with you harm?" she asked, her brows meeting as she puzzled over the intelligence.

"That is what we are attempting to discover." Wyatt spoke through gritted teeth as he struggled to a sitting position. "So far all we've learned is that he once served as my mother's secretary, and that he—" He broke off at the expression on Nia's face. "What is it?"

Nia pushed her glasses back up her nose, the fear she'd felt at seeing Wyatt falling from his horse returning tenfold. "Miss ... Miss Haverall told me there was a stranger in the village," she said slowly, forcing herself to speak carefully. "She says he was recognized as having once been employed in that capacity."

The news that Elliott was virtually on his doorstep drove all thoughts of pain from Wyatt's mind. "For God's sake, Nia, why the devil didn't you say something?"

She was so nonplussed she began to apologize. "I meant to, my lord, but it slipped my mind. And then—" She stopped as the inequity of the situation struck her.

"Why didn't *I* tell you? Why didn't *you* tell me?" she demanded, glaring at Wyatt as, with Mr. Royston's help, he staggered to his feet. "I must have asked you the villain's name a dozen times, and you fobbed me off with some nonsense about not having enough 'proof.' " She gave his bloodstained jacket a pointed glare. "Well, Your Grace, it would seem to me that you now have more than sufficient proof."

Wyatt sucked in his breath as the world swayed dangerously about him. He fought off the momentary weakness, his jaw rigid as he confronted her. "Blast it, Nia, you must know I'd have told you if I could!" he said, his voice clipped with fury.

"And pray, sir, how am I to know that?" she demanded querulously, furious to feel the sting of fresh tears in her eyes. "You've made it obvious on more than one occasion that you do not trust me!"

Her angry reply brought Wyatt's head snapping back, an action he quickly regretted. "Of course I *trust* you, curse it!" he snapped, ignoring the pain and nausea tearing at him. "I would have thought I had made that clear by now! Furthermore—"

"I beg your pardon for interrupting what sounds to be a most edifying conversation"—Ambrose's amused drawl cut into Wyatt's heated response—"but may I remind you that while we're standing here airing our vocabulary, Elliott is in all probability making good his escape?"

Wyatt glared at him, knowing he was right. "We will discuss this later," he told Nia in a strained voice. "In the meanwhile, it would probably be best if we returned to the house. Help seems to be rather late in coming, and I want to get started after Elliott. And of course I'll want my horse examined," he added, turning to run an anxious hand over Mahdi's flank.

"Oh yes, on no account must the horse be allowed to go untreated," Nia grumbled, mentally tossing her hands up in defeat. "What a pity his master isn't nearly so particular with his own hide."

Wyatt ignored her, his expression determined as he swung himself up into the saddle. The wound in his arm *was* no more than a graze, but that didn't stop the damned thing from aching with increasing ferocity. He'd also struck his head when he fell, and it was throbbing in tune with his arm.

Without another word they took off toward the house, each lost in his own turbulent thoughts. They were almost halfway back when Ambrose gave a sudden cry. "Look there!"

They stared in the direction he indicated with his whip, all spying the still figure lying on the ground at the same time. Wyatt gave a furious curse and raced his mount forward, reaching the stricken groom a few steps ahead of Nia.

"Is he alive?" she asked as Wyatt gently turned the younger man over.

"Yes, thank God," he answered, moving aside so that she could examine him more thoroughly. "I don't see any blood, so I don't believe he's been shot. But—" Before he could speculate further the groom groaned and opened his eyes.

"Your Grace?" The young man's voice was slurred.

"Yes, Harry," Wyatt said. "Where is Lady Amanda?"

Harry's eyes filled with tears. "He rode out of the woods, Your Grace. He—he said he would shoot her ladyship if I didn't let him take her. I tried to stop him, but I was afraid he'd hurt the wee one. I'm sorry."

"You did the right thing, Harry," Nia assured him softly, trying her best to remain calm. Inside she was exploding with rage and fury, but she knew now was not the time for emotion. "Did you see which way they rode off? Did he take her back into the woods?"

"I didn't see them, Miss Pringle," Harry replied, wiping his cheek with his fist. "The man told me to dismount, and then he hit me with something."

"His pistol, no doubt," Wyatt said. "Will you be all right by yourself, lad?"

"Y . . . yes, Your Grace," Harry stammered, regarding Wyatt with apprehension. "Will you be going after the blackguard?"

"Yes, but first we must ride to the house for reinforcements." Wyatt rose to his feet, dusting his hands on his breeches. "I'll send someone back for you, I promise. And Harry?"

"Sir?" The groom drew himself up as much as he could.

"Miss Pringle is right, lad, you did the only thing you could, given the circumstances. If you'd resisted, he might well have carried out his threat. This way, there is every hope we shall soon have Amanda back."

The butler and the housekeeper were enjoying a cozy cup of tea when Wyatt, Nia, and Ambrose burst into the kitchen. Their precipitous appearance sent the startled couple stumbling to their feet in alarm.

"Saints save us, Your Grace!" the housekeeper exclaimed, clasping her hand to her ample bosom as she took in Wyatt's bloodstained appearance. "What has befallen you?"

"Nothing of import." Wyatt impatiently waved his injury aside before turning to the gawking butler. "I want you to call in all of the servants and all of the tenants as well," he ordered. "Lady Amanda has been kidnapped, and I don't want a stone of this estate left unturned until she is found."

"My lord!"

Wyatt didn't wait to listen to the rest of the elderly man's shocked protestations. He hurried Nia out into the hall and took both her hands in his as he gazed down into her drawn features.

"Ambrose and I shall ride directly into the village," he said, wishing with all her heart that he could take her into his arms. Unfortunately, there was no time for such luxuries, and he prayed to God that it wasn't already too late to save Amanda. He pushed the panic back and forced himself to think rationally.

"Tell me everything you remember from Miss Haverall's conversation," he ordered. "There's a small chance Elliott hinted at where he might have taken her."

Nia repeated everything she remembered. When she finished, Wyatt's expression was grimmer than ever.

"Travlock runs the staging inn on the outskirts of the village. That is where we shall start." He turned to leave, but Nia caught his hand in hers.

"Will you not let me tend your arm?" she asked, her lips trembling as she fought back tears. "It's only a graze, but you ought to have it wrapped."

The concern in her green and gold eyes was almost Wyatt's undoing. "Not now, dearest," he said, the endearment coming unbidden to his lips. "In the meanwhile I don't want you taking any foolish risks. Have I your word you won't go tearing after Elliott the moment my back is turned?"

A strangled chuckle burst from Nia. "I might have known you'd be unable to resist issuing one final command," she said, blinking back tears. She knew he was out of his mind with fear for Amanda, and she wanted to do something to ease his terrible burden.

Her teasing jab seemed to have missed its mark entirely as his expression grew even more somber. "I have to know you're safe, Nia," he said, his hands sliding up her neck to cup her face. "Give me that much at least, or I swear I'll go mad."

A tear fell down her cheek at his impassioned plea. "I promise I shan't do anything dangerous," she promised, all but choking on the words of love she longed to utter. "Have I your word you will be equally prudent?"

In answer his mouth closed over hers in a fiery kiss, his lips telling her more than words ever could. When he raised his head, his ebony eyes were burning with the force of his emotions. "Wait for me," he ordered in a thick voice, and stepped back into the vestibule where Ambrose was waiting for him.

Chapter 13

ᘓᕲᖇᕲᐧ

It was late afternoon before Wyatt and Ambrose returned from the village, and the news they brought was far from good. They'd arrived at Elliott's rooms to find he'd already fled, leaving no indication as to where he might have gone. A message was sent out to the surrounding villages, but Wyatt doubted it would do any good. Elliott had the advantage of time and surprise in his favor, and he was familiar with the neighborhood. He could be anywhere, and the realization added to the icy fear growing inside Wyatt.

With nothing to do but wait for the searchers to return, Wyatt submitted to having his shoulder tended by Nia. While she was cleaning the wound, he and Ambrose discussed what to do next.

"I want the area already searched gone over again," Wyatt ordered, ignoring the stinging pain as Nia gently dabbed salve on the torn and bruised flesh of his upper arm. "I'm certain he's somewhere close by, and I won't rest until we find him."

"Why do you say that?" Ambrose asked curiously. "I should think he'd want to be as far from here as possible."

"He wants to see me suffer," Wyatt reminded him, his voice harsh. "He can hardly do that if he's miles away. No, he's here. We've just missed him, that's all."

They were still discussing various options when Jamesfield, Wyatt's bailiff, returned. "Still no sign of the scoundrel, Your Grace," the young man admitted, twisting his hat in his hands as he met Wyatt's gaze. "There's not an inch of soil on this estate I've not ridden over myself, and he's nowhere to be found."

"Then ride over it again," Wyatt snapped, "and while you're about it, have a horse saddled for me. I'm going with you."

"Do you think that's wise?" Ambrose suggested, sending Wyatt a worried look. "Elliott's already taken one shot at you. The next time he may not miss."

"At least then we'll know where he is," Wyatt retorted, thinking a bullet couldn't hurt any more than the pain already tearing at his heart. He turned back to Jamesfield. "Where did you first search?"

"The north field, Your Grace. Near the old hermit's cottage."

"The cottage?" Wyatt's eyebrows met in a frown. "I thought I'd given orders it was to be pulled down."

"Quite so, sir, but you arrived rather ahead of schedule, and there wasn't time."

"Never mind," Wyatt replied with a heavy sigh, deciding it hardly mattered now. "Well, what did you find inside? Any sign of either Amanda or Elliott?"

Jamesfield shuffled his feet. "I'm not certain, Your Grace."

"You're not certain?" Wyatt repeated incredulously. "The cottage *was* searched?"

The tips of Jamesfield's ears turned red. "Not precisely. There was no sign of anyone living there, and as there was so much ground to be covered we—"

"Do you mean you didn't even go inside?" Nia demanded, indignation finally loosening her tongue. "Why the devil not?"

"Because it's haunted, miss," Jamesfield answered, turning to her with an apologetic shrug. "Or at least that's what folk hereabout believe. No one goes near the place, and as I said, I saw no reason to search an obviously deserted cottage when there was dozens of acres waiting to be gone over."

Wyatt's heart began pounding as he pushed himself to his feet. "Call in the others," he commanded, his mind racing. "I want the cottage surrounded at once."

"You think that's where he's holding Amanda?" Ambrose asked, his expression grim.

Wyatt nodded, not bothering to question the matter. He'd never been more certain of anything in his life, and he accepted the knowledge with a deadly calm.

"Make sure the men are armed," he continued, his voice devoid of emotion. "While the rest of you are taking up your positions, I'll do my best to distract him. With luck I'll convince him to exchange Amanda for me, but if not, you may have to rush the cabin." He turned to go, only to find Nia blocking his path.

"I'm going with you," she declared, her hands on her hips as if daring him to object. "I won't let you leave me behind."

Despite the serious nature of the situation, the pugnacious look on her face made Wyatt smile. Unable to resist the comfort of touching her, he reached out to straighten her spectacles. "Somehow I never doubted that for a moment, my sweet," he drawled, his fingers lingering to caress her cheek. "Now, let us go. It will be dark soon, and I don't want to give Elliott any more of an advantage than he already has."

The cottage stood forlorn and alone in the small clearing, its tumbledown chimney and broken door adding to its melancholy air. Studying it, Nia could understand why the bailiff and the others hadn't bothered to search it, although she was of no mind to forgive them. Such dereliction of duty appalled her, and the moment Amanda was safe Nia fully intended ringing a peal over the servants' heads. She refused to contemplate even for a moment what she would do if Amanda wasn't safe.

"Now remember," Wyatt was saying, studying the cabin through narrowed eyes, "let me go up alone. He's liable to shoot her if he sees more than one of us."

"Are you sure that's wise?" Ambrose asked. "What's to keep him from shooting you and then Amanda?"

"Nothing," Wyatt admitted, having already considered this very real possibility. "I'm praying his need to see me suffer will make him incautious. If it does, we'll have him."

"And if it doesn't?"

Wyatt didn't bother to answer Nia's whispered question. Instead he inspected his pistol one final time before slipping it into the waistband of his breeches. "Give me five minutes and then begin moving in." He issued the clipped command to Ambrose. "The windows are boarded up, so I don't think there's a chance he'll see you, but to be safe I want you to keep low. Use the grass for cover."

"All right," Ambrose said, checking his own weapon. "Any other instructions?"

Wyatt's eyes rested on Nia. "Keep an eye on her," he said softly. "If anything happens to me, I want you to promise you'll take care of her."

Ambrose gave a solemn nod. "I will, Wyatt," he said quietly. "I give you my most sacred word."

"Good." Wyatt couldn't tear his gaze from Nia. She was wearing the same riding habit she'd worn that morning, and although it was stained and thoroughly disheveled, she'd never looked more beautiful. Her chestnut hair lay in an untidy knot at the back of her head, and he remembered the sweet, soft weight of it in his hands. Studying her, he finally accepted the truth of his own emotions. He loved her.

As if sensing his thoughts, she suddenly turned her head, and their eyes met and held in a moment of shared wonder.

The expression on Wyatt's face sent elation shooting through Nia. Her logical mind told her she was imagining things, but she didn't care. She loved Wyatt, and that love gave her the strength to set aside her pride. If she'd learned anything in her years with her father, it was that there were no guarantees, and that life could sometimes be appallingly short. Fearing she might never get a second chance, she gathered her courage and went to stand directly before the man she loved.

"Please be careful," she pleaded, her eyes moving over his face as she committed his features to memory. "I couldn't bear it if something were to happen to you."

Her low words filled Wyatt with happiness and searing regret. He gently cupped her chin in his gloved hand, his eyes burning with the words he could not yet say. " 'Had we but world enough, and time,' " he quoted with a rueful smile as his thumb brushed over the full curve of her lower lip. "Ah, Nia, the things I would tell you."

His unspoken promise made Nia tremble with hope. Ignoring the presence of the others, she rose on tiptoe and slipped her arms around his neck. When his arms closed around her waist in response, she pressed a shy kiss to his mouth.

"I love you," she said softly, her eyes meeting his without shame or remorse.

"Nia . . ."

"No." She lay a finger on his lips. "As you said . . . world enough and time. Amanda is what matters now. Bring her back safely, and then we will talk."

He longed to disagree, to speak the love burning in his heart, but he knew she was right. He gave her one final searing kiss and then turned away, closing his mind to everything but Amanda. He'd taken only a few steps when Ambrose moved to stand in front of him, blocking his path.

"Here," he said, handing Wyatt a second pistol. "He will expect you to come armed. If he relieves you of this, he may not think to search you for another."

Wyatt accepted the weapon with alacrity. "You're right," he said. "You dandies do have your uses. Remind me to ask you later how you came to be so devious." And he began making his way toward the cottage.

The broken door lay drunkenly on its rusty hinges, and as he crept closer, Wyatt could glimpse the gloomy interior just inside the doorway. He lay the flat of his hand on the rough wood and gave the door a shove as he stepped warily inside, Ambrose's pistol held in his hand.

At first glance there was no sign of recent habitation, and he was beginning to wonder if he'd made a mistake when a soft noise came from behind him. He whirled around to find Elliott sitting in the shadows, levelling a pistol at his enemy's chest.

"Ah, Your Grace, I wondered if you were going to honor us with your presence," he drawled, the lenses of his spectacles winking as a ray of watery sunlight pierced the dusty darkness. "Do come in."

Wyatt did as ordered, blinking as he fought to become accustomed to the shifting patterns of light and darkness. "So you've finally decided to show yourself," he said, his voice disdainful as he drew closer. "What have you done with my niece? I demand you release her at once."

"Demand?" Elliott repeated mockingly. "My dear duke, you are hardly in a position to demand anything of anyone, especially me. But if it will relieve your mind, your precious niece is safe . . . for the moment."

Shapes and details were finally becoming clear, and Wyatt could see a few pieces of shattered furniture laying on the dirt-packed floor. There was a crude pallet of sorts just behind Elliott, and on the pallet was . . .

"Amanda!" Wyatt leapt forward.

"Ah, ah, Your Grace." Elliott cocked the weapon

with his thumb. "No sudden moves, now. I should hate to kill you before I am ready."

"You bastard!" Wyatt spat the word with murderous fury, his body trembling with the need for violence. "You black-hearted bastard, I'll see you swing for this!"

"Will you?" the expression on Elliott's face was one of gloating triumph. "That is a distinct possibility, I suppose."

"What have you done to her?" Sweat beaded Wyatt's forehead as his anguished eyes rested on the tiny figure lying so ominously still. "If you've hurt her, I'll—"

"You'll what? You're no more in a position to utter threats than you are to make demands. There is nothing wrong with the child. She took a healthy dose of laudanum, that's all. Or should I say an unhealthy dose?" His thin lips curled in an evil smile. "I'm really not certain how much I gave the little imp."

"What do you want?" Wyatt roared, fearing he wouldn't be able to hold himself in check much longer. He knew Ambrose and the others would be arriving soon, and that all he had to do was to keep Elliott distracted long enough for them to rescue Amanda. It had sounded so simple at the time, but now he wondered if he would be able to do it. He was literally aching with the need to get his hands around Elliott's throat, and it took everything in him to remain where he was, passively listening to the other man's taunts.

"What do I want?" Elliott repeated thoughtfully, the pistol still trained on Wyatt's heart. "An interesting question. I want what I have always wanted, Your Grace. Revenge."

"Revenge?" Wyatt was genuinely puzzled. "Why the devil should you desire revenge against me? What have I ever done to you?"

"You?" Elliott gave a negligent shrug. "Nothing. But your family is another matter."

"I know you were once my mother's secretary, and

were very probably her lover," Wyatt said, and was pleased to note the information surprised the other man. "But I fail to see what that has to do with any of this."

"Don't you?" Elliott's expression was smug. "Ah, but I was more than your mother's lover. Much, much more."

Wyatt managed to hide his shock and revulsion at this confirmation of his worst suspicions. "Half the world was my mother's lover," he said, shrugging his shoulders to indicate his indifference. "She was never known for either her discretion or her taste."

"It wasn't her fault!" Elliott shouted, displaying emotion for the first time. "She was a loving, giving woman, but that cold fish she was married to was incapable of giving her what she needed! He was off on one of his precious diplomatic missions when I was first hired, and in all the months I was there he never even bothered to return. It was obvious he didn't give a feather for her!"

Wyatt caught a shadowy movement behind them, and knew the others were taking their positions. Just a little longer, he thought, bracing himself for action. Just a little longer.

"We were like innocents in paradise," Elliott was saying, his eyes closing as he lost himself in memory. "She was my first woman, and we loved each other without guile or guilt." His eyes opened, and in their dark depths Wyatt could see a wild madness burning. "Then your uncle arrived at the house unexpectedly."

"I take it he objected to his brother's wife dallying with the help?" Wyatt said, risking a glance toward the door.

"He beat me with his horsewhip!" Elliott shouted, leaping to his feet and sending his chair tumbling to the floor. "She tried to stop him, and then begged me to leave before he killed me. I implored her to come with me, but she refused, saying he was too powerful ... too dangerous. I vowed I would protect her, but she was too frightened to try."

Wyatt, who had vivid memories of his grasping, selfish mother, gave a bitter smile. "More like she didn't want to give up her silks and diamonds," he sneered, hoping to make the man see reason. "Face it, Elliott. She used you, just as she used every man unfortunate enough to cross her path."

"No!" Elliott pointed the gun at Wyatt again. "She loved me! We could have been happy together. Instead I was left alone, with no family, no love. Your uncle took all that from me, but I got even ... I got even."

"You kept the breach open between Christopher and me," Wyatt accused with fury. "He died because of your machinations, but even that didn't satisfy you."

There was triumph in Elliott's eyes. "Why should you have a family when I did not?"

"You—" Wyatt started forward impulsively.

"Hold there!" Ambrose leapt through the doorway, his pistol in his hand. "Throw down your weapon or I'll fire!"

A look of absolute rage crossed Elliott's face. "No!" he screamed. "I won't let you win! You may kill me, but I'll have my revenge first!" And he whirled, pointing his gun at the pallet where Amanda lay.

There was no time to think. Wyatt pulled the trigger, and the sound of the shot roared in the tiny cottage. Elliott staggered and then fell to the floor, the pistol slipping from his fingers.

Wyatt stepped over him without so much as a glance, his attention focused on Amanda. He gathered her up in his arms, his hands shaking as he brushed a piece of dirty straw from her tangled hair. "Amanda," he crooned, his voice hoarse with emotion. "My poppet. Are you hurt?"

Then Nia was there, kneeling at his side. "Let me see," she said gently, laying a hand on the little girl's throat. The pulse was slow but steady, and she bowed her head in relief. "She's alive," she whispered, tears in her eyes as she met Wyatt's gaze. "She's alive."

He reached out, his arm snagging Nia's as he dragged her against him. He closed his eyes and breathed a silent prayer of thanks that the two people he loved most were safe in his arms. He would have been content to remain there indefinitely, but the sound of someone clearing his throat brought him reluctantly to his senses. He glanced up to find Ambrose standing beside them.

"I hate to intrude," he said apologetically, "but what do you want us to do with our friend?"

"Is he alive?" Wyatt gently transferred Amanda to Nia's arms.

"Barely." Like Wyatt, Ambrose was indifferent to the other man's fate. "However, he does seem to want to talk to you."

Wyatt was strongly tempted to say to hell with Elliott, but he wouldn't leave even a dog to die alone. Sighing wearily, he pushed himself to his feet and walked over to where Elliott lay in a bright pool of blood.

"What is it you wish?" he asked, making no effort to hide his revulsion as he stared down at the man. "If it's forgiveness you're after, I am afraid I cannot grant it. Because of your machinations my brother went to his death thinking I wanted nothing to do with him."

A sickly smile crossed Elliott's pale lips. "Forgiveness?" He laughed, foamy blood appearing on his lips. " 'Tis not me who will be needing forgiveness, my lord. It is you."

"Because I shot you in the back?" Wyatt demanded, knowing his actions could well be deemed cowardly. "What other choice did I have? You would have killed an innocent child."

A film was covering Elliott's eyes, but it didn't mask his obvious hate. "Oh, 'tis much worse than that, Your Grace," he said, his voice so faint Wyatt could scarcely hear him. "My crimes may be great, but not so great as yours. You have committed the worst sin there is." His eyes drifted shut as the life slipped from him. "You have just killed your own father."

And then he was dead.

"Miss Pringle, will my uncle come today?" Amanda asked, her favorite doll clutched in her arms as she regarded Nia with solemn eyes.

Nia glanced up from the book she'd been pretending to read. "I don't know, dearest," she admitted, struggling to keep her tears from falling. "As I said, he is very busy with important matters, but I'm sure he'll come as soon as he is able. You must be patient."

Amanda's bottom lip quivered. She had been patient, but she wanted to see her uncle. It had been two days since the bad man had pulled her from her horse and taken her to the dirty cottage. He'd made her drink some perfectly awful tasting tea, and the next thing she knew she was in her own bed, her uncle and Miss Pringle sitting beside her.

Since then she hadn't seen her uncle for more than a few minutes, and when he did come he was so distant that she wondered if he was angry with her. Maybe he was mad because the man had taken her, she thought, her heart sinking to the toes of her slippers.

Nia saw the unhappy look on Amanda's face and drew her onto her lap. "It's all right," she soothed, running a hand through the child's soft hair. "I know you're worried about your uncle, but it will be all right, I promise."

Tears overflowed Amanda's eyes as she buried her face against Nia's neck. "I'm s-sorry, Miss Pringle," she cried, her shoulders shaking with grief. "I didn't mean to let the man take me away. I tried, I really tried, but he was so b-big . . ."

"Amanda!" Nia was horrified by her apology.

"Darling, no one blames you for what happened! You must never think that!"

"Then why won't Uncle come?" Amanda refused to be placated. "He stays in his room all day, and he comes to see me only because he has to. He doesn't love me anymore!" And she sobbed as if her heart would break.

Nia held her tighter, wishing there was some way she could relieve her anxiety. Since the moment he'd heard Elliott's dying declaration, Wyatt had retreated behind an icy wall, and there was nothing she or Amanda could do to breach it. Nia had heard from the servants that he'd moved out of the master suite into one of the guest rooms, and she wondered what his next step would be. Lord knew he hadn't been forthcoming with *her*, she thought, her smile bitter. Like Amanda, she'd scarcely exchanged more than a dozen words with Wyatt in the past few days.

Amanda continued crying, her fingers clutching the front of Nia's gown. "I don't want Uncle Wyatt to go away." She sniffed, rubbing at her eyes with her fists. "You won't let him go away, will you?"

"Oh, Amanda." Nia sighed, her heart breaking at the plea. As much as she longed to reassure the little girl, she didn't want to make promises she couldn't keep. "I wish I could help, but—" Her voice broke off abruptly.

Blast Wyatt! she thought, her eyes kindling as her grief flamed into anger. She knew he was going through hell at the moment, but what about Amanda? She was just a little girl, and she needed the reassurance only her uncle could give her. It was time he stopped dilly-dallying and resumed his duties, she decided, her jaw clenching with determination as she gently set Amanda to one side.

"Where are you going?" Amanda asked, wiping her nose with the sleeve of her dress.

"To get your uncle," Nia said, straightening her glasses and stuffing her hair back under her cap.

She'd started wearing caps again, and she felt invulnerable in her prim blue gown and starched apron. She pulled her shoulders back, and with her chin thrust out at a militant angle, she stalked off to fulfill her promise to Amanda.

"So you see, Your Grace"—the newly hired solicitor's voice was firm but apologetic—"there is no way you can renounce the title in your niece's favor. The laws of primogeniture would never allow it."

Wyatt rubbed a hand across his face, wishing he could say to hell with everything and simply walk away. In the past two days he'd gone through so many emotions he felt drained and empty. The only thing he cared about was setting matters to right; he didn't have the energy for anything else.

"What about my fortune?" he asked wearily, dropping his hand as he met the other man's gaze. "Can I at least sign that over to her without Amberstroke's permission?"

"Certainly, Your Grace," the solicitor replied, shuffling his papers nervously. "But I do not understand why you would wish to do so. You are a young man, and you will doubtlessly want to pass on your wealth *and* your title to your heirs."

The words were like a lance through his heart. The mention of heirs brought Nia's face to mind, and the enormity of his love lay heavy on his heart. Thank God he hadn't told her of that love, he thought bleakly. Now at least she wouldn't have to feel obligated to a bastard ... the son of a whore and a man who had kidnapped a helpless child to serve his own evil purposes.

The solicitor shuffled the papers on his desk and nervously cleared his throat. "If you will forgive my asking, Lord Tilton," he began diffidently, "why do you wish to renounce your title? It is among the oldest and most honored in the country."

Wyatt rose from behind his desk and began to restlessly prowl the room. This was the hardest part of his decision, but after careful consideration he knew it was his only choice. "I have decided to leave England," he said, his calm voice giving no indication of the wrenching pain inside him. "And since an absentee landowner would be the death of Perryvale, I've decided it would be in the best interests of the estate if I surrendered complete control to my heirs."

"I can understand that, Your Grace," the solicitor conceded with a frown, "but why give that control to a child? And a girl at that? Would it not make more sense to—"

The door to the study was suddenly flung open and Nia stormed inside, her eyes glittering with challenge as she marched over to where Wyatt was standing. "There you are," she said, bending her most formidable look on him. "Amanda is in her room sobbing because she thinks you blame her for Elliott's atta—" Her voice broke off as she became aware that Wyatt was not alone. "Who the devil are you?" she demanded, whirling around to glare at the stranger sitting at Wyatt's desk.

The solicitor drew himself up haughtily, his plump form fairly quivering with indignation. "I am Mr. Cranshaw, His Grace's solicitor," he announced, glaring at Nia down the length of his nose, "and I will thank you to leave at once. We are in the midst of some highly confidential negotiations."

Nia's snort was eloquent. "A solicitor, are you?" she asked, her eyes moving over him with obvious disdain. "Well, I hope you're better than the last one. He was one of the vilest creatures I have yet to meet. In the meanwhile, your meeting will simply have to wait. His Grace is required elsewhere."

Wyatt gave a weary sigh, his eyes closing as he pinched the bridge of his nose. He'd known a confrontation with her was inevitable, but he'd hoped to avoid it until he was in better control of himself. "Nia, I haven't time for this right now," he said, his tone heavy. "Go back to Amanda and tell her—"

"No," Nia interrupted, refusing to grant him any

quarter despite the anguish on his face. "*You* tell her. The poor child is beside herself because you've been so busy licking your wounds you've forgotten she exists! I insist you leave off this maudlin behavior, and resume your duties as her uncle."

Mr. Cranshaw appeared about to swoon at such brazen behavior. "How dare you address His Grace in that overly familiar manner you ... you jade!" he accused, his chins quivering. "You deserve to be dismissed ..."

"Oh, do be quiet," Nia grumbled. She didn't have either the time or the patience to soothe the man's outraged sensibilities. She felt she was on a dangerous precipice, and that one wrong step could send her plummeting over the edge. As she always did when she was afraid, she grew even more bellicose, her eyes sparkling with determination as she continued her attack.

"Well?" she snapped, jabbing her finger against Wyatt's chest. "Are you going to do you duty, or are you not? Everything else aside, you are still Amanda's uncle, and she loves you."

"His Grace hasn't time for these unbecoming melodramatics," Mr. Cranshaw said before Wyatt could reply. "He will be leaving the country soon, and we have a great deal—"

"You're *leaving*?" Nia gasped.

"Nia, I was going to tell you—"

She had heard enough. Unmindful of Mr. Cranshaw's presence, she lashed her hand against Wyatt's cheek. "You ... you coward!" she accused, tears streaming down her face as her heart shattered. "I wish I never loved you!" And with that she turned and fled out into the garden.

She ran without direction, her one thought to put as much distance between herself and Wyatt as possible. When she reached a stone bench, she collapsed onto it, burying her face in her hands as she gave vent to the anguish that was tearing her apart.

"Nia, are you all right?" Wyatt was suddenly

kneeling before her, his touch gentle as he reached out to take her hands in his. "Don't cry, my love, please. It is more than I can bear."

She brought her head up, her face wet with tears as she studied him. "How can you do it?" she asked, her voice shaking with emotion. "How can you turn and run rather than stay and fight for what is yours?"

Wyatt flinched at her words. "It's not mine," he said, forcing the words past his clenched teeth as shame overwhelmed him. "You heard what Elliott said. He was my father. I don't deserve Perryvale."

His obtuseness infuriated Nia. "Elliott was a scoundrel and a liar!" she snapped, pulling her hands from his and surging to her feet. "He hated your family and did everything in his power to destroy you. What the devil makes you think he was telling the truth?"

Wyatt, rising to his feet, froze at her furious demand. He gave her a startled look. "But—but he was dying," he protested, lowering himself to the bench. "He wouldn't have lied at such a time."

Nia had seen too much of death to put much faith in Elliott's dying declaration. "Why not?" she demanded crossly, hands on her hips as she faced him. "He knew he was dying, saw his last chance for revenge, and grabbed it with both hands. You have only his word he is your father. Are you going to give up everything on the basis of *that*?"

Wyatt stared at her, his heart and mind in turmoil. When he'd heard Elliott's dying taunt, it had shattered his world, but he'd never thought to question the veracity of the words. Now ... he rubbed an hand over his face, unable to think what he should do next.

Seeing his pain and confusion, Nia's anger dissolved. She returned to his side, reaching out and turning his face toward her. "Even if by some horrible twist he is telling the truth, nothing changes," she said softly, willing his eyes to meet hers. "You are still Amanda's uncle, and you are still the man I love. What does it matter who your father was?"

Wyatt lay a shaking hand on her cheek. "But if I'm not the duke . . ."

"Do you think I love you because of your title?"

"Of course not, but—"

"Would you not like me if you discovered my father was a gambler or a wastrel?" She continued, praying she could make him see the error of his ways. "Would you demand I leave Perryvale if it came out my mother was a common camp follower?"

Wyatt's expression grew inexplicably fierce. "Never," he vowed, his hand coming up to cover hers. "I would love you if you were the daughter of the devil himself."

For a moment Nia couldn't believe she had heard aright. But when Wyatt's mouth closed over hers in a kiss of searing passion, she knew her ears hadn't played her false. She returned his kiss with all the love and desire that burned inside her.

"Nia, I love you," he whispered urgently, holding her in a fierce embrace. "I love you more than anything in this world. Don't ever leave me, or I would die."

"My love." Nia felt more tears streaming down her cheeks, but she was too blissfully happy to care. She pressed herself closer, giving Wyatt all the love she'd held inside for so long.

He groaned softly as he felt her response. Her sweet touch was a balm to his tortured soul, and he accepted the comfort she offered with rising fervor. He wanted to make love to her more than he wanted to draw his next breath, but first there was something he must do. Giving her breasts one final caress, he managed to draw back. He met her dazed stare with stern determination.

"Marry me," he commanded, his voice shaking with desire. "If you love me, if my parentage truly doesn't matter, I want you to marry me the moment I can obtain a special license."

"M-marry you?" Nia's hopes soared even as her common sense made a belated appearance. "B-but that is impossible. You are a duke, and I am a governess. It would never do."

"Why?" he pressed, adroitly turning her own arguments against her. "You said you don't love me for my title. Do you mean you will refuse to marry me because of it?"

"Of course not!" Nia denied, straightening her spectacles with hands that weren't quite steady. "But you must know it can never be. Such a misalliance would cause a dreadful scandal."

Her sudden concern with the proprieties made Wyatt grin. "Since when have you cared a brass farthing what others might think?" he asked with indulgent amusement. "If you really cared for such nonsense, you'd never have crept into my carriage posing as a doxy. Enough prevaricating now," he warned when she opened her mouth to protest. "Are you going to marry me or not?"

Nia knew she should refuse; everything she had been raised to believe told her so. Wyatt had his duty, and she had hers, and even though they loved each other, she couldn't see how they could reconcile those conflicting responsibilities. Then she met his eyes, and the love and fear she saw there was all that mattered.

"Yes, Wyatt," she said softly, leaning forward to press a kiss to his mouth. "I will marry you."

Wyatt gathered her against him, his eyes closing in relief. "I love you, Nia," he said, his arms holding her tight. "I pray you never have cause to regret that decision."

"I won't," she said, her hands tangling in his thick hair. "So long as you love me, I'll never regret anything."

They continued kissing, revelling in each other and in the joy of their love. Finally Wyatt forced himself to be practical, and drew away from her once more.

"I still think I should relinquish the title," he said. "It's not really mine, and—"

"Beg pardon, Your Grace, but it most certainly is."

A gruff voice sounded behind them, and Wyatt jerked around to find Hemsley standing there. "Hemsley!" He gave the agent a furious glare. "How long have you been watching us?"

"Not long, sir," Hemsley assured him, his rough face lit with a saucy grin. "Allow me to offer my felicitations on your marriage. The two of you are well-matched."

Nia ignored that. "What do you mean the title is his?" she demanded, peering around Wyatt's broad shoulder. "Have you proof that Elliott lied?"

"Aye." Hemsley drew a piece of paper from his jacket and examined it with studied care. "Elliott was your mother's lover, true enough, but you was born almost eighteen months after your uncle drove him off with his whip. He couldn't be your father."

Relief made Wyatt weak. "Are you certain?"

"As the grave. What's more, I've proof Elliott spent those eighteen months out of the country clerking at a shipping firm in Charleston. There is no way he could have continued his affair with your mother from that distance."

"Then he *did* lie," Wyatt said quietly, his arms slipping around Nia. "Perhaps he lied about everything from the start."

"There's no doubt in my mind," Nia said with a firm nod. "You are your father's son. You may not have his hair and eyes, but you have his chin. And his arrogance," she added challengingly, and was rewarded by his reluctant smile.

"Perhaps," he said, and for the first time in more years than he cared to remember, he felt a deep sense of peace.

Hemsley was wise enough to see he was *de trop* and slipped away, leaving Nia and Wyatt alone.

"What now?" Nia asked, after Wyatt had remained silent for several minutes.

"Now I ride to London and obtain a license from the courts," he said. "I should manage to make the trip and back in a day or so. Will that give you enough time to handle matters here?"

She drew away, her cheeks pinking with confusion. "I ... you still wish to marry me?" she asked uncertainly.

He frowned. "Of course. I thought I'd made that obvious."

Her color deepened, but she was determined to do the honorable thing. "But at the time you made the offer you were still uncertain about your future. Now that you know—"

"Now that I know, I am more certain than ever that I want you in my life," he said firmly. "Blast it, Nia, if my title is all that's keeping you from marrying me, I'll renounce the damned thing tomorrow! Although I must warn you," he added with a sudden grin, "my cousin Amberstroke would then inherit, and he is the biggest idiot you can imagine. Do you really wish to see Perryvale in his dubious care?"

A slow smile spread across Nia's face as she finally accepted the reality of Wyatt's love. "No, I suppose I do not," she said, her arms once more twining around his neck as she tilted her face up to his. "Very well, Your Grace. I shall marry you, and then you may do your noble duty by Perryvale."

"Oh, I will, my angel, I will," he replied, his eyes bright with promise. "And since a duke's first duty to his estate is to guarantee the continuation of the line, you may be sure I intend carrying out those duties with the greatest of pleasure."

And he proceeded to demonstrate that willingness with stunning efficiency.

Avon Regency Romance

Kasey Michaels

THE CHAOTIC MISS CRISPINO
76300-1/$3.99 US/$4.99 Can

THE DUBIOUS MISS DALRYMPLE
89908-6/$2.95 US/$3.50 Can

THE HAUNTED MISS HAMPSHIRE
76301-X/$3.99 US/$4.99 Can

Loretta Chase

THE ENGLISH WITCH   70660-1/$2.95 US/$3.50 Can
ISABELLA   70597-4/$2.95 US/$3.95 Can
KNAVES' WAGER   71363-2/$3.95 US/$4.95 Can
THE SANDALWOOD PRINCESS
71455-8/$3.99 US/$4.99 Can

THE VISCOUNT VAGABOND
70836-1/$2.95 US/$3.50 Can

Jo Beverley

EMILY AND THE DARK ANGEL
71555-4/$3.99 US/$4.99 Can

THE FORTUNE HUNTER
71771-9/$3.99 US/$4.99 Can

THE STANFORTH SECRETS
71438-8/$3.99 US/$4.99 Can